THE HOBYO
AFFAIR

Dick Jacobsen

ISBN: 0692355383
ISBN 13: 9780692355381

ACKNOWLEDGEMENTS

Writing a novel is, to my mind, fun, revealing, brain-busting, regenerative and satisfying. Publishing a book is quite another matter. There are those who take it in stride, however, and reap their own rewards for their efforts.

First to acknowledge is **my wife Joyce,** who puts up with the endless hours staring at the back of my·head at the computer, ceaseless nagging to get chores done, limitless generosity of her thoughts and ideas and selfless dedication.

Secondly, the editors need to be acknowledged. Even though I have personally read the book eight or nine times, looking for errors and changes and each time finding them, before I handed over the task to the professional, my good friend **Jim Reimer**, also an author, reads the book for change development and content. We also swim the publishing and marketing swamps together and buoy each other through the social media miasma. Thanks Jim.

Thirdly, a new friend, **Delanee Bourland**, took on the task of the professional edit. She earns a fee, but also earns my earnest thanks. She has to read the book three times, once to find out what it is about, next to make the corrections and finally to help create a better book.

Fourth, **Kate Bourland**, mother of Delanee, has shined a very bright light into the cavernous crevasse known as marketing. She often had to bang my thick skull against my computer to knock some savvy into me, but she was relentless to the point where I can twitter with the best of the birds out there. I am probably in a session with her as you read this. We will get there Kate, I can feel it in these old bones.

Lastly, *Mark Owen*, thank you for opening my eyes to the world of the US Navy Seal, and to **Jay Bahadur**, for daringly revealing some of the secrets of Somalia. Get their books, they are fantastic reads.

DEDICATION

This book is dedicated to the men of the **United States Navy Seals**. What an honor it is to have them in our midst, working silently, courageously, indefatigably and in anonymity against the horrors that exist in this world, what they call 'nefarious activity,' and deal with it all for little financial reward.

We should thank the gods, all of them, that these men are on this Earth, on constant watch and on our side.

HOOYA!

PROLOGUE

John Wingate has worked a long, successful and prosperous career, starting as a cabin boy on his father's ships, to his current position as president and CEO of Double O Shipping Company. He toiled inexorably to build one of the most successful shipping companies plying the seas, and John is now at the point in his working life where he wants to name his nephew, JT Wingate IV, the current operations chief and second in command, as his successor.

John's road has been long, and has not been without serious and severe twists and turns. *The Chabahar Incident*, the first of a trilogy, chronicled John's experiences as operations chief dealing with very difficult shipping situations and performing his work in the midst of the Iranian Islamic Revolution in late 1978 and early 1979. He barely escaped the event with his life.

Six years later, in 1985, his father, JT Wingate III, turned the company over to John and he has been at the helm ever since.

The Hobyo Affair, the second in the trilogy, takes place in the period from 2000 to 2002, as John Wingate nears the end of his presidency and moves up to chair the Board of Directors.

His years of leadership came with a cost, however, as John never found the opportunity to settle, marry and raise a family. Constant travel, erratic schedules, and hands on requirements robbed him of any committed, conventional personal associations. He saw the void as a necessary evil, and tried to plug the gap with myriad women of similar lifestyles, tastes and means.

Now, with time to reflect, he feels there is a deep hole hollowed out of his life's experience. A chance meeting with a young stranger begins to turn his world completely upside-down, only to be threatened again by the rigors of his work and the largest threat ever known to the shipping industry in the Arabian Sea and the Gulf of Aden.

ACKNOWLEDGEMENTS

Writing a novel is, to my mind, fun, revealing, brain-busting, regenerative and satisfying. Publishing a book is quite another matter. There are those who take it in stride, however, and reap their own rewards for their efforts.

First to acknowledge is **my wife Joyce,** who puts up with the endless hours staring at the back of my head at the computer, ceaseless nagging to get chores done, limitless generosity of her thoughts and ideas and selfless dedication.

Secondly, the editors need to be acknowledged. Even though I have personally read the book eight or nine times, looking for errors and changes and each time finding them, before I handed over the task to the professional, my good friend **Jim Reimer**, also an author, reads the book for change development and content. We also swim the publishing and marketing swamps together and buoy each other through the social media miasma. Thanks Jim.

Thirdly, a new friend, **Delanee Bourland**, took on the task of the professional edit. She earns a fee, but also earns my earnest thanks. She has to read the book three times, once to find out what it is about, next to make the corrections and finally to help create a better book.

Fourth, **Kate Bourland**, mother of Delanee, has shined a very bright light into the cavernous crevasse known as marketing. She often had to bang my thick skull against my computer to knock some savvy into me, but she was relentless to the point where I can twitter with the best of the birds out there. I am probably in a session with her as you read this. We will get there Kate, I can feel it in these old bones.

Lastly, *Mark Owen*, thank you for opening my eyes to the world of the US Navy Seal, and to **Jay Bahadur**, for daringly revealing some of the secrets of Somalia. Get their books, they are fantastic reads.

"I have no other way of saying it John, but you have first stage testicular cancer," was the doctor's bad news. "The good news is that we caught it very early and it is curable. Your tumor is very small, has not metastasized and everything looks well contained. The tumor is so small we nearly missed it."

John sat staring at the wall, momentarily frozen. There was no expression on his face and he was obviously deep in thought.

"John, the first thing most of my patients do when they are initially told about their cancer is to bog themselves down in thoughts of doom. What about my family, my business, what about this, what about that, and I would like to caution you against doing that. That sort of thing only produces more, exacerbating stress."

John snapped out of his musing and looked at the doctor. "Okay. Where do we go from here Doc?" he asked bravely with the beginnings of his trademark dimpled smile forming on his handsome tanned face.

"I recommend that we begin a three cycle BEP regimen of chemo and see where that takes us. If that does it we are done, if not we continue," the doctor said. "You are otherwise as healthy as a horse and you should respond to the chemo well, without a lot of side effects."

"What are the possible side effects, Doc?"

"Worst case scenario there is hair loss, mouth sores, loss of appetite, nausea, diarrhea, easy bruising and tiredness which you are already experiencing."

"Sounds like the cure is worse than the disease!" John chided.

"In the case of cancer, often it is, John, often it is," Doctor Wilson ruminated.

"When do we get started?"

"I recommend we start this week, let's set Thursday," he said.

"If you don't mind, I'd like my assistant to contact your scheduler to set up the continuing regimen. She knows more about me than I do. I'll have her call as soon as I return to my office."

"John, I want you to have a good outlook on this. We can, no, we will beat this, and we will have you in remission in no time," the doctor added.

"That will be wonderful Doc, I just turned sixty and I want to tick off a whole bunch of items from my bucket list before I go," John said with a concerned look starting to return.

"Don't even think about going. The only going you will experience is *going* to be here, on this planet, for a long, long time to come," the doctor finished.

"See you Thursday Doc!" John sat up and hopped off of the examination table and stood to leave. He teetered slightly and he used the doctor's shoulder for support. "Whoa!"

"Don't be alarmed John, that was a normal, physical reaction. You just got up too fast."

"Charles, I'd like to drive around for a while if you don't mind," John asked of his driver.

"Anywhere special?" Charles asked.

"No. Just drive around, give me about half an hour before we get back to the office."

John wanted to think. Clear, concise, analytical thought usually brought him to a better state of mind. His inner engineer's mental process needed to sift through the realities to put everything in its proper place and make sense of it all. He needed to understand what was happening to him. He needed to put the doctor's words in proper perspective.

The thing he liked most about Doc Wilson was his no-nonsense approach, his thoroughness and his wisdom. Because of John's MIT Civil Engineering degree, the doctor always talked to him in technical terms, which made John more cognizant of his situation. John had complete trust in Doc Wilson; he had been the family cancer doctor for as long as John could remember. John suddenly felt relief in the knowledge that he would be taken care of properly.

Change is what he needed now. John needed to steer his ship a good ten degrees off of its current heading and take a hard look at what lies ahead. He would beat this thing like he had beaten everything else that had threatened him, challenged him or caused him harm.

2

CHANCE ENCOUNTER

John maintained his jogging regimen for the next two days, and his mind was full of thoughts. The Central Park trails were soothing to him, but he thought he noticed that his breathing was slightly labored.

A particularly attractive young woman passed him on his left. She looked up at him with a lovely smile.

"Good morning!" she offered in a happy, breathless lilt. She was obviously enjoying her day.

"Good morning yourself," John said as she passed and she kept on jogging, her thick, natural golden blond ponytail bouncing from side to side as she ran on. John couldn't help but notice her trim, shapely, muscular body in the skin-tight running suit she wore. *Oh to be thirty again!*

He kept going, and, up ahead, noticed the girl who had passed him was on her hands and knees in the middle of the trail about fifty yards away. He picked up his pace and ran to her side. Kneeling next to her, he asked "Are you okay?"

"I'm so embarrassed." She answered. "I stubbed my toe in a crack back there and went down like a rocket. I feel so clumsy!" she said.

"Don't be embarrassed," He said as he helped her to her feet. "Happens to the best of us. Are you ready to stand on your own?" he said, supporting most of her weight.

"Yes, I feel okay," she answered, but she fell toward him as he began to release his grip.

He noticed that her palms were scratched, cut and bleeding and her leotard was shredded at both her knees. "You're sure you are okay? Those scrapes on your hands and knees look raw and painful," he repeated.

"If you don't mind, I think I'll jog at your pace with you to the end; I do feel a little woozy."

"Glad to have you along, we can walk if you prefer," John said.

"That would be better, thanks," she said.

They got to the end of the trail and the girl smiled and thanked John for his consideration, kindness and concern and started off in the direction of her apartment. "Thanks again!" she said, and she was gone.

Charles was waiting for him and John climbed into the back of the limo.

"Good run?"

"Yes it was, Charles." John said, deep in thought. "Let's go directly to the office, I'll clean up there."

Thursday morning John woke, showered and dressed casually for the day he knew was ahead. His first chemo session was at nine AM and he was mentally ready to begin. Charles dropped him off at the clinic and he entered, registered with the receptionist and found a seat in the waiting room.

There was a seat next to a young woman and her charge, who sat facing her in a wheelchair. The little girl looked to be eight years old, with an angelic, smiling face and an Aunt Jemima head scarf encircling her ivory white brow, tiny blue veins at her temples. She beamed up at John with round, crystal blue eyes and said, "Hello mister! My name is Jennifer, what's yours?"

John stuck out his soft, tanned, well-manicured hand and replied, "My name is John, and I am very pleased to make your acquaintance

Jennifer." He glanced casually at Jennifer's mother with a smile. "The girl from the trail Monday! How are you?" he asked.

"I'm fine, thanks to you! What a wonderful coincidence," she replied. "Jennifer, this is the nice man I told you about who was so kind to me when I fell the other day."

"It was very nice of you to stop and help my mommy. You should see the scrapes on her knees and hands," Jennifer said.

John looked at her hands and noticed that in addition to the cuts and scrapes, they were red, rough and used to continual housework. The beautiful young woman looked tired beyond her years and certainly pushed beyond any normal daily stress and struggle.

"I was happy to do it Jennifer. Besides, your mommy is a very pretty woman, and I have made it my life's quest to always help pretty women in distress," John added. "By the way, I know another Jennifer. She is a particularly beautiful woman, a model, as a matter of fact, but she can't hold a candle to you and your radiant smile, sweetie."

Jennifer smiled and looked down at her lap in girlish shyness. "Why are you here John?" Jennifer finally looked up and asked.

"I have a cancer, and I'm here to begin my chemotherapy today," John said outright. "I'm a little nervous about it."

"Me too. I'm not just starting though, I have been here many times, and I want to tell you that it is not that bad, and there is nothing for you to worry about," Jennifer offered with a very serious, knowing and concerned look on her face.

"That's good to know." John said, reaching forward and taking Jennifer's small hand in his. "I only hope that I can be as brave as you obviously are."

All three were smiling and talking when a nurse came out to wheel Jennifer back to the therapy room.

As the nurse began to wheel her around, Jennifer stopped her and turned back to John with a very serious face to say, "John, don't worry about anything now, and when you come back to the therapy room I'll be there to help you if you need me. I will be there for you, just like my mommy is for me." And off she went.

John's eyes began to well up as he looked at Jennifer's mother. "What an amazing little girl you have there. You have done a fantastic job with her; she is perfect, bright and happy in spite of all her issues."

"She is that way, and has been since she was old enough to talk. I really don't think that I have had that much to do with it. She wants to protect everyone, help everyone, and befriend everyone. She is a constant inspiration to me."

"How is she doing?" John pressed.

"Not so well, I'm afraid." The young woman's eyes started to tear up. "She is stage four, and it is only a matter of time now. Her cancer has metastasized to several areas of her little body. They have tried extremely hard but can't seem to stop it."

"I am so sorry to hear that," John said, looking at the young woman. "May I introduce myself? My name is John Wingate," he said while offering her his hand.

"Carrie Latham, John. Nice to finally make your acquaintance," she said, narrowly smiling into his warm, handsome and dimpled face. "It seems we have known each other for some time now."

"I feel the same way," John replied.

They sat silent, looking at the floor and the walls for a few awkward moments. He finally looked at her and took her hand in his.

"Is there anything I can do, anything she needs?" he asked, still holding her rough hand and looking into her tired yet gorgeous blue eyes.

"That's kind of you, but we are okay, we will make it," she said, looking into his sincere and beseeching eyes.

"What I meant was, is there anything special she wants to do, or has a passion for?" John pushed.

"Well, she does love horses, and for a little girl from New York City, where she got the passion is beyond me." She went on to explain how Jennifer cuts pictures of horses from magazines and pastes them into her many scrapbooks. She continued to say that Jennifer, just eight years old, has taught herself drawing and sketching horses in every position. "You should see her sketch pads, they are brilliant. Where she gets it from I have no idea, I can't draw a decent stick man," Carrie said.

"Has she ever spent time with horses, does she ride?" John asked.

"No, I'm afraid that is just too far beyond our means, and she knows and accepts that. All she wants is an occasional car trip to the country to observe them or pet them at their fences. It breaks my heart to watch her, she loves them so. I would love to be able to do more, but I just can't," Carrie concluded.

"Yes you can," John said, seizing the opportunity. "What are her requirements here at the clinic for the immediate future?" John instantaneously launched into his take charge, problem solving mode.

"This is her last session. The doctor is saying that if we go too much further her remaining quality of life will be severely at risk and I really think that I want her to leave us happy and smiling," Carrie said, her lovely face clouding with the dark thought.

"Here is what I would like to propose. I have a very close friend who has a horse ranch in South Carolina. She breeds race horses. I would like you and Jennifer to go there, as my guests, and spend as much time there as you wish, or that Jennifer is physically able to do. There are no time restrictions; when you return is completely up to you. My friend also has a deep passion for horses and children, and I know she would certainly enjoy having you and Jennifer as her guests for as long as you like. She is an old girlfriend of mine, and one of the kindest, gentlest, life-loving people I know."

Carrie turned and looked at John square on. "Why would you want to do this? You don't know anything about us," a hint of skepticism creeping into her voice.

"That's not true, I do know you. I know that you are a clumsy jogger," he chuckled as she smiled. "I know you are a top notch mother, who is struggling to raise a top notch child who has been kicked in the gut by a nasty bully, and I have the means and I want to intervene and help with that. Besides, I am wealthy well beyond my needs and would enjoy assisting you and getting to know you and Jennifer better. My offer includes paying your ongoing bills here while you are gone and out of work, as well as providing you with spending money while you are away and out of work."

Carrie looked down at her knees and stared for a moment. "As much as I would like to take you up on your kind and generous offer John, I really can't afford to lose my job. Her medical bills have me chained to the time clock."

"May I ask what you do?" John asked.

"I'm a night-schooled and certified public accountant and I work for a major retail store," Carrie answered.

"I know this is rude beyond belief, but may I ask what your salary is?" John pursued.

She looked him in the eye and proudly said, "My salary is $45,000 per year, plus medical and dental."

"Here is my further proposal," John went on. "If your present employer wants to terminate you because you want to make your daughter's last days joyful, you will come and work for my company, and we pay our accountants substantially more money than that. I will cover you from all sides," John offered. "And there are no strings attached," he ended emphatically. "I want nothing but your and Jennifer's happiness in return."

Carrie looked at John in complete disbelief. Why should this man who she just met want to be so kind? She knew that there were people out there who did this sort of thing routinely but just couldn't believe that it was happening to her.

"Look, take some time and think about it. Not too long though. Here is my card, and I am on the trail just about every day at the same time," John said. "Behind those tired and overwrought beautiful blue eyes of yours there is a gorgeous, young, energetic woman, and I want you to take some time to rest and treat that exceptional little girl of yours to a dream come true, and most of all be happy. From this day forward I don't want you to worry about anything but making you and

Jennifer happy, which, by the way, will make me very happy. I do get something personally out of this."

The nurse called John's name to come to the therapy room. As he rose he looked down at Carrie. "Please consider my offer." He smiled and walked away, his six-foot-four frame upright, forthright, rigid and determined.

3

A LOVE AFFAIR BEGINS

A s he entered the therapy room he saw little Jennifer, sprawled out in her La-Z-Boy chair, foot rest extended, soundly sleeping. She looked completely stress free, like a rag doll that had been thrown there by a hapless child. He asked the nurse to be seated next to her.

"Is she okay?" John asked the nurse.

"Sure. Jennifer is a rock, but the therapy can take a lot out of you and it's easy to doze off," was the nurse's reply. "Feel free to do the same, by the way."

John had particularly large protruding veins and preferred the peripheral line to a vascular access device. He leaned back and let the nurse do her job. She took his blood pressure, which was a steady 125/70. She drew blood for blood counts and other serology. Finally the infusion was started.

"How long will this take, Nurse?" John asked.

"From two to three hours, usually," she answered.

John leafed through a few magazines he had at hand, but he wasn't overly interested in their content. So many of the magazines in doctor's offices were tremendous wastes of time. Celebrity worship, gossip rags, health and exercise magazines featuring airbrushed eighteen-year-olds; he just couldn't get interested.

Jennifer stirred next to him. She opened one eye and saw John broadly smiling at her. She wakened, smiled and stretched as if she hadn't a care in the world. She reached over and asked John to hold her hand.

"You are going to be just fine," she said. "We will get through this together, and we will win."

"Yes we will, sweetheart, yes we will," John answered. "I want to get to know you much better. I want to know all about your horse scrapbooks. I want to see your sketch pads, and I want you to teach me how to draw horses like you do."

She beamed up at him, her expression strong, clear and engaging. "Who told.....Mommy told you about those things, didn't she?" Jennifer smiled.

"She did, and she is so proud of you! As she told me about your drawing ability, she almost burst her buttons," John said.

Laughing, Jennifer said, "Everybody seems to think so, but it's not really that hard to draw. You just have to see what you are drawing in your head, and then make your pencil follow the lines of your vision. It's simple really. Look, I'll show you."

She opened her sketch pad and began drawing a horse's head. As she sketched she looked up as if glancing at an image in front of her, and then back down to the pad to guide her pencil accurately. Within minutes she produced a lifelike sketch of a proud horse's head and neck, a star blaze on its forehead with a long flowing forelock and mane.

"Beautiful," John said. "Absolutely perfect."

She ripped the sketch from her pad and handed it to John. "It's for you to tack on your bedroom wall."

John knew the importance children placed on their bedrooms, their solitary places.

John smiled down at her. He wanted to pick her up, hold her tight and somehow squeeze the menacing cancer from her young body.

"I will cherish this young lady. I will have it framed and hang it in a prominent, worthy place in my bedroom," John said. "Will you sign it for me?"

Jennifer was overcome with feeling as she signed her name.

"John there is a Carrie Latham on the phone for you, line one." Patricia relayed over the intercom.

"Carrie I am very happy you called. How are you and that little charmer of yours?" said John.

"Hello John, we are both as well as can be expected," Carrie said.

"Have you come to a decision on my offer?" John asked, getting straight to the point.

"We have, and I'd like to speak with you about it."

"Wonderful, let me send my driver for you and we can have lunch together. Can Jennifer join us?" John offered.

"She can, and we would both love to see you again." Carrie rang off.

"How is my beautiful new girlfriend?" John said picking up Jennifer gently and hugging her as tightly as he thought he could without causing her cancer-ridden body any further pain.

"I'm just fine," Jennifer said smiling and giggling, her bandana jostling on her head.

"Well you look just great to me. You look a lot better than this tired old grandpa," John said.

"Carrie, you look wonderful as well. Come, let's get our table."

John pushed Jennifer's wheelchair to the table and helped Carrie with her chair.

"Carrie I can't wait a moment longer, what have you two decided?" John asked, sliding his chair closer to the table.

"We have thought long and hard, about thirty seconds to be exact, and have decided to take you up on your offer. Jennifer hasn't thought or talked about anything else since I told her. I hope you won't be insulted, but I looked you and your company up on the computer and what I found pushed me right over the top of our decision. You are quite something in your world, and this isn't the first time you have done this."

"Not insulted one bit; in fact I would have worried had you not looked into things. I told you I would be most excited and pleased to be a part of this for you and Jennifer."

"How many horses does your friend have?" Jennifer asked impatiently.

"At last count, she has fifty three, and coincidently, when I spoke with her last night, she said she has a special one year old horse which she hasn't named yet, and she wants you to take special care of her and give her love and a name."

John could see that Jennifer was beside herself with joy and excitement. Her radiance was all encompassing. *There are few things more thrilling than seeing real joy on a happy, satisfied child's face,* he thought. It was infectious, and both Carrie and he were beaming. John was already seeing a return on his investment.

"When would you like to go?" John asked.

"Soon," Carrie said. John noticed the cloud that momentarily crossed her face and she quickly regained her smile.

"When we finish our lunch we will go back to my office and get started on the arrangements immediately," John replied.

"Patricia, please get Samantha Capers on the line for me," John requested into his intercom as the three settled in to his office.

"Very nice office you have here John. I like the heavy, masculine, nautical feel of the space, and the view is breathtaking!" Carrie remarked.

Jennifer wheeled herself around the office looking at the ship models and pictures, and she noticed the horse head picture she had drawn for John was hanging in a prominent space on his wall. It even had a light trained on it.

"How do you think it looks hanging there Jennifer?" John asked. "I don't spend much waking time in my bedroom and decided that I would be able to look at it more if it was here in my office."

She raced back to his desk, threw her arms around his neck and kissed him on the cheek.

"I'll take that to mean you like where I have hung your drawing." John smiled.

John's call rang through.

"Sammy, I have Carrie and Jennifer Latham with me in my office and I'm going to put you on speaker," John started.

"Hi ladies," Sammy said brightly.

"Hi Sammy, this is Jennifer and I am so excited to come and see you."

"I have everything ready for you sweetie, and I want you and mommy to come right away. I have so much to show you and I have a very special friend that can't wait to see you as well," Sammy went on. "She doesn't have a name yet, and I expect you to take care of that problem when you get here."

Jennifer threw a barrage of questions at Sammy who told Jennifer that she would answer every one of her questions when she arrives.

"They are to arrive day after tomorrow, Sam. Are you ready for them?" John asked.

"John, I am always ready, you know that," Sammy retorted.

The next day was an eternity for Jennifer, who spent her time gathering up her drawing supplies, pads and scrapbooks.

"I don't think you have to take them all honey, one or two scrapbooks should be enough; pick your very best ones. Take enough changes of clothes for a week; we can do our laundry there."

"Yes mommy," Jennifer said.

The following day, Charles dropped them off at the airport and John's pilot took them to the Greenville-Spartanburg, South Carolina, airport where a driver was there to meet them and take them the rest of the way in Sammy's limo. Carrie had never experienced such luxury, and she and Jennifer's very first airplane ride was quite an experience.

4

THE THRILL OF A TOO-SHORT LIFETIME

A tall, beautiful, southern woman walked out on the front porch of the antebellum, plantation-style South Carolina home to greet her guests. Her hair was lustrous grey blond and tied back in a thick pony tail that bounced playfully as she walked and turned her head. She wore riding clothes that fit her slender, shapely, athletic body perfectly.

"Hello there, my name is Sammy and I am so happy to see you both!" The hostess said in a rich, round southern aristocratic accent. "My old friend John has told me so much about you, I can't wait to get to know you and see all of your horse pictures and drawings. I didn't realize there was someone else on the planet who loves horses as much as I do."

Jennifer beamed and Carrie smiled as the houseboys took their bags and belongings to their rooms. They pushed Jennifer up the wheelchair ramp that Sammy had had her men construct for the visit. The house was completely transformed into a 'Jennifer-ready' heaven.

"The boys will take you to your rooms. Why don't you take your time and rest after your trip and come down when you are ready?" Sammy offered.

"I'm afraid that won't be possible Sammy. Jennifer is so excited, if she doesn't pet a horse in the next five minutes, I think she will explode," Carrie said.

"Well we can't have that now, can we?" Sammy replied while nodding to one of the boys.

The young stable hand soon returned with a sleek, muscular, one-year-old chestnut Thoroughbred filly. She was snorting and bouncing her head up and down, and she appeared restless as she pranced up to the group. Her sleek, shiny coat was rippling over her Thoroughbred racehorse's muscles. When she saw Jennifer in her wheelchair she immediately calmed and slowly, curiously and cautiously walked up to her.

"Don't be afraid dear, she just wants to get to know you," Sammy offered.

"I'm not afraid," Jennifer said. "I'm just so scared she won't like me and my dumb old wheelchair."

The stunning animal calmly lowered her head to Jennifer and gently nudged her on her shoulder. Jennifer reached up to pet the horse's nose and the yearling nuzzled and sniffed her hand. The boy gave Jennifer some carrots. Jennifer and her new horse became instant friends.

"I have got to say that I have never ever seen that before," Sammy noted, looking at Carrie. "Horses are very sensory animals and have keen perception. I have seen many horse/child relationships begin but I have never seen one develop that quickly."

"Jennifer this is your horse for as long as you stay here with us, which I for one am hoping will be a very, very long time. She obviously likes you and I hope your feelings are the same," Sammy offered. "She has no name yet, as you know, and she wants you to think of a good name for her. Will you do that for her?"

"I will," Jennifer said, smiling up at her new friend.

"Carrie, do you ride?" Sammy asked.

"A desk chair is about all I'm afraid," Carrie replied.

"Would you like to learn?"

"Oh yes, most certainly," Carrie cheerfully responded.

"Good, we'll get started on that in the morning, but for now why don't you and I go in and have a glass of wine and chat," Sammy offered. "Jennifer you and the boys can walk your horse, or whatever you want to do with her. We have a special motorized chair for you so you can keep up with her. The boys will show you and teach you how it works."

Jennifer learned the workings of the Bounder, an all-terrain, motorized power chair very quickly. She was surprised at how fast, maneuverable and stable it was. The joy-stick drive allowed her to move along and hold the horse at the same time. At first her horse was a little skittish around the chair, but soon calmed down, trusting Jennifer completely. She walked the horse as far as the graded, gravel path would take her. She was even able to safely get up to a slow trot and the young horse loved the exercise and the attention.

"Jennifer, the chair is an all-terrain vehicle, you can take it anywhere on the property," the stable boy said.

"What will I name you?" Jennifer asked the filly as they stopped in the shade of one of the many weeping willow trees, near a picturesque pond on the property. "Should I name you after a famous personality, like Cinderella, or Wonder Woman? How about a famous lady race horse, like Zenyatta, or Azeri, or how about Ta Wee, which means *beautiful girl* in Sioux? You sure are a beautiful girl. What if I named you after a city or a county or a state, like Dakota, or Carolina, or Selma or even Salem? What will it be?"

It was almost as if the horse understood her as she nudged Jennifer several times, snorted and looked at her. The animal bounced her head up and down several times and stomped her right front hoof.

"Do you want me to name you Jennifer too?" Jennifer asked, smiling broadly.

The yearling stopped its antics and snorted at Jennifer, then nudged her shoulder again.

"Then Jennifer Too it is!" Jennifer said gleefully, handing her a carrot.

☙

The women went out on a large old brick paved, open veranda with its slate tile roof in the rear of the mansion that overlooked the white rail fences, pastures, ponds, weeping willows, ancient yews, elms, grassy expanses and the many pedigreed horses grazing below the main house in a bucolic setting.

"What type of wine would you prefer Carrie?" Sammy offered.

"A chilled white wine would be wonderful."

Sammy instructed a house girl and ushered Carrie to a plush white-cushioned deck chair. Carrie was in awe of the woman: her home, her life style, her taste and her obvious, ageless beauty.

"Sammy, this is such a beautiful place. I feel so relaxed and comfortable here, and the setting, my God, is spectacular," Carrie said.

"Thank you Carrie, I hope you and Jennifer will enjoy yourselves here. John instructed that I am to spare no expense to see that you have everything you need and want and I am to hold nothing back. He wants this to be one of the best experiences of your and Jennifer's lives. Please let me know if there is anything you want or need. First thing tomorrow we are going to get you some riding attire, cap, boots, crop, jodhpurs, the works. With your figure you will look absolutely smashing!" Sammy graciously offered.

"You are too kind, and John is such a wonderful man," Carrie said.

"How did you meet?" Sammy inquired.

"The first time I had fallen flat on my hands and knees on a jogging path in Central Park, and like a knight in shining armor he picked me up, dusted me off and walked with me back to my apartment," Carrie said. "The next time was at a cancer treatment clinic where he was beginning chemotherapy and little Jennifer was finishing hers. We talked for a few minutes and the next thing I know I'm on my way here."

"Very persuasive man, my Johnny. He can charm birds from the trees, fish from the sea, deer from the forests and the panties off of any woman he meets. Trust me, I know! On top of that he is a one-man Make A Wish foundation. Jennifer isn't the first child John has sent to me," Sammy confided. "I love that man fiercely and have all my life. Neither he nor I ever married. Our wants and desires and careers differed drastically and we couldn't see a way to get together."

"Were you an item?" Carrie asked.

"I was, and still am actually, along with a dozen others. I have never minded as long as when he is in my vicinity, I get the call," Sammy said. "Does Jennifer have a father figure in her life?"

"No. Like an idiot I got pregnant when I was seventeen. He turned out to be a deadbeat jerk, and Jennifer and I have been alone ever since," Carrie looked away momentarily and then back and continued. "It turned out to be a good thing though; I was able to complete my high school education and graduated from night school with an accredited degree in accounting. I certified a few years later. I have been able to provide Jennifer with what she needs, and we have become the best, dearest and closest of friends. She excels in everything she attempts and has never felt sorry for herself. She is a marvelous young lady, who is getting an extremely bad deal from life. I don't honestly know what I will do when she is gone," Carrie confided as tears came to her eyes. "She is all I have."

"There, there. We will have this little cry together," Sammy choked. "But when this one is over, you must promise me to be positive, positive, positive. It is my hope that little Jennifer loses herself completely in her passion for horses and fulfills all of her childhood dreams while she is here. I have seen it happen several times before and so has John, and we both sincerely want that for you and little Jennifer."

All of a sudden, Jennifer wheeled up in her new motor chair, whirled around and parked directly in front of Sammy and her mother. "Mommy, mommy I came up with a name for my horse!" Jennifer breathlessly screamed.

"Wonderful, what is it sweetie?" Sammy asked.

With a big smile she said, "Jennifer T-O-O. I was thinking and thinking to myself and all of a sudden I said 'I'll name her Jennifer Too.' Get it mommy?"

"I do sweetie. How clever you are," Carrie said with a maternal smile.

Jennifer spun back around and wheeled off as fast as she had come in. Head scarf blowing in the breeze behind her, smiles and enthusiasm lighting her way, she was back to the stables in a flash.

"That horse has never had this much attention and care. What a perfect child. God, it is sometimes so unfair," Sammy cursed.

The next two weeks went by in a flash. Carrie was becoming quite a horsewoman and Jennifer was one with Jennifer Too. She rode her every day, sometimes two and three times, in her specially constructed and padded saddle that held her weakened figure comfortably upright at all times without chafing or bruising her tender, young, cancerous body. Jennifer looked tired, but Carrie couldn't remember a time when she had seen Jennifer happier, more sprightly or more enthusiastic and alive.

"How much longer do you want to put up with us Sammy?" Carrie asked one evening.

"Are you kidding me? I don't want you to ever leave, and I'm not kidding. You and that little girl have grabbed me by my heartstrings and I don't want to ever let you go. I'm serious now," Sammy enthusiastically responded in her deep, aristocratic southern drawl. "I've never had children of my own, and even though I have had many children in and out of my life, I am overwhelmed with my love for your Jennifer. You have done such an amazing job with her. I hope I'm not ingratiating myself, by the way."

"Absolutely not Sammy, we love you dearly. I spoke with Jennifer last night and she doesn't want to leave, but we can't go on being a burden to you," Carrie confessed.

"That's utter nonsense!" Sammy scoffed. "You can stay here for as long as you and she like. Besides, I am enjoying your company and I won't hear another word."

Sammy's driver met John at Greenville-Spartanburg Airport. The thirty mile trip to Sammy's estate wound through tree covered county roads and around antebellum plantation homes with white rail fences as far as the eye can see. Seeing the Thoroughbred horses grazing in the tall, green grasses gave John a feeling of calm and serenity that he seldom, if ever, felt in New York City.

As John's limo pulled up in front of the early 19th century mansion, he saw the girls in front, lined up and ready to receive him. His smile grew.

"John, John!" Jennifer screamed as she raced toward him in her new motorized chair. She stopped dead in front of him and threw her arms up at him in impatient eagerness and love, waiting for his strong arms to whisk her from her chair.

"Jennifer, my little beauty," John said as he dropped his bag and gently held her close to him. "You look radiant my little princess!"

She hugged him tightly around the neck with all of her strength and kissed him several times on the cheek. "I love you so much, and I can't wait to introduce you to my new very best friend ever, Jennifer Too."

"I can't wait either," he answered.

"How is your chemotherapy going John?" Jennifer asked with seriousness and concern.

"I'm getting along fine. I have finished one round and start the next in a few weeks and the doctor thinks that might be enough,"

John said. "My only problem is I miss my Jennifer time, but we can catch up now ok?"

Sammy and Carrie took up their places behind Jennifer, welcoming John with open arms, hugs and kisses.

"Wow, I'm going to have to come here more often! With a welcome like this, I think I want to leave and come back all over again," John smiled.

Jennifer rode next to John, holding his hand as they all walked, first thing, to the stables. Jennifer Too stood majestically in her stall, staring anxiously while waiting for Jennifer to arrive. She bent down and nuzzled Jennifer's head, knocking her vanity scarf to the ground. Jennifer momentarily froze, and immediately frolicked on as if nothing had happened. Carrie tenderly replaced the scarf as Jennifer formally introduced John to Jennifer Too.

"She is such a perfect friend," Jennifer said. "She is always here waiting, she always wants to play, she always wants to be with me, and she ALWAYS wants her carrots!" Jennifer proclaimed as she took out a handful, giving some to John.

"What a stately animal you have here Jennifer. You must be very proud of her," John said.

Jennifer let her horse out of her stall all by herself, and showed John how she walked and trotted with Jennifer Too. He was impressed by her lack of fear and her complete confidence and daring in handling the animal many times her size and weight. John noticed that the spirited filly was very aware of Jennifer's presence and followed her commands with obedience and love as Jennifer led her off.

"Well that's the end of her for a while. We will be lucky to see her for dinner," Carrie remarked dryly.

"Let's go in for lunch then," Sammy suggested.

Later that evening, after dinner, they retired to the veranda. Little Jennifer rolled up to John. "I would like to sit on your lap now please," she said to John demurely.

"Jennifer, give John some time to himself!" Carrie admonished as Jennifer looked down at her lap apologetically.

"Are you kidding, I flew 600 miles for this, and I'm not going to miss a minute of cuddle time with this one," John announced.

He rose and picked her up gently, and the two sat with their arms around each other.

"I have some new drawings I want to show you!" There were several amazing likenesses of Jennifer Too and a sketch of the house and the surrounding fields and fences. They were near professional resemblances.

"Where do you get time to do these things sweetie?" John asked.

"At night," she said. "I get in bed and my body is very tired, but my brain is still going full power."

"Do you draw from pictures you and mommy have taken?" John further questioned.

"No silly. I told you, I see the pictures in my mind and then I sketch them," she answered.

"The house as well? The detail and perspective are perfect!" John said.

"What is perspective?" she asked.

John could only hug her and shake his head. "If you don't know, and can draw like this, there is no need to confuse you with obscure nomenclature," he said with a knowing smile.

John spent the next three days with the girls, enjoying every minute. He was relishing his time with all three and didn't want to leave.

"John, do you have to leave?" Jennifer asked.

"I do sweetie, I have business in New York that needs tending to. I want to ask you a special favor though. Would you call me Grandpa or Papa?" John asked.

"I like Papa. I will call you Papa from now on. I have never had a Papa before and I think you are the best one a little girl could have," she said, smiling up at him.

He bent over and kissed her on her cheek as she threw her arms around his neck and kissed him several times on his cheeks. "Will you come back soon Papa?" she asked.

"I will come and visit twice a month, maybe more if I can get the time, how does that sound?" John said.

Jennifer, Carrie and Sammy clapped their hands in excitement and their smiles told John everything he needed to know.

Two months later Jennifer and her stable companion were out riding together, and Jennifer suddenly slumped in her saddle, dropping the reins. Jennifer Too stopped, immediately sensing something was wrong with her rider. The boy tried to wake Jennifer but she appeared to be out cold. He took the reins and led the horse slowly back to the stable, Jennifer's head wobbling and her body safely shifting side to side in her special saddle. The stable hand unbuckled her and lifted Jennifer up off of the horse and out of the saddle, then carried her back to the house.

"I don't know what happened ma'am. We weren't riding very fast. I turned around and there she was slumped in her saddle," the stable boy said, shaken and worried.

"I have a doctor on the way Carrie; he will be here in minutes," Sammy said. "Don't worry Jimmy; you are doing a wonderful job being Jennifer's friend and companion." Sammy noticed his acute grief.

Jennifer lay still on her bed, breathing shallowly as everyone fretted around her. The doctor came and gave her a thorough examination.

He said he would need a scan and an x-ray, and that he would have it arranged for tomorrow as soon as they could get to the clinic.

The scan showed that there had been an increase in the growth of the tumor, but still nothing of life ending proportions.

"It's a combination of anemia, cell expansion and of course her energetic lifestyle. Let her rest up a little and give her these medications. She should rally in a day or two; she is a mentally and emotionally strong little girl," the doctor ordered. "She will be back and ready to go in no time."

The stable boy brought Jennifer Too to Jennifer while she was convalescing on the back veranda. Jennifer Too snorted and nudged Jennifer, and Jennifer rallied rapidly. She was back on her horse three days later.

Two more months passed and Jennifer was out riding again, and again she slumped over in her special saddle. The doctor's news wasn't as good this time. The tumor was advancing rapidly and Jennifer needed hospitalization. Carrie knew she would have to return to New York and give Jennifer what she needed.

"Mommy do I have to?" Jennifer beseeched her mother that evening.

"I'm afraid so sweetie."

"Do we have to go right away? I want to be able to say goodbye to everyone, especially Jennifer Too," Jennifer said bravely.

"It is Wednesday; we will leave next Monday morning," Carrie relented. "How about that?"

"Thank you, thank you, thank you mommy!" Jennifer squealed, hugging her mother with jubilation.

"John, Jennifer has taken a turn, and the doctor wants Carrie to take her back to New York for observation and treatment by her regular doctor," Sammy reported to John.

"Oh no," John sighed. "Tell her that Charles and I will be there to pick her up at the airport. Does she know what is going to happen from here?"

"All she knows is that the tumor has made a rapid change, but I don't think she knows what the doctor has in store," Sammy replied. "They have decided to return to New York on Monday."

"I'll contact our doctor here, and grease the skids for her and Jennifer. She will get the best care money can buy. And Sammy, I can't thank you enough for what you have done." John rang off.

As Carrie and Jennifer drove down the long, tree-lined drive to the main road below the ranch, Jennifer Too ran alongside the fence. Jennifer rolled down the window and shouted, "I love you Jennifer Too!" as the car drove slowly on. Jennifer Too trotted side by side with the car, looking over at Jennifer, saying her goodbyes and trying hard, in her way, not to let Jennifer get away. Carrie could not hold back. She burst into uncontrollable sobs.

5

THE WORLD COMES CRASHING DOWN

"Carrie, I would like to stay in close touch with you and Jennifer. Please call me at any time, at home or at work. I'd like to have you two for dinner at least once a week if that is okay with you," John asked as he and Charles dropped them off at their apartment.

"We would definitely enjoy dinner with you, if you let me reciprocate on occasion. I'm a decent cook and we would love to have you in," Carrie answered.

Three weeks later John was jogging at his usual hour, and he came across Carrie on the side of the path. She was kneeling slouched and bent next to a tree sobbing deeply, her body wracked with each outpour. Other joggers ran by, uninterested and gawking as John ran up to her, knelt and put his arms around her.

"She's gone," Carrie said as she looked up at John, her eyes red and swollen from hours of crying. "She left us early this morning, I had to come out and run to try and gather myself together, and I can't seem to stop crying."

"Oh God no," was all that John could say. He picked her up by her shoulders and walked her to a nearby bench where he sat with his arms around her, comforting her.

"I don't think I can go on John," Carrie finally said after long minutes of weeping. "She was my life, my heart, my soul and my only reason for living."

"Certainly you can go on Carrie. It is going to be hard at first, I agree, but you have me to lean on, and I guarantee that no matter what or how long it takes I will stay with you and keep you safe," John promised.

"You have done enough for Jennifer and me. I can't accept anything more from you," Carrie said.

"Oh yes you can, young lady, and I won't hear any more of that talk," John commanded in as comforting and as stern a tone as he dared. "What are you doing about a funeral?" he inquired, changing the subject and the mood.

"I haven't done anything; I don't know where to begin," she said, shaking. "I just want it all to be over."

"Where is Jennifer now?" John asked.

"She is still at home; I can't bear to let her go."

John suddenly realized the depths of shock and despair to which Carrie had fallen, and knew what he had to do. Pulling her tightly to him, holding her head in his hand and pressing her cheek to his, he softly said, "Carrie, I will have everything taken care of, I don't want you to worry about anything. I want you to be involved in everything, but not to worry. You, young lady, have been through enough. You must let me assist you now," John said. "Besides, I have big changes coming up in my life, and you are a big part of it."

They both got up and slowly walked arm in arm back to Carrie's apartment.

John picked up Carrie's phone and called Patricia. He quickly explained the situation to her and then issued a long list of orders while Carrie went to Jennifer's room to place a blanket over the dead girl's face.

"Patricia, I'll wait here until the Coroner and funeral people are finished. We have a lot to do and not a lot of time in which to do it. I'll be back to the office as soon as I can," John said.

The Coroner arrived and dealt with Jennifer's remains. John held Carrie's trembling body as firmly as he could; she was very weak and was heavy in his arms. They watched the funeral people, dressed in their suits and ties, place Jennifer on the gurney and wheel her out of the apartment. "We will take care of everything Mr. Wingate. Please come to our offices when you are ready, and we will make arrangements from there. Please accept our deepest sympathies Miss."

Carrie reached down with a mother's touch and caressed the lifeless shape leaving her forever. Somehow she seemed to come back from her lassitude and appeared to be gripping the finality of the scene unfolding in front of her. Still at her side, John could feel her body gain control of itself, as suddenly she stood stronger and more erect, as if to let Jennifer know nothing was wrong and that everything was okay again.

The doors closed behind the solemn, dignified group.

"I want you to pack a few things and come and stay with me," John further ordered. "I have a three thousand square foot apartment of which I use one third. The rest is yours."

John wanted Carrie close to him, within eyeshot and earshot. Nothing was going to happen to her on his watch, nothing.

She threw some clothes and toiletries in a suitcase and they walked down to Charles and the waiting car.

"John, again, why are you doing this?" Carrie asked. "Why don't you just let me go?"

"I see in you a woman of unlimited worth, who is temporarily knocked off her pins and teetering a little, struggling hard to catch her balance, a woman on a tight rope without a net," he returned. "I see a woman with character, honor, immeasurable love and energy; in other words, someone with a great future. I want to see you flourish, and I won't let you go to waste."

As if sobering or coming out of a coma, she looked at him and smiled with acceptance. "If I hadn't stubbed my toe and fallen to my knees, where would I be today?"

"Charles, please take us to JM's Boutique. Carrie needs some work clothes to start her new job tomorrow."

They arrived at the Double O offices around two in the afternoon and John introduced Carrie to his brother Joe Jr. and Joe's two sons, JT IV and Richard, as well as Patricia, John's assistant.

Taking full charge, John began, "First of all I want you all to know that Carrie will be staying with me at my apartment for a while until she can get back on her feet. She needs new surroundings and all of our support. Secondly, Joe, Carrie is a Certified Public Accountant, and I would like her to start work here under your care and tutelage," John announced to the gathering. "Patricia, we have a funeral to organize first thing and I would like you to work closely with Carrie to accomplish that. Please see that she has whatever she needs, nothing but the best."

John called JT, Joe, Richard and Patricia into his office while Carrie was being enrolled with the company. He told them that Carrie had just lost one of the most precious little girls he had ever known, and that Carrie had no one in her life to lean on.

"I look at Carrie as a daughter," John announced. "I would appreciate all of you working with her, getting to know her and giving her a sense of family here. She spoke to me of not wanting to go on this morning. I know we can help her see her way past that. Let's all rally around her and show her who the Wingates and the Harcourt-Simpsons are.

With resolve, the group rose and started to leave John's office. "Joe, what do we pay our accountants these days?" John inquired.

"If I'm not mistaken, we pay seasoned accountants around 60K." Joe answered.

"Eventually she will be wearing several hats once she gets the hang of things around here, so let's start her at 65K after taxes. I know she has a backlog of medical bills to pay, and she stubbornly won't accept my help with that, so we'll do it this way," John said. "Patricia, the funeral will be at my personal expense so spare nothing." Patricia nodded and made notes on her steno pad. "Talk with Carrie and see if she is ready for a funeral this Saturday. I'll get a hold of Father O'Malley and see if he will officiate. I'll let you know."

They all left and tended to their allotted tasks. John saw genuine concern on all of their faces and he was sure that they would take Carrie into their hearts, just as he had.

"Carrie, what faith denomination are you?" Patricia asked.

"I'm afraid none," Carrie answered. "I had my daughter baptized a Catholic, and saw to it that she had some faith training in her life."

"Fine, we will plan along those lines then. Will this coming Saturday be a suitable day for you? That gives us the rest of the week to prepare," Patricia patiently and delicately went on.

"I don't see why not," Carrie said, feeling Patricia's empathy.

"John has contacted a good friend of his, a Father O'Malley who wants to speak with you this evening. John will take you there, and you will be able to get a look at the church and choose a burial plot," Patricia said.

The two women selected flowers, a casket and clothing for little Jennifer to wear. Carrie faltered at several junctures during the process but Patricia guided her through with hugs, pats and more hugs and the two women grew close. Carrie wrote the obituary and the funeral date was announced using John's name as Carrie's patron. It would guarantee a packed congregation.

The remainder of the week seemed an eternity, and Carrie stood the task. She healed quickly in the Double O environment. She felt much stronger, surer and safer than she had ever felt before in her young and challenging life.

The day of the funeral arrived and John walked Carrie through the crowd of mourners to their pew. She wore a black, two piece suit, black hose, a black hat and a fine mesh veil to mask her grief. She sat weeping softly in John's arms as Father O'Malley began the requiem mass in his violet vestments.

At the appointed time, Carrie rose to face the mourners. She stood next to the three-foot-wide by five-foot-tall framed photograph of Jennifer, smiling, astride Jennifer Too. She glanced at the photograph, reeled slightly and caught her balance on the dais as nearby attendees softly gasped. John immediately went to her side and held her around the waist. She looked up at him and smiled, which he parentally returned. She pulled back her veil and unfolded the eulogy she had prepared, and bravely began to deliver her speech.

"My daughter was blessed with the ability to feel, comfort and care for virtually every living thing in her world. She always thought of others before herself. Since she first began talking she wanted to do for me and care for me and she was selfless in all her relationships.

"She was diagnosed, too late, with cancer at age five and last weekend, in my arms, at age eight, she died," Carrie hesitated, stammered, sniffled and caught her breath.

"She asked for nothing, and yet those who met her and knew her bent over backward to give her everything in the hopes of continuing her stay here on Earth. I did the best I was able until one day Providence brought this beautiful man into my life," again she faltered slightly and buried her face in John's chest. "John instantly fell in love with Jennifer and he turned her last remaining months into a meaningful thrill of a too short lifetime. She died a happy, fulfilled and contented young girl, and where people like this come from is a mystery to me, but I thank God every day for John's presence in our life."

John gave her a squeeze and smiled down at her.

"I have lost my best friend, my heart and my soul. I am severely bent, bruised and beaten," she slowly and deliberately said, looking up into John's tearful eyes. "But I'm not broken. Please, all of you, accept my deepest thanks for surrounding Jennifer and me with your generosity and love and buoying us through this horrific time." She needed to blow her nose and John offered his handkerchief. "Please remember my little star in your prayers. Thank you." She looked at John, and he led her back to her seat.

Several other mourners, including John and Sammy and even Sammy's stable boy Jimmy, rose to give their final words. At the completion of the mass, the congregation filed out to the waiting hearse and assembled limousines. Carrie could not believe the gathering. She counted twenty three cars in the procession. They were mostly Double O employees showing their support for their newest and neediest family member.

John and Carrie rode in the first car behind the hearse. It was a four and a half mile trip up Madison Avenue to E. 59th Street, over the Ed Koch Queensboro Bridge along NY25, and ending at 48th Street, Queens. The slow, solemn, and NYPD-escorted procession took twenty minutes. John held Carrie close the entire way, and escorted her to where she sat graveside, legs crossed at the ankles, gloved hands holding a single light pink rose in her lap, veiled face looking straight ahead at the tiny coffin, eyes tearful.

Father O'Malley said the final words over the grave as Carrie stood and brought her floral offering to the casket. She kissed the pink rose, laid it on the coffin and softly murmured, "I'll see you in heaven my dear sweet child. Go quickly now, God is waiting. I love you."

She turned bravely away from the grave and walked back to John, who always seemed to be within arm's reach. She took his arm and the two led the procession back to the waiting limousines.

John marveled at her strength, courage and determination. This was a new person on his arm. She looked up at him.

"I'm ready now. Thank you for this closure," she said. "Jennifer and I have been alone for so long it is impossible to remember what it is like to have a complete family, people who love you, care for you, trust you and see you through to the other side."

He squeezed her arm in understanding.

"After the family get-together, I want to spend the rest of the evening alone with you, holding you and feeling you close to me. When that is over, I know that I will be whole again," she said and walked bravely into the crowded room of mourners, head held high.

At John's apartment, close family gathered to be with Carrie. They had all accepted her completely. After the meal they prepared to leave, each giving Carrie a long, warm and consoling hug. John watched his family do what they all did so well, giving inspiration, confidence, buoyancy, resilience and comfort. Joe Jr. and his wife Peg, JT's parents, were the last to leave.

"Anything you want or need from me or my family is yours. Even though we didn't know little Jennifer that well, we knew her well enough to know that you must be a very special young woman. We welcome you into our hearts," Joe Jr. said.

Peg gave Carrie a long hug and kissed her several times on the cheeks. "I'm here if you need to talk, walk, shop, whatever. The Wingate men can be overpowering at times and it's good to have another woman in your corner," Peg smiled and they left John and Carrie standing at the apartment door, arm in arm.

Inside, John told Carrie to go wash her face and get into her PJ's and meet him in the living room for a nightcap. She walked to the bathroom, kicked off her heels, took off her dress and slip and looked in the mirror. Her eyes were red and mascara was everywhere it shouldn't be. She put her hair back in a ponytail, washed her face, and went into her bedroom for her night clothes. She returned to the living room and found John sitting on the couch with two snifters of brandy on the coffee table in front of him. He patted the seat next to him and asked her to join him. She sat and tucked her strong, long runner's legs under her. She took a swallow of her brandy and shuddered.

"It's better if you take small sips, and roll it over your tongue several times before swallowing," John said with a knowing smile.

"I've never had this before, what is it?" she asked.

"It is two-hundred-year old Napoléon Brandy, which means it was produced in 1800 just for your enjoyment!" John playfully answered.

John put his arm around her and she nestled into his shoulder. They sat like that, silently sipping their brandy for an hour or more when Carrie placed her empty glass on the coffee table and stood offering her hands to John. He stood and they walked back to her bedroom.

She stood with her back to her door and looked up into his handsome, dimpled face and those dazzling blue eyes.

"There is nothing more I can think to say, except thank you," she said as she stood on her tip toes and kissed his lips. Then she turned and went into her room.

6

THE BEST LAID PLANS.......WORK

With the funeral well behind them, John announced that he wanted to have a party for all of the office employees.

"Patricia, I want you to set the plans in motion for a formal dinner and dancing affair at Henri's. Closed function. Henri will understand, we have taken over his place before. Husbands and wives need to attend," John directed.

"When you say formal, how formal are you thinking?" Patricia asked. "Most of the men will be in business suits, and some of the women in business attire, so make it semi-formal?"

"I want everyone to feel special," John concluded.

"So, business suits and cocktail dresses?" Patricia asked.

"Between you and me, I have something more splendid and special planned for Carrie. She will be dressed to the nines, and I don't want her to look too much out of place. Jennifer Middleton's shop can give you some details. Talk with Margo, Jennifer is out of town," John said. "You could give all the working girls the afternoon off to go home and get dressed."

"I'll figure it out," Patricia commented and went off to begin her efforts.

The day before the function, John gave Carrie a spa day and had Jennifer Middleton's boutique fit her in the evening gown he had selected for her. He had purchased appropriate jewelry. On the evening of the event, Carrie came out of her suite and John's jaw nearly dropped to the floor. The strapless gown with the small train fitted her lovely young body perfectly. Her smooth, glowing, South Carolina tan flattered the sky blue gown and soft white ruffles at her breast. Her rich, natural blond hair was piled on her head in a new hair-do that impeccably completed her made-over look.

"Ta-da!" Carrie announced with arms spread wide and a big smile on her face.

"My God, let me look at you. Turn around for me," John requested. The back plunged to below her waist, revealing a flawless, taut and toned figure. "You, my dear, are going to be the Belle of the ball this evening. I am going to be so proud to have you as my date tonight. I feel truly sorry for the other guys," John praised on.

"John, I can't remember a time when I have felt so good about myself, my life and my surroundings. I have you to thank for all of that," Carrie said.

"No Carrie, and you need to understand this. You have only yourself to thank for that, my beauty. All I did was give you the place, time, space and the means for it to happen. It is you that you look at in the mirror, not me. This is you, the drop-dead gorgeous, gregarious and intelligent woman I knew you were," he spun her around. "Come on, Charles is ready, and I can't wait to show you off to the crowd."

John and Carrie entered the gathering arm in arm. All heads turned to them, and John beamed with pride. John noticed that JT was taken with Carrie's beauty, poise and self-assuredness, the reaction John was looking for. As the evening began, JT worked his way over to Carrie.

"May I get you a drink?" JT asked.

"Oh, thank you JT, I would really enjoy a glass of champagne," she answered. "For the first time in a long while, I feel in a party mood."

He hailed a server and ordered the drinks.

"I don't want to be out of line, Carrie, but I am dazzled with your presence," JT blurted out.

"Well thank you kind sir," she answered with a curtsy. "With remarks like that, you can be as out of line as you wish."

JT smiled and led her to his table. As he handled her chair, her hair brushed his cheek and her scent made him a little lightheaded. JT monopolized her time as they talked and danced until John intervened.

"JT, let me borrow Carrie from you for a moment, I have an announcement I want to make. You may have her back later," John winked.

Both JT and Carrie blushed slightly as John led her away.

John stood at the front of the room and tapped on his glass for attention. It took a few moments, but everyone finally quieted down.

"I have an announcement to make," he said with Carrie at his side. "I am stepping out as president of Double O effective tonight, and stepping back in as Chairman of the Board in two months." The people in the room buzzed and twittered for a few moments, and then John continued.

"JT will be stepping into the presidency beginning tonight, and I know you all wish him well."

Everyone in the room clapped and cheered. JT was well respected and appreciated by all the Double O employees. Carrie was inwardly elated at the news that JT was moving up and she clapped excitedly.

John tapped his glass again. "I'm not done yet," John injected in a sing song voice. "Beginning Monday, I am going on a 'bucket-list' vacation trip, and will be gone between one and two months. I'm taking this absolute stunner with me as my assistant, travel companion and caregiver, if need be. So all of you, eat your hearts out," John highlighted Carrie's aura as he spoke. "As you all know, I have come to look upon Carrie as my daughter and I want to show her some of the world she has never seen and I can't think of anyone I would rather travel with." Everyone nodded and clapped in agreement.

Carrie stood astounded in delight, eyes wide, beaming a gleaming, white toothed smile with hands on either cheek. She looked up at John and he smiled at her schoolgirl-ish reaction and pleasure.

"Okay JT, you may have her back now!" Everyone laughed and John knew he had gotten the reaction he wanted all around.

"You will have the time of your life Carrie," JT said as he seated her back at his table. "Uncle John knows everyone, has been nearly everywhere and could write a book about traveling in style. I don't know where he is taking you, but you can bet it will be a world class trip and a time to remember."

"When he announced it I was dazed. He hasn't said a word to me about it. I have rarely, and only recently, been anywhere outside of New York City, except for Mineola where I was born, and the few trips my daughter and I have taken to the western New Jersey countryside," Carrie admitted.

JT monopolized Carrie's time the entire evening. He reluctantly gave others a chance for her attention, but let it be known he was the top dog in the fight. He sat next to her at dinner, danced with her and sat talking with her for long periods. He noticed that John looked at them from time to time with a knowing smile. *Did he plan this, or is he just happy to see Carrie in such great form and enjoying herself?* JT thought to himself.

"Come my dear girl, it's time to go," John said, walking up to JT's table.

"John, I'm happy to see Carrie home if you would like," JT interjected.

"Oh, I'm sure you would be, but we have a lot to do before we leave," John said.

Carrie stood and walked over to John's side. He covered her shoulders and back with her wrap and began to lead her away.

"Carrie, have an absolutely wonderful time!" JT said, shaking John's hand in a gesture of bon voyage.

On the way home, Carrie had a million questions for John that she asked rapid fire.

"Whoa, hold on there. I can only talk so fast," John smiled.

They arrived home and went to the living room for a last nightcap, which was where she cornered John and began her interrogation.

"Where are we going?" she asked like a child on a Sunday outing.

"First we are going to London to see a very close and dear lady couture friend of mine," John went on to say that from there they would travel to Tuscany and meet Sammy again. "She has a small horse ranch and a beautiful villa near Siena."

"Then it's on to Lake Como and Venice; Sitges and Mijas, Spain; Samos, Greece," John continued. "Then finally, we will travel to Tiburon, California where I have a home," John concluded.

"My God, that sounds like a trip of a lifetime!" Carrie said excitedly.

"Carrie, I hope it will be the first of many trips we will take together," John confessed.

"Where is Tiburon?" she asked.

"It is just north of San Francisco, across the Golden Gate Bridge," John informed. "It is a bayside community devoted to the water and the beautiful views it creates. I will show you my retreat and we will sail and fly my plane, cook together at home and dine in San Francisco and Napa Valley."

"I don't know if I have the proper clothes for this type of trip," she said.

"Not to worry, I have that covered as well," John replied. "Now let's get off to bed, we have final preparations to make tomorrow and then the next day we are off."

John raised himself from his easy chair. He stood to his six-foot-four inch height and stretched his still strong, slender and flat body. He was still extremely handsome despite his years. He was beginning to feel the aches and pains of his age, but he maintained his extraordinarily good physique.

Carrie went to her bedroom and prepared for bed. She stood in front of the full length mirror in her panties and looked at herself from head to toe. "I am beautiful," she said, smiling at herself. All of the years working so hard and raising and caring for Jennifer had gone now in the luxury of John Wingate's world.

I did the very best I could during my years as a single mother. I was happy, given my circumstances; satisfied, given my station; pleased, given my beautiful, challenged child; and nearly beaten, given my grief, she thought. *The changes in my being since meeting John Wingate are life altering, but I have done it myself. This IS my world. This IS me. This IS who I am. I will continue to grow as a woman. I look forward to tomorrow.*

She dozed off thinking how lucky she was and how wonderful her newfound father was to her.

Carrie rose early the next morning and cheerfully prepared a breakfast of scrambled eggs, bacon, toast and a bowl of fruit, all the time humming a mindless tune. John awakened to the smell of fresh coffee and joined Carrie in the kitchen.

"You're up early, my pretty," John said.

She put his coffee next to him and kissed him on the cheek with a bright and excited smile.

"I can't wipe this ridiculous damned smile off my face!" she said. "It's like it is painted on. I am so happy."

John looked at her beaming face. "It is only just the beginning," he replied.

"I am packed, and have a few things I need to wrap up at the office. Pack lightly. Bring what you need in the way of cosmetics, lotions and the like. We will be in the sun a lot, and we will be with people from all over the world," John said. "I'll send Charles by to pick you up around 6:00 PM for dinner. We need to make it an early night, we have an early start in the morning."

John left, and she wandered into the living room to finish her coffee. Her head was spinning. The phone rang.

"Hello," Carrie said.

"Carrie, this is JT."

"Good morning JT, have you recovered from last night? Have you jumped into the Presidential saddle yet?" Carrie playfully asked.

"You don't jump into the saddle around here Carrie. The saddle hunts you down, picks you up and off you ride, holding on for dear life," JT kidded.

"Sounds like fun," Carrie retorted.

"Carrie, I want you to know that I had a wonderful time last night, and I hope that I didn't monopolize your time too much," JT pleaded.

"Well you did," Carrie confessed with mock irritation. "But I enjoyed every single minute of it. You are dashing, articulate, a fantastic dancer and a gentleman. Not much more a girl can ask for in a monopolizer."

"That's wonderful, I thought maybe I was pushing too hard," JT said.

"Not at all," she consoled.

They talked on for a good fifteen minutes or so about the trip before Carrie finally interrupted. "JT, or should I say 'Mr. President', isn't it about time you got back to work?" Carrie said.

"You are right. Carrie, have a wonderful time and I will see you when you return," JT finished.

"I will JT, and thanks again for last night," she ended reassuringly.

7

HELLO JENNIFER

"**J**ohn do you realize this is the first long, trans-Atlantic flight I have ever taken, let alone the first First Class flight?" Carrie confessed in the United First Class lounge.

John smiled and took her hand in his. "I am so excited that I am the one who gets to take you on your first long flight."

On the plane, they sat in the new side-by-side pod seating and Carrie marveled at the luxurious accommodations.

"I don't feel like I'm on an airplane," Carrie said. "This is decadent comfort."

"Carrie, when you are six-foot-four and fly the number of miles that JT and I do, it is a necessity, not a luxury. I have flown hundreds of thousands of miles and I would be a bent and broken old man today if I had to do it in economy seating," John confessed.

Carrie delighted in her comfort and, with a satisfied smile on her face, promptly fell asleep an hour after the meal service.

They got off the plane in Heathrow and a man with John's name written on a placard was there to meet them. A United representative retrieved their bags and brought John and Carrie through customs and baggage check. The driver took them to the Connaught Hotel in Central London where John had reserved the Library Suite. A hotel representative and bellman strode to the car to help John and Carrie out and see to their bags.

"Mr. Wingate, it is so nice to see you again sir," the day manager said. "It has been a while. I hope all is well and that you enjoy your stay with us."

"Thank you Wilfred. I'd like you to meet Carrie Latham, my assistant and traveling companion."

"Good day, Miss Latham," the manager said, clicking his heels and bowing slightly from the waist. "We are so happy to have you, if there is anything you need, just let me know."

"Thank you so much," Carrie smiled as they walked off to the Library Suite. The rooms were an eclectic mix of modern decoration and old world charm. The two bedrooms were very large and the living room with its gas lit, wood burning fireplace, extensive library and overstuffed furniture was particularly comfortable. Built in 1815, the hotel has entertained celebrity and royalty for the better part of two centuries, and it was evident in the design of the room.

"I need to make a few phone calls, Carrie. Why don't you clean up and get some rest and we can meet each other for a drink at six-thirty with dinner at eight. If you are hungry or need anything, call the concierge. There is a full bar en-suite so help yourself, don't be shy. Pretend like we are at home."

John went off to his room and Carrie strolled around the library, looking at the books and the paintings the room housed. She couldn't believe that people lived this way. She yawned and realized that she was tired and went to her room to lie down. Before she knew it, John was knocking at her door.

"You don't want to sleep too long because you won't be able to sleep tonight and it will slow the acclimation process. Get up sleepy-head, drinks in the library in one hour," John chided outside her door.

The next morning John again had to wake Carrie. "You are acclimating quickly, must be the youth. I didn't get much sleep last night at all," John said. "We have a great day ahead of us, so get up and meet me downstairs for breakfast."

Carrie walked down the ageless mahogany wood staircase, mouth slightly open, gazing at the pictures on the walls; touching, almost caressing the rich mahogany balustrade as she descended. John saw the childlike wonder in her eyes, and he marveled at her still-youthful curiosity, wishing he was twenty five again.

"You look as though you have just seen the Queen herself coming down the stairs," John said smiling.

"It is *soooo* beautiful here. Everything is so tasteful and perfect. There is a richness about this hotel that seeps into your pores," she remarked.

"I stay here when I come to London, which isn't that often of late," John confessed. John wore pleated tan slacks with a vertically striped brown and cream long-sleeved shirt and a kelly green cashmere v-neck sweater draped over his back with the arms crisscrossed in a loose tie in front.

"I feel a little under-dressed, judging by you and the rest of the guests," Carrie said.

"We will just have to take care of that feeling, and today I have someone I want you to meet who can help with that. She has a shop just two blocks away," John answered.

They walked into the well-stocked and elegant boutique. John wanted to surprise Jennifer so he hadn't told her he was coming, but he had cleared his plans through her New York shop and sworn them to secrecy.

"John, oh my God!" Jennifer screeched as he and Carrie walked through the door. Every head turned to see what the excitement was about. Jennifer hopped up and down on her toes several times and clapped her hands together at her breast in exhilaration. She ran to him, threw her arms around him and kissed him hard on the mouth. "You are a sight for these sore old eyes. Oh my god, my heart is going like a trip hammer!" Jennifer mock punched him on his shoulder as she broke her embrace. "You shouldn't do this to me."

"It is so wonderful to see you too, Jennifer," John said, noticing that she was wearing his emerald ring.

"Jennifer, I have someone I would like you to meet. Jennifer, this is Carrie Latham. Carrie, this is …."

"Jennifer Middleton, I know. Oh my God, *the* Jennifer Middleton!" Carrie said, agog. "*The* supermodel Jennifer Middleton, *the* award-winning clothing designer Jennifer Middleton," Carrie went on.

"I'm guilty," Jennifer smiled, reaching out to Carrie with both hands. Jennifer looked at Carrie up and down. "What a gorgeous young lady you are. But then I wouldn't expect anything else, given the company you keep," she winked at John.

"Oh my God," Carrie blurted again. "Until I met John I owned one piece of your clothing, a scarf that I had to save for months to buy at your New York store," she said excitedly.

"That's all about to change Carrie," John began. "Jennifer, Carrie and I are embarking on a trip that could range from six weeks to two months and my young lady companion needs a suitable wardrobe," he announced. "She needs several cocktail dresses, an evening gown or two with a wrap, chic day wear, horse riding wear, bikinis, one piece suits, like the one you wore to the pool in Bahrain; some cover-ups, blouses, slacks, shorts, underclothes, accessories, the works," John listed. "Spare no expense. She will need a full set of Hartmann luggage as well. You have my full attention." John sat back, crossed his arms and legs and smiled at the thought of what was to come.

Jennifer looked up from her notes and said, "What bathing suit did I wear in Bahrain?"

"The black, one piece, wafer thin Gottex. I can still see you in it," John reminisced. "The vision is forever etched in my memory."

Jennifer escorted Carrie back to the changing area. "Let's start with the swim wear. That will loosen him up for the rest of garments I have in mind for you," Jennifer suggested. "We can gather the under-garments and accessories as we go, fitting the outer wear."

For three tireless hours, Carrie paraded possible choices in front of John, who would shake his head or smile and nod with each new selection. There were many more nods than shakes.

Jennifer watched John from behind the dressing screens. She wondered at the attention and love that John was showering on this lovely young woman. Jennifer also saw that John was assuming a fa-therly bearing with her. When Carrie finally came out in her evening gowns, Jennifer thought she saw tears well up in John's eyes.

"Hey big fella, what's going on with you?" Jennifer asked John, sit-ting down on his lap as Carrie modeled the final gown.

"Isn't she beautiful?" John choked.

"That's an understatement, but what is it to you?"

"It's a bit of a long story, but she just recently lost her eight-year-old daughter to cancer. She was a single mom who worked very hard to make something of herself after mistakenly giving birth at age seventeen," John told her. "I had a great deal of affection for her little girl, who was named Jennifer by the way. I want this young lady to succeed, and I will do whatever it takes to see her through. I want her to know the good things in life, and I don't want her to struggle just to get by anymore."

"How long are you in London?" Jennifer asked.

"As long as it takes for you to finish her wardrobe," John replied.

"It should take me another three or four days, if that's okay," Jennifer replied. "I don't carry some of your requests here in the shop, but I have access to it all and will gather it all as quickly as I can. There will also be several fittings."

"Don't be too quick. How is your social schedule for the next four days?" John pried.

"Let's see. Hmmmmm. I just happen to have all four days available."

"Dinner at seven sound good to you?" John asked.

"Are you at the Connaught?"

John told Jennifer that they were in the Library Suite and that they should start there with drinks and then dinner at Espelette at eight.

"Wear something sexy and short and maybe bring a toothbrush if you have a mind to," John winked.

"I have a mind to," Jennifer smiled back.

That evening there was a knock at the door and John went to open it. Jennifer stood there in a stunning mid-thigh length cocktail dress. Her legs were still smooth, tan, long and lustrous. Her nearly white hair was up in a sexy 'do, and she wore her emerald ring to go with her clear green eyes and metallic, emerald green and body-caressing cocktail dress. John invited her in, hugged her and handed her a gin and tonic, neat. She sat opposite John and crossed her lovely legs without tugging and pulling at her revealing hem line.

"Where is your charge?" Jennifer asked.

"She's not quite ready yet, she told me she wants to look perfect for you."

John asked Jennifer if she could scare up a blind date for Carrie. She said that she knew a male model that was straight, and she was sure that he would be glad to escort Carrie. Jennifer said that he was a much better-than-average, very handsome young British man working his way through university by modeling men's clothing. She had used him several times escorting models for her spring and fall line showings.

"See if you can make that work, and tomorrow we will do dinner and a show. Is there anything good going on?" John asked.

"*42ND Street* is playing at the Palace," Jennifer said.

"I'll set it up and call you tomorrow," John agreed.

Carrie appeared at the far end of the library with a "Ta-da," holding her arms out to the side and playfully shaking her shapely backside.

Both Jennifer and John turned to look at her at the same time. She was spectacular in a royal blue mid-thigh cocktail dress with pearls at her revealing neckline and spike heels.

"What do you think?" Carrie asked John, but looking at Jennifer.

"If I was thirty years younger you wouldn't stand a chance young lady," John boasted.

"And I can attest to that!" Jennifer quipped.

They all chuckled. John got Carrie a drink as she sat down next to Jennifer and crossed her legs.

Jennifer and John related the story of their first meeting, their days in Chabahar, and the years of their, life lonely love affair that followed. Jennifer with her world based career and John with his globetrotting business brought them together on a catch-as-catch-can basis. They continued the discussion over dinner at the hotel. The evening went extremely well and they all went back to the suite for a night cap.

Carrie went to her room to change into something more relaxing. Jennifer walked up to John, who was pouring Camus Cognac Cuvee into three Waterford snifters, and draped her arms around his neck and kissed him hard on the lips. "I want you now," she hissed, pressing her still firm, flat and taut body to his.

"I want you now too, but decorum for the moment, my love," he kissed her back. "The night is ours after we complete our babysitting job."

Carrie returned to the room and saw John and Jennifer nuzzling each other at the bar. He was ruggedly handsome with his snow white wavy hair and deep tanned face in his shirtsleeves and tie.

"Sit and have a cognac with us," John said.

"Just one and then I have to go to bed, I'm bushed. Still working on the jet lag I guess," Carrie said.

"John, I'd like to have Carrie for a several fittings tomorrow, and then I was thinking we could all meet for lunch if that suits everyone? I also have some girlie things I want to do with Carrie tomorrow afternoon at my spa," Jennifer asked.

"Fine by me girls. I can keep myself entertained, but only for so long, and then I'm on to greener pastures," John returned with a grin.

"As if you could find any pastures greener than this," Carrie quipped.

The next four days flew by, and Carrie was in a whirlwind of complete elation, ecstasy and delight. Her wardrobe was complete and she and John were off to Tuscany that morning.

"Jennifer, thank you so much for stepping up this week. I think Carrie's head is still spinning," John said to her at the airport.

"John, you know I love you and would do anything for you. Besides I had a great time, and you get the bill."

"The feeling is shared, my beauty, see you soon," John said as he and Carrie boarded their flight.

8

CIAO SAMMY

S ammy met them at Florence International Airport. Carrie was beyond happy to see Sammy again and they hugged each other warmly. Sammy kissed John on the lips, grabbed his arm and put her other arm around Carrie and together they walked off to her waiting limo as her driver gathered the bags. Sammy had local Chianti wine and antipasto for them for the forty-five mile, one hour and fifteen minute drive, south to her farmhouse and villa outside of Siena.

"Carrie, I hope you remember your equestrian training, I have several horses and the countryside is beautiful here this time of year. I have never been able to get this big galoot on a horse, but that won't stop you and me," Sammy joked. "John you can lounge by the pool."

Sammy went on to lay out the week she had planned for them.

Her sister's two sons, Jerod, twenty-five, and Richard, twenty-seven, were in country and would be there at the villa for the rest of the week. "Carrie, you will have your hands full of men while you are here, and I refuse to help you, with the exception of keeping this one busy, of course," Sammy smiled wryly.

"Bring 'em on," Carrie said defiantly. "I can conquer the world today."

Sammy laughed and John looked on with a tender smile. His plan for Carrie was working well.

The young men took Carrie on day trips to San Gimignano; Arezzo and Montepulciano; Florence; Lucca, and Pisa and lastly Siena. She marveled at the concentration of old world beauty and charm that filled the Tuscan countryside.

It was ordered that everyone would be back at the villa no later than 6:00 PM for evening cocktails and dinner al fresco, where Carrie would talk at length, until breathless, of the sights she had seen that day. Dinners under the stars on balmy summer evenings were irresistible and the conversations, loosened by the food and wine, were engaging.

"There is more beauty and ambiance here in Tuscany by accident, than I think exists in most places in the modern world combined," Carrie sagely remarked to the group.

"Tuscany was the seat of the Renaissance, so it is no doubt we have more beauty here than most," Sammy added.

Sammy and John spent their days together by the pool, taking short trips to town to buy groceries and fresh baked bread, cured meats, cheeses and fresh vegetables, and making beautiful love in Sammy's breeze-cooled bedroom overlooking her vineyards and the surrounding Chianti countryside.

John had not relaxed to this level in months. "Sammy you have turned me into a jellyfish! I am so relaxed."

"That is a good thing," she said. "All work and no relaxation makes Johnny an uptight man, or haven't you heard?"

John sighed with tranquil joy.

"Do you want to travel around and see some of the sights?" she asked him.

"I have all the sights I can take in here with you in your exquisite, romantic and welcoming bedroom," he answered.

She smiled as he drew her naked body to him and she kissed him hard and long.

The week ended with a trip back to Florence Airport and Sammy holding John's hand in a death grip all the way. John needed to rent a car for the remainder of their stay in Italy.

"I'm sorry, but I hate it when you leave," she said with tears beginning to form on her lower lids. Sammy felt a finality in the parting that she had never felt before.

"Sam, it's not goodbye," John said, embracing her and trying to comfort her. "It is 'see you soon.'"

9

CIAO MIRANDA

Miranda stood at the front door of her walled estate on the stone-walled banks of Lake Como as John's rental car pulled into the long, circular driveway. The old world gardens were immaculately tended by a crew of four gardeners on a full time basis, and it showed. Carrie almost stumbled as she walked, gawking at the lush surroundings.

"Miranda, darling, I'd like you to meet my assistant and traveling companion Carrie Latham," John said.

"I am so happy to meet you," Miranda said in her thick Italian accent, embracing Carrie's shoulders and kissing her on each cheek, European style. "Come in and let's get you settled."

Marble tile floors, stone walls and frescoed ceilings from ages past gave Miranda's home a Renaissance Era atmosphere.

"Do what you need to do and lets all meet on the terrazza in half an hour," Miranda suggested.

Miranda was a very successful avvocatessa (lawyer) in her early years. She handled all of John's legal dealings in Italy when Double O started operations there and had continued working with them through the years. She later went into politics where she was also very effective. She enjoyed entertaining and opened her home to John and Carrie unreservedly.

Three days of eating, swimming and private boat trips up and down the beautiful lake visiting Como, Villa de Este, Grand Hotel Termezzo Palace, Villa del Balbianello, Villa Carlotta and Villa Serbilloni in Bellagio were eye-opening testaments to the grandeur of glorious times gone by, all thankfully preserved from the ravages of war. Carrie felt as though she was living in another time and John could see that she was basking in the old world traditions and grandeur.

"Miranda, everything here feels so solid, lasting and permanent. How old is this house?" Carrie asked.

"It was started in 1585 by a bygone family member, and has been built and rebuilt many times to become what you see today. It was one of the first structures built on the lake, and its gardens are world renowned. I am obligated to keep the property in perfect condition at all times. It survived the wars and you are correct, it does give you the sense of sturdiness, strength, resilience, permanence and durability," Miranda agreed.

"Some of the art you see on the walls is over three hundred years old. That is over seventy years older than the United States itself!" Miranda said. "The tapestries are older than that, and over the years our family has collected much of the Roman period statuary you see in the gardens."

"Do you live here year around?" Carrie asked.

"I didn't until recently," Miranda answered. "My law practice was in Milan, where I made my permanent home and came here only for the summer. I retired and moved here permanently two years ago."

"Miranda, darling," John said, kissing her and caressing her nakedness. "Tomorrow we must go. You have been a perfect hostess, and I know Carrie has enjoyed her stay with you."

"When and how did Carrie enter your life?" Miranda asked as she rolled over on her side to face him and toy with the graying hairs on his chest.

John explained his relationship with Carrie and her deceased daughter, and the fact that he wanted Carrie to grow and live a successful life after losing everything she had and wanting not to go on.

"That poor girl," Miranda said.

"Actually she is a very resilient young lady, and you shouldn't feel sorry for her," John answered. "She has picked herself up again on this trip, and has found renewed enjoyment in life. I see her as a daughter."

Miranda waved goodbye from her front porch as John drove off toward Milan to intersect the E70 which would take them to Venice. Carrie looked back through the rear window and noticed Miranda wiping her eyes with a tissue.

10

ALONE AT LAST

In Venice they stayed at the Hotel Danieli on the Grand Canal and visited all of the sights. Hand in hand they walked through Saint Mark's Square and Saint Mark's Basilica and Ducal Palace; where from the thirteenth century on the powerful Doges had made their presence known through banking, power broking and the arts.

Breakfast in bed, lunches from twelve noon to two and three in the afternoon, dinner at nine or ten at night at Ristorante Terrazza Danieli, walks along the Grand Canal, boat trips to Murano and Gondola rides through the somewhat fetid canals were all a wonder to Carrie. She enjoyed three beautiful days alone with John before heading off to Sitges and Mijas, Spain. Carrie enjoyed the chance to monopolize John's time, not having to share him with one of his beautiful lady friends.

In Spain, John wanted Carrie to see how the beautiful young people lived in Sitges (pronounced Seeches) with three days in the sun on the Gold Coast beaches. They roughed it in a suite near the beach at the four-star Hotel Alenti, and sunbathed on the somewhat crowded seashore. Beach boys gathered chaise lounges, umbrellas and cool drinks for the visitors for tips. The majority of the young girls and women wore only their bikini bottoms and frolicked gaily on the sandy tracts, wind surfing and playing volleyball, badminton and Frisbee. Carrie joined in whole heartedly and John took it all in stride. She thought it must be his worldliness and his worldly women, but she felt extremely comfortable with him being at her side.

Many of the young men looked at John with wry smiles as if to say 'dirty old man', but John smiled right back behind his aviator sunglasses as if to say 'eat your hearts out'. Their bodies were taking on the beautiful color produced only by the Gold Coast's sun, a rich golden brown.

They dined, al fresco, at Ristorante Mare Nostrum where Carrie was introduced to a marvelous selection of Mediterranean seafood. She was also introduced to Andalusian Salad, which consisted simply of two nearly over-ripe Roma tomato halves, four large, pungent Italian garlic cloves, three slices of grilled country crostini and salt.

"First you rub the top of the bread with a garlic clove like this," John instructed, covering the entire slice, wearing the whole clove down to a nub. "Then you rub the bread with the sliced end of the tomato half until the bread turns a rich pink color. Then you sprinkle a little salt on top and *voila*, Andalusian Salad."

"My God John, this is such a wonderful taste," Carrie raved. "Phew, the garlic will ward off everything though."

"The Italians, Spaniards, and the Greeks do amazing things with tomato, garlic and fresh baked bread, a cucumber, olive oil and Feta," he said.

"We are going to have to start jogging in the mornings," Carrie announced. "I'm beginning to feel a little tightness at my beltline."

"You are on, because I'm having the same feelings. We start tomorrow," John agreed.

11

HOLA GABRIELA

Further down the Gold Coast toward Marbella, they spent the remainder of the week with Gabriela Garcia Montoya at her hillside villa near Mijas, nestled in the hills overlooking the port villages of Fuengirola and Torremolinos to the north.

Gabriela was a fiery Spanish lady of classic Castilian beauty. Her jet black wavy hair, rich olive skin and black eyes gave her an air of elegant excitement. She had been one of Spain's top models in her younger days, and later became a very popular television actress. John had been at Torremolinos on vacation many years back when he met Gabriela at a party at a friend's house.

She greeted John and Carrie on horseback at the front gate of her rambling six hundred acre estate of olive trees, grazing pastures and vineyards. She cantered, sitting the horse perfectly, just ahead of John's limo, up a winding gravel road to a whitewashed Spanish villa, perched on top of the highest hill in her realm. She dismounted at the front entrance of her beautiful home where a stable hand took her horse away at a trot.

"Gabby, Gabby! You are a vision," John said, arms outstretched, inviting an embrace.

"Juan, que maravilla es verte," Gabriela greeted in Castilian Spanish.

"English, Gabriela, I have forgotten almost every word you taught me," John confessed as they warmly embraced. "Except 'yo pierde mi amor.'"

Carrie picked up on the 'mi amor,' remembering her high school Spanish.

"Gabriela, please meet my assistant and traveling companion, Carrie Latham," John said.

"A great pleasure," Gabriela said in a heavy Spanish accent, offering both her hands and, in European style, kissing Carrie on both cheeks. "Please come in," She ushered John and Carrie into her stately home. "Let us go out to the veranda for a cool drink."

"Do I call you Gabriela or Gabby?" Carrie asked.

"My Juanito is the one who gave me that name, and he is the only one I know who calls me that. I love it when he calls me Gabby, it is so American. When I hear that name I know he is here with me, do you know what I mean. You may use whichever name you feel comfortable with," she answered.

Gabriela walked ahead of them, her spurred riding boots clapping on the Spanish tile floor like flamenco shoes, spurs jingling like the bangles on a dancer's wrists.

She swung around as she reached the sitting area, and waved her arm, gesturing for them to sit.

"Gabriela, what is that in the haze off to the south?" Carrie asked.

Shading her eyes and peering far into the horizon she said, "Believe it or not that is Ceuta, Morocco, North Africa; it is a particularly clear day today, no?"

The houseboy arrived with a pitcher of Sangria and tapas as they sat.

"How long will you stay, John?" Gabriela asked.

"Long enough to see your beautiful countryside and short enough not to overstay our welcome," John replied tactfully.

"Then you must give me at least one day's notice before you wish to leave, it is your choice," Gabriela said, reflecting her rich Castilian spirit of gracious hospitality. "You may stay as long as you wish."

John smiled and sipped his Sangria.

"Careful with this elixir Carrie, it has a way of sneaking up on you," John warned. "Especially on a warm afternoon like today."

"John, before dinner this evening, I would like us to go down to the square in Feungirola and stroll the paseo, it is particularly beautiful this time of year. I think Carrie might enjoy it."

John escorted both Gabriela and Carrie, one on each arm, as they walked around the market square, the lights in the trees illuminating their way, Spanish music wafting through the arboreal tree branches caressing their ears, smells of food and the sea air filling their nostrils. Señoras pushing baby carts, proudly smiling as they passed; niños y niñas running in the grass as parents looked on; young lovers caressing on benches without care or shame, a panorama of Spanish life paraded by.

Gabriela's driver picked them up at the end of their walk and drove them back up to the villa where a sumptuous dinner awaited them on the partially moonlit veranda. A large Paella pan filled the center of the thick, solid oak round table, with small tapas plates of olives, cheeses, salads and breads placed all around the candelabra lighted offering, everything within easy reach.

"Paella is our signature Spanish dish Carrie. It is chicken, chorizo, shrimp, how you say *langouste*, mussels and clams in a bed of saffron and tomato rice," Gabriela said.

"Lobster," Carrie said, answering Gabriela's question. "It looks marvelous; I can't wait to try it."

"These are my aceitunas--olives," Gabriela said. "We grow them mainly for the oil, but we also cure and finish them here at the villa."

"They are delicious, do you market them?" Carrie asked.

"Only locally, to the better restaurants and tapas bars," Gabriela said.

After dinner, Carrie begged off to bed for a read, leaving John and Gabriela to themselves on the veranda. An hour or so later Carrie heard the two of them enter Gabriela's room for the night.

Gabriela took John and Carrie on yacht trips, to the bullfights, and organized picnics in the hillsides where John relaxed in the Andalusian sun as Gabriela and Carrie rode horses through the vast countryside. Carrie wore one piece bathing suits in deference to Gabriela's propriety. Even though Gabriela still had her model's figure, she was very dignified and suitably dressed at all times.

Their last day and evening were spent on Gabriela's three million euro yacht, cruising up and down the Gold Coast and stopping for dinner onboard in Fuengirola harbor. The captain and crew was a young Australian couple, Alan and Glenys, who worked for Gabriela the entire sailing season and then returned to Brisbane for the summer season there, escorting divers on the Great Barrier Reef near Townsville. They were fun-loving, hard-working people, bent on making John and Carrie's cruise one to remember.

The next morning, Gabriela had her driver take them all to Malaga International Airport, a seventeen mile trip back up the Spanish coast. Gabriela uncharacteristically threw her arms around John's shoulders and kissed him goodbye. For some reason she thought this might be the last time she would see him. Her woman's intuition sensed a settling in his manner.

Gabriela embraced Carrie and said, "Juanito, take good care of this one, she is the best." She winked at John, and turned back to the waiting car as John and Carrie were escorted to the Olympic Air lounge.

12

Χαιρετώ SOPHIA

There was one last stop on their European trip, Samos in the Greek Islands. Their hostess was Sophia Eleni Stavros, a leggy Greek beauty who was obviously one of John's longtime lovers.

Sophia's father, Demetrios Papadakis, was a big presence in the shipping world. He had a fueling and outfitting concession at most of the Aegean ports of call. John's father, JT III, had done business with him for years and had taken a liking to the jovial, hardworking, hard living Greek. JT introduced him to the Papadakis family on one of their trips together and John and Sophia had hit it off from a very early start, remaining sophisticated lovers over the years.

She was alive and vibrant, like her father, and stunningly beautiful, like her mother.

She had been unlucky in love, losing her husband in a terrible light plane crash only two years after they were married. She vowed not to remarry and she raised her son Christos alone. Her parents loved them dearly and protected them from the hardships of life. She inherited her father's two billion euro business and ran it for years with the same iron fist her father had wielded. She recently sold the business as Christos had no interest. She made sure that the concessions that Double O had been given by her father were carried on by the new owners, a gesture John was thankful for.

She had a vast villa that hung on the edge of the rocky western hillside overlooking the town and harbor below. The thick stone and white plastered walls had been hand raised a century before. Even on the hottest of days, the house was cool and airy.

The ambiance was splendid and Carrie felt rich and opulent. She swam in the crystal clear Aegean and sunbathed in the warmth of the Greco-Turkish sun. Sophia's handsome, twenty-three-year-old son Christos kept her busy motorcycling around the island, eating and dancing at the local restaurants. Ouzo made her head spin, but she soon became an aficionada.

For the five days they were on Samos, John and Sophia never left the βίλα (pronounced veela). They sunned, swam at the private beach near the house, talked, ate and made beautiful love. Like John's other lovers, Sophia also sensed that this might be John's last trip to her Aegean paradise.

"So good of you and Christos to share your beautiful home with us. I have had an unforgettable time," Carrie said, embracing Sophia and her son Christos, three years her junior.

"You are most welcome my dear. Take care of my Γιαννάκης (pronounced Yaneece, meaning Johnny)."

John and Carrie stood waiting on the pier for the private sea shuttle back to Athens. Carrie stood with her arms around John's waist hugging him, and he stood looking up the far cliffside at Sophia's magnificent villa. Sophia stood at the railing of her veranda, hair and dress blowing in the breeze, arm raised in a wave. John returned the wave and a sense of finality gripped him.

13

TIBURON - I LOVE YOU, MY SWEET, DEAR FATHER

At Athens International Airport they boarded a Swiss Air flight to Zurich and from there a flight to San Francisco. John particularly liked the Swiss Air flights. The crew was overly courteous and efficient, the food and the beverages were of exceptional quality and the first class passengers were seasoned and astute travelers, knowing what to do and when.

Carrie could not believe that she was being asked by the stewardess to use the rest room to change into the airline provided pajamas. She settled in and the next thing she knew she was being awakened by the same stewardess to prepare for breakfast and landing. Carrie knew she would remember the trip for a lifetime. John had a limousine waiting at SFO to take them to Tiburon.

"Is this the famous Golden Gate Bridge?" Carrie asked John on the way.

"It is, and over there, just on the other side, is Tiburon," John replied.

"John, what a beautiful home," Carrie said

"For the last thirty years I have enjoyed it Carrie, and I want to share it with you now. You should feel that this is your home as well. Something has come over me these last few weeks, and I want you to know how much you mean to me. My generosity has not been entirely unselfish."

She looked at him questioningly. There was nothing more this man could possibly do for her or give her. *Where was his selfishness?*, she thought.

"Why have you settled here, rather than one of the east coast areas like the Hamptons or Cape Cod? This seems so removed from the rest of your life," Carrie asked.

"You have hit the nail on the head again. I needed to be removed from my life on occasion. In this day and age of communication, however, you are never fully removed from your life, but at the time I first moved here I felt completely isolated from everything. It was and still is my haven." He went on to explain that constantly traveling around the world, living out of suitcases, hotels, airplanes and shuttles takes an emotional toll as well as a physical one. "The need to root is inherent in all of us, some more, some less. One week here, for me, carries me mentally through the months and months that normally follow," John explained. "Eventually I will retire here."

"Do you feel that your life is whole?" Carrie asked.

He looked her straight in the eye and said, "The first time in my life I felt whole was the day I held your little girl's hand in the chemotherapy room in New York," his bottom lids welled.

She looked at him with a knowing smile and stroked his hair. He had just confessed to her something he had never divulged to any of his lovers. She was reverential of his openness and felt highly honored to be his confessor.

"Enough of this deep chatter," John said. "We came here for a reason, let's get on with it."

For two weeks, John sailed her and flew her around his beloved Tiburon. She saw a homey side of him that she had never seen before. This was obviously the place he felt most relaxed, most safe and most himself.

One night, out on John's veranda, overlooking Paradise Cove, she looked over at him and asked, "What about all of your lady friends? How do you all cope?"

"If you noticed, all of the ladies I introduced you to are self-supporting, gregarious, resourceful, capable and very successful women. To a woman, none of my independent, free acting lovers wanted kept men or hangers-on. Several, like Sammy, Gabriela and Sophia, have inherited wealth, but all of them have used their wealth wisely and have, selfishly or not, placed their business lives above their personal lives. Although I came close many times, I never asked any of them to marry me. I think that would have been the end of our relationships," John explained. "I am cut from the same cloth. I have always placed Double O above self, and I have done it with joy and can think of no more fulfilling or rewarding a lifestyle."

"Was there ever one that you held in higher regard than the others?" Carrie continued to probe.

"Yes and no. All in my flock are sovereign souls. I admire and respect each one for different reasons, but being of the same breed I see them all as lovers. When we are together it is as though we have never parted. It is difficult to explain, but I love them all equally, with the exception of Jennifer Middleton. For some reason that I don't fully yet understand, she holds a special place in my heart, has since the first time I met her on that Iran Air flight from New York to Tehran, nearly twenty-one years ago," John said.

Carrie reached across to John and grasped his hand, then squeezed and said, "This whole trip I have marveled at the relationships you exposed to me. I could see that you were completely with each different person, and when it was time to leave it was always a very clean break."

"It has to be. I know it and they know it. Can you imagine the misery we would have to bear if it was any other way?" John concluded. "I know full well that I am not the only man in their lives," he said. "It's getting late and tomorrow it's back to the salt mines and seeing how the working people live," John joked. "We have an early start in the morning. Are you packed and ready?"

"I'm sad to say that I am," Carrie sighed.

They rose from the chaise lounge and John went through his ritual closing down of the house for the night. They went upstairs and each their separate way to bed.

John lay on his side, back to the door, reminiscing about the trip. He knew it was a good thing that he had done for Carrie and he felt that Carrie was fully back in control of her life.

The door opened quietly behind him and Carrie walked in wearing nothing. She slinked into bed and put her arms around his chest and pulled herself firmly to him. John was at first stunned by feeling her naked body against him, but quickly pulled himself together.

"Carrie, what's going on? Are you okay?" he asked softly over his shoulder.

"These last seven weeks have been undeniably the most wonderful time of my life. I have grown to love you as the father you want to be, but the woman in me has also emerged and is conflicted with the daughter you want me to be," she said almost as if rehearsed. "My desire to give myself to you stems from an overabundance of inner confusion I have regarding my feelings for you."

He lay there motionless. A moment or two later he turned toward her and drew her to him with his still powerful arms.

"Your offer is more than any man could possibly imagine. You are a beautiful, sexy, saucy, smart and oh-so-desirable young woman, and as I have said, if I were thirty years younger, you wouldn't have a chance of getting away from me," John put forward.

John's eyes began to tear. "We will have this nearly naked embrace together, and we will remember it as a confused yet joyous, warm and close yet filial moment and will always cherish it in our thoughts. Your embrace is the entire gift I need, and I want you to know that I love you with every fiber. You have made me so proud and I can't wait to watch your continued growth," John said, whispering into her ear.

Carrie kissed him on the lips firmly and moved to leave. She started to proudly and sexily get up and walk out when she reached the door and turned to him. "I love you my sweet, dear father," and she softly closed the door behind her.

On the flight back to New York John leaned over to Carrie. "There is something I want to propose to you, and you need not answer me now."

"What can be so serious?" Carrie asked, leaning forward.

"Everyone who has met you has told me how highly they regard you. You have managed to join my family and seamlessly have become an important part of it. I love you like a daughter as you know, and I have an overwhelming desire to have you in my life and care for you. For many reasons, financial coming first to mind, I think it would be most beneficial for both of us if I were to formally adopt you and give you my name if you want it. Your future would be sealed. You would be a woman of wealth beyond your imaginings, and I would be the proudest father I know," John said.

Carrie fell back into her seat and looked up at the ceiling. Within moments, she bounced forward again and took John's hand.

"There is no need for me to think about your wonderful proposal. I can think of no other person in my life now who is more meaningful to me than you, and being able to call you my father would definitely put everything back into perfect order for me. To hug you on Father's Day, to curl up with you on Christmas morning, to walk down the aisle with you, to proudly bring you grandchildren. I have dreamt of fulfilling this one need, this void, all my life. I had no father growing up, as you know, only an overworked, functioning alcoholic mother who still has no idea where I live or if I am even alive. She disowned me when I got pregnant," she kissed his hand and held it to her cheek. "Thank you," was all she could say before the tears choked off her words.

"I'll have our attorney begin the process tomorrow. Bless you. You have completed my life," John said. "We can announce our decision at our next family get together."

14

BACK IN THE SADDLE AGAIN

JT was the first to meet John and Carrie back at the New York office.

"Well I see you have taken over my office in fine fashion," John remarked.

"You taught me well. 'The first thing you do is snag the biggest office,' your words exactly. Your new office is completed and ready as well by the way," JT returned. "I can see, by your San Tropez tans, your trip was a howling success."

"We had a marvelous time, and you were absolutely correct. He does know everybody, he has been everywhere and he really does know how to travel in style. I've had the time of my life, and I wouldn't trade one second of our time together," Carrie said, looking knowingly and lovingly up into John's eyes.

The three talked at length about the trip, where they went and who they met. JT was a little surprised at the news that his uncle had taken Carrie to Tiburon, his sanctuary. JT knew that John traveled west to get away from the rigors of the Double O presidency, and rarely shared his off time with anyone, not even his lady friends. *Very strange indeed,* he thought to himself.

"Well I think it's about time you both got back to work," JT said in a mock huff. "But first, I have a proposition for you Carrie. I'm just going to blurt this out; I don't know any other way. I would like you to be my assistant if that is acceptable to you. It comes with a substantial increase in salary, but there is substantially more responsibility that goes with it."

"If it is okay with you two, I'm going home to clean up and shake off some of this travel dust," John interrupted. "I'll leave you two to your working life misery." They hugged and John left the room.

"JT, I would be honored to take the position, assuming your father is agreeable to letting me leave his accounting staff. I think that you and I have clicked, and I believe we will work well together," Carrie responded.

"Marvelous!" JT said. "I knew from the first time we met that I wanted you for the job. It has been a little hectic around here for the last seven weeks waiting for you to return. It will be good to start to bring some order to this office. By the way, it took some effort and I even had to pull a little rank, but Dad has reluctantly agreed to let you go."

"I can see by this mess that you must have some really festering saddle sores," she joked, pointing to the stacks of files and boxes strewn around the desk and office.

"Neatness and orderliness are not my strong suits," JT needlessly confessed.

JT and Carrie spent the remainder of the day discussing JT's expectations and Carrie's wants and needs to carry out her tasks as assistant to the president. She was very interested to see how decisive, open-minded, knowledgeable and commanding JT was. She was amazed by his knowledge of the shipping world and the position that Double O held in it. She felt very comfortable with her tall, handsome and brilliant new boss. Evidently, the Wingate genes flowed strongly in his veins.

"Carrie, your office is the one next to mine through that private door. There is a second door for you to use when you don't want to deal with me. You are not to take on any reception or secretarial responsibilities except in dire emergencies, and I mean that. I have gathered several pamphlets and publications documenting the company's history, business plan and mission statement along with the current financials. I'd like you to absorb them as soon as possible and then I will introduce you to all the people I work with and the companies we do business with. You will accompany me on the majority of my business trips and meetings, especially in the beginning," JT said. "I'm going to give you a crash course on Double O, and there will be a test later!" JT finished with a smile.

Carrie dove into the challenge with abandon. The world of bankers, mega-construction companies, ship builders, ship repairers, harbor masters, politicos and regulators was astounding to Carrie. She and JT went on numerous trips, both home and abroad, and met some very interesting and prominent people.

Carrie saw that it would be necessary for her to become his eyes, ears, heart and soul. She would need to attend meetings alone if JT couldn't, entertain clients, make presentations to prospective clients and participate at shipping industry expositions. He even expected her to wine and dine clients and their families and employees.

She had, all of a sudden, found herself in a position where she couldn't wait to get to the office and perform.

Many nights, she would stay late and study the books to learn all she could about the activities of Double O and its various clients. She studied shipping rules and regulations, protocols, maritime law and rules on the high seas. She studied world geography and knew the location of virtually every port Double O ships entered. She put push pins in a world map identifying every port of call Double O used and hung it on the wall for instant reference. She would stay up working past one in the morning and still be refreshed and ready for the following day.

There was only one personal routine that she refused to break, her morning runs through Central Park, which more often than not she would do with John at their usual time. She rose at six am, dressed in her running clothes and the two headed off to the park before sunrise.

"How is the new job going Carrie?" John asked as they jogged along the well-lit pathways.

"I like it very much," she said. "In the last three months I have learned more about this old world than I had in the previous twenty five years combined. What a journey."

"It is a life-long Wingate journey, and JT has it in his blood as thickly as I have and my father before me had. I am happy to see your interest level. I look up at your office window each night as I go home and smile."

15

JT AND CARRIE

Three months into her new job, Carrie was in full control of the president's office. JT was impressed with the speed with which she had taken over, and let her know in some way or another on an almost daily basis how much he respected her and marveled at her capabilities. With John's blessing, she had since moved out of his apartment into her own, which was nearer to the office. She was happy, independent, prosperous and growing by leaps and bounds.

"Carrie, if this comes as a shock to you, then forget what I am about to say," JT said somewhat nervously to Carrie, who stood surprised and confused in front of his sprawling desk. "I would like to take you to dinner."

"I would love to have dinner with you," Carrie replied. "I think it is perfectly appropriate for presidents and their assistants to dine together on occasion." They had eaten together many times on their various trips, but always with others in attendance. This was the first time he had asked her for the sole purpose of spending time with just her.

"Right you are," JT said, somewhat relieved. "Would this evening be acceptable to you?" he asked, almost reticently.

"Ahhh, certainly," Carrie replied in a girlish, almost giddy voice. She had a date with girlfriends that she could easily bow out of.

"Great, I'll pick you up at seven."

Carrie walked out of JT's office, her heart beating more rapidly than it should. Where had this come from? She couldn't wait for the evening to begin.

At the Capitol Grill, which was sandwiched between skyscrapers on 42nd Street just a mile from the office, the valet took JT's car. JT seated Carrie at their table and walked around to his right, seating himself a little nervously. Carrie was dressed in the black, mid-thigh length body hugging cocktail dress that John had purchased for their trip. She was striking, and JT, like most of the other males in the restaurant, couldn't take his eyes off of her.

"May I say you look extraordinary this evening?" JT began.

"Well thank you sir," Carrie beamed. "A girl always likes to hear that."

They dined and talked and laughed and smiled together the entire evening. JT was dazzled by Carrie's wit, intellect and charm. For a first date, JT thought, Carrie seemed very composed and relaxed. He, on the other hand, was antsy and wasn't sure if it showed or not.

They talked very little about work, and for most of the conversation JT directed questions like "What are your favorite things to do when you are not at work?", and "Do you like Broadway shows?" "Do you have a lot of girlfriends?" Her answers were lengthy and complete. It was as if she wanted JT to know all about her. He, on the other hand, stayed fairly private with his answers when she countered with similar questions, and was open only as far as he knew how to be. He wasn't hiding things, he just wasn't embellishing.

"An amazing meal and wonderful conversation," Carrie said as she finished her crème brule. "If you will excuse me, I need to visit the ladies' room."

JT almost toppled his chair trying to stand, and she smiled over her shoulder as she walked off. *Is he a little nervous?*, she questioned. *Is that a good thing or a bad thing?* She hadn't dated in ages, and had trouble reading the signs. She did notice, however, that she was very happy and satisfied, and that certainly had to be a good sign.

On the way home, JT couldn't help but notice the lovely turn of Carrie's runner's thighs, calves and ankles. Her scent was light but heady, reminiscent of his mother's perfume. He now felt more relaxed and at ease and he knew it was her demeanor that put him there.

At her door she thanked him for a wonderful evening.

"I would like to do this again very soon," he said probingly.

"If you feel it appropriate, I would like that very much as well," she replied.

She playfully kissed him on the cheek, bounced into her apartment and closed the door.

The whirlwind had begun.

Within two months JT was seeing Carrie two or three times a week and one evening he invited her to his country home for the weekend. JT had several riding horses and asked Carrie if she would like to try.

"That sounds like fun," she said. She knew this would be a defining time together; it was their first over-night date.

They went to the stables and JT saddled their horses as Carrie, seemingly a novice, looked on. With the chores completed, JT helped Carrie onto her horse. JT made a last few adjustments to her stirrups as she adjusted the reins and sat the horse perfectly. They exited the barn and started off at a walk toward the riding trails. Once on the trail, Carrie picked up the pace to a trot, and JT followed behind. He slowly moved up beside her, but before he could, she broke into a gallop and sped away. JT watched her ride off in amazement. Was there nothing in which this woman wasn't skilled?

"Where did you learn to ride like that?" JT asked, catching up to her.

"John has a friend," Carrie answered.

"Say no more, I get it," JT interrupted. "I should have guessed."

The day went well and JT cooked Carrie a delightful meal of filet mignon, mushrooms and onions, asparagus and baked potatoes with a marvelous Pinot Noir. It was a hearty, masculine repast.

"You Wingate boys are quite the chefs," Carrie toyed, playfully rubbing her tummy.

They finished their meal, cleaned up together and JT took Carrie's hand and led her out to the porch where he sat with her on the porch swing finishing their wine.

"What a beautiful day and evening JT, thanks for sharing your private place with me. I'm enthralled, impressed and delighted."

JT leaned in and kissed her firmly on the mouth. She kissed him back and nuzzled her head into his neck, smiling to herself. They rocked back and forth in silence. Carrie finally got up and took JT by the hand and led him to the bedroom. She slowly took off her clothes and slithered onto the bed. JT gazed at her remarkable nakedness as he, clumsily, took off his clothes and got on the bed beside her. She took his hand and placed it on her firm, pert, still fully tanned breast. He caressed her and kissed her from head to toe. Their bodies intertwined as one and they made passionate love long into the night.

Carrie rose late the next morning, stretched and went naked to the window to open the curtains. JT, on one elbow, watched in wonder of her aura, beauty and self-confidence.

"Come back to bed," he pleaded.

She playfully ran to him and pounced on him. "I bet I can pin you in thirty seconds," she said, giddy with happiness.

"You're on."

They wrestled playfully in their nakedness and she finally cried 'uncle' and kissed him hard on the mouth. They got up several hours later.

"Don't you think we should do something today?" JT asked.

"I thought we had been 'doing something,'" she retorted in a sassy voice. "Where have you been?" she accentuated with a broad smile.

The relationship was changing, and both of them felt it.

They decided to go horseback riding again and went to the barn to saddle the horses. John was acting a little sheepish as they went into the barn. He went for his saddle as Carrie approached hers. On her saddle was a small black velvet box with a big, bright and silky red bow. She was hesitant to touch it, but finally picked it up. Inside was a heart shaped, blood-red, six carat, diamond studded, crystal-clear ruby in a twenty-four-carat gold setting.

"Oh my, JT, it is stunning, thank you so much!" she cried, throwing her arms around his neck. "What's the occasion?" she asked.

"It is the occasion of me giving you my heart," he said, romancing her further. "I want you to know that I am hopelessly and helplessly smitten, a lovesick school boy, and I have been ever since my uncle's step down party. I hope you will wear it often."

She kissed him again and put it on the ring finger of her right hand, promising to wear it always.

The weekend was a complete success and JT told her he loved her several times, holding hands across the console of his XJ8 Jaguar, smiling and happy, on the way back to the city.

For the next six months their relationship flourished. They took trips together to the country, spent several weekends in the Bahamas and spent most evenings at one or the other's apartment after their ten to twelve hour stints at the office. They couldn't get enough of each other's company.

On one particularly late working evening, JT and Carrie strolled up the street to Henri's for a late dinner. Henri greeted them warmly and led them to their table. They were becoming very regular guests. At their usual table there was a small vase with a single red and a single white rose. Carrie knew the meaning of the pair of roses but had never seen that particular arrangement at Henri's before, and she was curious.

No menu was offered, and Henri served cocktails with a small plate of deliciously prepared calamari. Again Carrie was curious, but JT seemed to be expecting the service.

"Since when have you been a Cosmo fan?" Carrie asked JT.

"Since tonight I guess, Henri is running the show," JT answered. "I called him and told him it was his choice for everything."

They completed the calamari, and Henri brought a small niçoise salad with a glass of chilled Pinot Gris.

Next Henri brought an entrée of beef loin medallions with black truffle butter, fingerling potatoes and French green beans. A tasty beef stock reduction with sautéed Baby Bell mushrooms accompanied the beef, as did a rare, twelve year old bottle of 1990 Beaulieu Vineyards George de Latour Private Reserve Cabernet Sauvignon.

"Wow, this is splendid," Carrie smiled, beginning to feel the alcohol. "You really don't even have to chew this meat. It is melting in my mouth."

"It is wonderful isn't it?" JT answered. "Henri knows his business."

"How is everything so far?" Henri asked as he neared the table.

"You have outdone yourself as usual Henri. Compliments to the chef," JT answered.

"My comments exactly," Carrie echoed.

"Your choice for desert tonight is crème brule or chocolate soufflé," Henri said, nodding and smiling at their praise.

"I couldn't eat another bite," Carrie announced.

"I'll have the chocolate soufflé, and bring two spoons just in case," JT said.

"Very good," Henri said. He winked at JT and was off to the kitchen.

JT explained to Carrie that Henri cooked his desserts from scratch, to order, and it would take at least twenty minutes to return with the sweet course. They had plenty of time to finish their entrees and wine.

They chatted lightly and relished the perfectly cooked chateaubriand in savory mushroom sauce.

Finally Henri returned with a bottle of Moet & Chandon, Dom Pérignon and the dessert, and a second plate with a small silver dome cover which he placed close to Carrie. He ceremoniously popped the champagne cork and filled their glasses.

"Enjoy," was Henri's one word wish as he left the two alone to enjoy the remainder of their evening.

JT held up his glass. "To John for introducing us, to the Gods for bringing us together and to the smartest, most beautiful woman I know," JT toasted.

The term 'woman' resonated in her already buzzing head, and it brought feelings of belonging, esteem and love deep in her chest. He wanted her as a woman.

"And to the most wonderful man I know," Carrie clinked his glass and drank.

"Let's try the desserts," JT said. "You first."

"I didn't order dessert. Remember?" Carrie said.

"I took the liberty to preorder this especially for you," he said as he pushed the domed plate closer to her.

Carrie put down her champagne glass and tentatively reached for the handle on the dome. Slowly she lifted it, not knowing what might be beneath. She revealed a small black velvet box with a white silk bow.

"Will you please marry me?" JT stammered slightly, reaching for the box, removing the bow and opening it.

The flawless ten carat, emerald cut diamond in a simple platinum setting gleamed out at Carrie. She caught herself in the onset of a swoon and jerked slightly as she looked at JT. Tears started to form in her lower lids. She blinked and reached for JT's face with both hands and kissed him.

"Oh my God, certainly I will marry you!" she quavered slightly as she spoke. "To spend the rest of my life with you would be marvelous …no perfect ….no perfectly marvelous," she said, beaming.

JT removed the ring from its container and placed it on Carrie's left ring finger. She held out both of her hands, showing her ruby promise ring and her diamond engagement ring together.

"You are serious, aren't you?" she said, looking at both of her rings.

"As a train wreck," JT answered, kissing her on the cheek.

"You are going to have to invest in a body guard at this rate darling," she quipped.

"I am your body guard and will be to eternity," JT romanced.

They thanked Henri for the beautiful evening and walked back to the office, and then Charles took them to JT's apartment.

"You Wingates are a bundle of constant wonders," Carrie said to JT as she took his hand in hers. "I vow to you this moment that I will be shocked and amazed every time you feel the need to surprise me."

"Be careful what you wish for, and be prepared. I intend to keep you on your beautiful toes for the rest of your life."

They melted into each other's arms. Carrie slipped into a reverie. So much had happened to her this last year, and she tried to take it all in at once and couldn't. *My God, what more can come from this amazing family?* She thought.

16

THE HONEYMOON'S OVER

John Wingate called his first annual Board Meeting, and JT threw a lavish dinner party afterward for all of the Double O New York executives and their wives. Carrie hosted the dinner with perfection and John praised her in front of the entire group. In a very short period of time, she had engaged the venue, ordered the caterer, the piano, cello and violin trio, the flowers and centerpieces and set the theme of the evening. She concentrated on John and his first annual Board Meeting. She had place cards made with a caricature of a baby boy with a photo of John for a face, saying "There is a first time for everything." Her playfulness didn't go unnoticed.

JT tapped his wine glass and announced he had something to say to the group. "I must be the happiest man on the planet today," he excitedly exclaimed to the gathering. "I have no idea why, but this smart, astute, efficient, drop dead gorgeous assistant of mine has, for some reason, and probably in a moment of weakness, agreed to marry me."

Carrie smiled demurely, did a small curtsy, walked to JT's side, put her arm around his waist, sassily cocked her head on his shoulder and held her engagement ring hand high up in the air, waving it back and forth for all to see.

"We have set a date; you will all get your invitations soon," JT continued. "I'd like you all to join me in a toast to the most beautiful woman in the world, my lover, my assistant and my soon to be wife."

"To the bride," "Here, here" and "Way to go JT" rang out from the crowd. They all rushed to hug her, admire her ring and pat JT on the back.

John sat back in his chair and beamed at JT and Carrie as they danced. *You crafty old bastard,* he said to himself. *I love it when a plan comes together.* He got up to cut in on JT to dance with his protégé. "I am so happy for you my darling daughter. You have made me a very happy, satisfied and smug old man."

"Oh stop," she said. "You are not old, but you are definitely smug. You have had all this in mind all along, haven't you?" she asked in a non-questioning statement.

"I have," came his simple two word answer.

She hugged him warmly and kissed him on the cheek. "Thank you for believing in me."

"Here's to little Jennifer, the sweetest little girl I have ever known, and here's to more little Jennifers to come," he said with a broad smile. "If you can do that, my grand scheme will be complete."

Holding back a sob, she hugged him with all of her strength.

Joe and John Wingate threw a lavish wedding affair for the young, hardworking couple. John proudly walked Carrie down the aisle. He wore his pride on his sleeve. She was beautiful and calm, serene and sexy, glowing and knowing and very happy to have JT as her new husband. John had persuaded her to wear a traditional white wedding gown that Jennifer Middleton had designed and made especially for her.

"It will symbolize the freshness and newness you have created for yourself and have shared with the Wingate family," John had told her.

At the reception, Carrie lit up the room and all of the men wanted to dance with her. They wouldn't let her sit down.

"This is your day sweetheart, and it looks as though you are taking it all in stride," John said to Carrie as they danced.

"I am on cloud nine John, and I don't know if I will ever come down!" she answered.

"Where are you going on your honeymoon?" John pried.

"He is taking me to Tel Aviv and then to Eilat, Israel for a few days, then on to a place called Sharm el-Sheikh in Egypt for scuba diving, something I have always wanted to try. There we are supposed to board one of the company Ro Ro's for a relaxing cruise to Bahrain. The cruise is to take a little over seven days. JT said he has some business there he has to attend to," she answered, smiling. "He also wants to introduce me to the swashbuckling, rumbustious, cavalier side of the Wingate life on the high seas."

John shuddered inwardly, but kept on dancing. He made a mental note to have a talk with JT about his routing.

"I hope you have a grand time, it is a very exotic part of the world. I have sailed it many times in my youth," John smiled down at her.

The time came to leave, and JT and Carrie, now changed into their traveling clothes, ran from the ballroom under a traditional hail of rice and rose petals.

Carrie turned, waved and blew a special kiss to John as Charles opened the rear door of the company Mercedes S600 Sedan for their trip to the airport. John winked at Carrie, who was smiling at him through the rear window. He smiled broadly, proudly and anxiously and waved as the limo left the curb.

The United Airlines flight to Tel Aviv was uneventful, and JT and Carrie rested along the way. They stayed at the Tel Aviv Hilton, their honeymoon suite overlooking the Mediterranean yacht harbor. JT showed her the Holy Land that she had previously only seen in pictures, movies and travel brochures. They visited the Baha'i Gardens in Haifa, Bethlehem, Galilee, Matulla, the Golan Heights, Via Dolorosa,

The Western Wall, Temple Mount, Dome of the Rock, Al Aqsa and Al Sakhrah Mosques, Church of the Holy Sepulcher and Mount Zion. They strolled along Dizengoff Street to see and be seen, ate the local foods and drank the local wine. They visited the diamond district in Ramat Gan, and Carrie flushed from the brilliance of the stones she saw there.

"You know your way around here, don't you?" Carrie said.

"I have been here many times on business over the years. I am always in awe when I come," JT confessed. "There is something about this place."

"You know what I'd like to do next?" Carrie announced. "And don't get me wrong, I have enjoyed all of the sightseeing so far."

"What is that?" JT said.

"I want to go back to our beautiful hotel, get naked and lay out on our balcony," she replied.

"You're on," JT said with an ogling glance.

The next day, the short 240 mile Elal flight from Tel Aviv to Eilat was bumpy and thankfully quick. Eilat's beaches and hotels were lovely and Carrie enjoyed the topless sunbathing, even if JT was initially a little uncomfortable. Sharm el-Sheikh met all of her expectations as well. Scuba diving and snorkeling proved to be very enjoyable sport. The waters were crystal clear and the sea creature assortment was widespread and varied.

The Gulf Queen arrived in port at Sharm el-Sheikh the day before they were supposed to leave. The ship's crew took on fuel, water and fresh provisions and the following morning they boarded the newly renovated RO RO ship. The Gulf Queen had been refitted with all new engines, refurbished and updated staterooms, the latest in sonar and radar and other electronics and completely outfitted with the latest in safe space technology, anti-hijacking detection and defense systems, a precaution John and JT had taken with their entire Middle Eastern fleet and the high cubes that serviced the Arabian Gulf. This was to be the Gulf Queen's shakedown cruise.

The three day cruise down the Red Sea to Djibouti was very re-laxing. Carrie enjoyed the lazy pace of the trip, with the beautiful rock formations, quaint and modern lighthouses and flocks of exotic birds. A novice bird-watcher and bird lover, JT pointed out the White Eye Gulls, Storks, Egrets, Spotted Eagles, Honey Buzzards, Steppe Eagles and Black Kites. Most of the species appeared to be large birds of prey.

The Gulf Queen was just passing Perim Island off the southwest coast of Yemen and venturing into the Arabian Sea and the Gulf of Aden. JT and Carrie were in the wheelhouse when the captain tuned into the pirate alert radio. The announcer was citing the day's activity and said that there were no sightings or activity reported today. JT looked at the captain and asked him to call Combined Task Force 150 and get their take on the pirate activity in route. The captain did so, and reported the area had been quiet for the last week to ten days.

"I also reported our course, speed and current location," the captain said.

"Are we in danger?" Carrie asked, with a worried look on her face.

"The reports say that the area we are traveling has been quiet lately," JT told her. "These waters are always a threat, but the odds of safety are heavily on our side. We are well equipped and prepared. Please don't worry. Last year there were some one hundred and ten pirate attacks of which forty-two were successful, and there were upwards of thirty thousand ship movements through the area for the twelve month period. Forty-two out of thirty thousand is slightly over one tenth of one percent. Pretty slim chance, so please relax and enjoy the cruise," JT said.

"Everything will be fine ma'am," said the Pakistani captain. "I have sailed these waters all my life."

"Thank you for the reassurance, gentlemen," Carrie said with a smile.

The Gulf Queen sailed on for a fourth day, and was now approximately eighty miles south and east of Masirah Island, off the coast of Oman, when JT got a call to come to the wheelhouse.

"Our radar is picking up three blips, approximately two miles off our starboard bow," the captain advised.

"Very good," JT said going to the radar screen. There were three dots in close inverted 'V' formation coming from the direction of Mumbai India, a classic hijacking pirate formation. There was another larger dot a few miles behind the three dots. "Let's kick it up to full speed, and turn hard to port for Masirah Island," JT ordered the captain; the maneuver would place the pirates at their rear, starboard quarter. The pirates would have to chase now, rather than meet nearly head on.

"Yes sir," the captain agreed.

"Captain, don't forget to have the radioman report our new course, position and speed," JT reminded.

Carrie was jarred in the stateroom by the sudden change in speed and direction. She quickly put on a pair of jeans, flannel shirt and tennis shoes and ran up to wheelhouse, leaving her jewelry, Rolex watch and everything else behind in the safe in her haste. She needed to see what was happening.

"Is everything okay dear?" she asked excitedly, entering the bridge and somewhat out of breath.

"Everything is fine sweetie. We have picked up a radar indication, and I have decided to take evasive action for safety's sake," JT said.

"Radar indication of what?" Carrie fired back.

"The dots are a classic pirate attack formation. Here, have a look for yourself. They are about two miles away, and we are now about sixty five nautical miles from Masirah Island off the coast of Oman, here," JT said, pointing to the chart. "They have speed advantage over us, but not much. They can cruise at a top speed of nineteen knots, while our top cruising speed is seventeen and a half to eighteen. If they are pirates, they will catch us eventually, but will have great difficulty boarding us at our top speed. Attempts like this, at these speeds, often times if it is too difficult for them to board, they will call off the chase."

Carrie watched the radar screen intently. She was nervous, but felt safe at JT's side. He was calm, commanding and self-assured. She told herself to be strong and not give JT reason to worry about her.

Suddenly there was a loud crunching and grinding noise from the bow of the ship.

JT looked at the captain as the ship suddenly and rapidly lost speed.

"Forward, starboard engine is out," shouted the captain as he shut power to the engine. "All engines three quarter," he called to the engine room.

"What is our speed?" JT shouted at the captain.

"Thirteen knots sir," the navigator yelled out.

JT glanced at Carrie with a very serious look on his face and told the captain to have all hands man their attack stations.

"Can you squeak any more speed out of her Nabeel?" JT asked.

"She is shuddering even at this speed sir, but if you order it I will try," came the captain's reply.

"No, keep her steady as she goes," JT ordered.

The blips were getting closer at a much faster rate now.

"Captain, call Combined Task Force 150 and give them our position, heading and speed. Let them know we are under imminent attack," JT was still unruffled and thinking straight. "Carrie, with the engine out, we are assured of being attacked. I can imagine what you are thinking right now, but you should know that Somali pirates typically do not harm their victims, their sole purpose is ransom."

"Captain, Combined Task Force 150 reports that the closest help is the USS Roosevelt and she is located just south of Bahrain in the Gulf, some 1200 nautical miles away," the radioman reported.

"Call them and give them our position, course and speed," the captain ordered. "Let them know we are under imminent attack and have lost our forward starboard engine."

17

LIKE BANSHEES THEY CAME

The Somali pirate captain stood braced in the center of his skiff. Though bouncing, lurching and pounding the waves wildly he was able to notice that the ship he was chasing had slowed substantially, and wondered if he wasn't getting into some sort of trap. He thought it would be better to have the mother ship closer at hand in case there was a covert trick being played. He radioed the skiff to his right to go back to the mother ship and help her catch up.

The Somali pirate maintained his top speed and peered through his binoculars at the Gulf Queen. Smoke was streaming through her stacks, and he thought that it was blacker than it should be. This was either going to be the easiest attack he ever made or he was going to be the dupe in some elaborate ploy. He decided to slow down and wait for the mother ship and the third crew to arrive before he continued his assault on the Gulf Queen. He radioed the second skiff to his left to reduce speed to just keep up with the quarry. He scanned the 360° horizon, looking for interlopers and flankers.

JT noticed the speed change in the pursuing boats as well. He too wondered what was going on. He noticed that a skiff that had broken away from the group was now joined with the bigger boat to their rear. Soon he observed that the bigger boat was moving faster toward the forward two skiffs with the third boat following behind, probably in tow.

"Captain, I'm not sure whether or not we should put up a fight. At this speed we are sitting ducks for a pirate and any real resistance we offer could be cause for bloodiness, or end up being bloody. What do you think?" JT asked.

"At the very most, I think I could push another one to two knots out of the three remaining engines. That is still not enough to give them a run for their money. I think that we succumb to their attack with some, but not too much resistance, and hope the USS Roosevelt can get to us in time. Whatever happens, the pirates will have to travel to their home port at our speed, giving us a chance of being rescued."

"I guess it does depend on where the pirates will take us, doesn't it?" JT remarked. He was momentarily upset with himself that he hadn't thought of that.

"Very much so sir," was the captain's reply.

JT noticed that the skiffs and the larger boat were gaining on them again but still at the slower rate. He looked through his binoculars at the attackers. He could make out the two forward skiffs now, and he saw that there were three men in each. He quickly calculated that the total attack force was between ten and twelve, depending on how many were on the larger boat.

"Something is going on with that ship," the pirate captain radioed to the mother ship. "We will attack slowly and cautiously. Skiff two and I will speed up and circle the ship out of rifle range and have a look. Depending on what we see, we will radio you accordingly." The pirate captain had survived many years and many attacks by being cautious, stealthy and wary. In his early days he had seen too many attacks go awry from the use of Khat-fueled cowboy tactics.

The pirate captain noticed that the smoke from the Gulf Queen now burned a more normal gray color. He pushed his skiff to full speed and prepared for the flanking movement.

They gained ground rapidly and began their circling maneuver. They kept circling and looking for any sign that would let them know what was going on. The pirate captain noticed the starboard bow-break was different than the port. It wasn't as strong. He also noticed that the wake was shifted more to port, indicating that the two stern engines were offset slightly starboard, causing the ship to crab to port to compensate for the damaged and inoperative starboard bow engine.

Pleased with his analysis of the situation, he announced to his crews, "I think they may have lost their starboard bow engine." He radioed back to the mother ship and the other skiffs. "We will mount a standard attack. We will re-group, and skiffs two and three will attack from starboard and stern, and I will attack from port," he commanded. "Mother ship is to keep up with us and all-out attack if this proves to be some sort of ruse."

"Let's go all out full with the remaining three engines and give them the impression we are trying to get away. Set the anti-boarding devices (ABD's). Deploy the long range acoustic anti-boarding devices (LRAABDs)," the captain ordered. "Turn on the water cannons and activate the slippery foam dispensers. At my order, deploy the razor wire fence canisters," he confidently ordered.

All of the defense systems were passive and, with the exception of the razor wire, they were frustrating and debilitating rather than life threatening. The industry rationale was that taking the humane approach would inspire humanity in the pirate aggressors.

JT was impressed with his captain's knowledge of the available deterrent systems with which the Gulf Queen had been armed. The canisters, when deployed, formed a razor wire wall on the side of the ship that made climbing onto the ship very risky, treacherous and much more difficult. The long range acoustic device produced a loud, high-pitched noise that was above the average human's hearing range and induced severe pain. They were typically destroyed by gunfire very quickly because of their size and the requirement that they be placed in a wide open location within the line of sight of the attacker. The water cannons sprayed a two-inch diameter, high pressure, gyrating stream of sea water and mist which made it very difficult for the pirates to see and stung their eyes. All of the systems were non-lethal.

"Captain, I am remaining in the wheelhouse," JT said.

"I am staying with you JT, whatever happens, I want to be at your side," Carrie insisted.

The captain called to two of the men in the wheelhouse to each grab a dazzle gun and be prepared to use them if the pirates were able to get beyond the other ABD's and seize the upper hand.

"Deploy canisters, all non-essential crew go to the safe room and batten down," the captain ordered.

18

THE ARABIAN SEA, EXOTIC NO MORE

"Attack, attack!" the pirate captain screamed into his radio. As the LAABD's came on, he ordered everyone to quickly use their ear plugs. He was prepared for this eventuality after having been thwarted once before. They circled the ship like the Indians of the Old West, looking for weakness in the ship's defense systems. "Skiffs two and three pull down the razor wire with your gaff hooks."

This was a very dangerous maneuver. The razor wire nets could pull away, and if the pirate skiff was in the way it could blanket the skiff and rip the skin from anyone beneath. It had to be done very carefully and the skiffs needed to stay upstream of the razor wire nets at all times.

The two Gulf Queen crew members came out on deck and fired their dazzle guns at the approaching skiffs. The skiffs had to drop back and reorganize themselves. The pirates put on very dark glass goggles which drastically decreased their vision but greatly diminished the adverse effect of the dazzle guns and the salt water spray. They made a second run at the Gulf Queen, this time successfully ripping down one razor wire canister from each side of the ship. One of the canisters of wire came down on top of skiff number two and seriously cut two of the pirates, forcing the skiff to retreat back to the mother ship. The attackers were down to six men, four of whom could board.

"Skiff three, take skiff two's place," the captain screamed into his radio above the din of his and the Gulf Queen's straining engines as he positioned himself for a stern assault. Bow and wake spray, ABD spray, engine smoke and churning wakes seemed to make the attack impossible, but the modest pirate skiffs, sailed with daring and skill, kept up with the hair-raising skirmish.

"Roosevelt, Roosevelt, we are under full scale attack by pirates. Over," JT called out over the radio. He gave the USS Roosevelt their current coordinates, course and speed.

"Gulf Queen, we are 1200 nautical miles north and west of your current position, and we know of no other task force ships in your vicinity. We are under way and will do what we can to assist you. Over."

"Thank you Roosevelt, we are crippled on three engines and can barely maintain the 13 knots. Over," JT added.

"Roger, Gulf Queen that will actually be of help to us, the slower you go, the better chance we have to catch up to you. We are on our way. Out," came the USS Roosevelt's final message.

"God's speed. Out," JT prayed his final reply.

Carrie stood frozen to her position near JT. She knew she had to be strong, brave and ready to lend a hand to JT, and support him in any way she could. The only thing she wasn't willing to do was leave his side.

"Carrie, sit by this radio and listen for contacts," JT said. "Let me know if you hear anything."

She sat, put on the headset and listened intently, but heard only static.

She could hear her heart pounding in the headset and she took deep breaths to calm her anxiety. She knew that she would be worthless to JT if she let herself fall apart with fear. In that moment, she realized that they were all in the same predicament and would all suffer the same fate. She had to conquer her fear and do her part, after all JT had said that the pirates usually didn't harm their victims.

"Get your ladder attached," the pirate captain shouted at his crew as he pulled up to the Gulf Queen's stern. The Gulf Queen's twin engine wake was difficult to maneuver, but the pirate captain's years of experience, his crew's bravery and their wily agility allowed them to overcome the adversity and hook their ladder over the aft unloading ramp and climb aboard the Gulf Queen. He and his crew looked like monkeys, barefoot with AK-47s strapped across their backs, helter-skelter, wildly clambering up the ladders. The trailing mother ship picked up the crewless skiffs and drivers and took them in tow.

The other crew was successfully boarding on the starboard side of the Gulf Queen. The two pirate crews moved forward to the wheelhouse on foot. The slippery foam made it necessary for them to hold on to railings and anything else they could grab, making it impossible for them to shoulder their automatic weapons on the run. One of the pirate captain's crew slipped and went overboard and was picked up by the mother ship.

"Wait until we are both in place before you enter the bridge. We are down to only three men now, we need to be overly cautious and watch what we are doing," the pirate captain ordered.

19

THE INEVITABLE CURSE

The remaining three members of the two pirate crews reached the wheelhouse without further resistance or losses. The ship was slowing as the pirate captain and his crew burst through the wheelhouse hatch. He stopped, surveyed the room and pointed his AK-47 at each person in the room in turn.

"Very good fight. I am impressed with your defenses, but I am the winner today. Everyone here needs to understand that. There will be no more resistance. Do you hear me?" said the water-soaked, wiry, diminutive, ebony-black Somalian with a brownish-green stained tooth smile.

"We hear you," JT replied, looking around at everyone.

"Now we might as well get to know each other," the pirate captain offered. "My name is Raaxo, which means in English, 'the pleasant one,'" he said with wry sarcasm. "So it is everyone's job here to help me live up to my name. Am I clear?"

Everyone nodded and looked down at the deck.

"You," Raaxo pointed at JT with his AK-47. "What is your name?"

"My name is Joseph Thomas Wingate. People call me JT."

"You are the captain of this ship JT?" Raaxo further inquired.

"No, I am the owner," he replied, instantly realizing his mistake. "Actually I am president of the company that owns this ship," he quickly corrected.

"And what have we here?" Raaxo said, pointing his automatic weapon at Carrie, who stiffened in horror as the barrel of the AK-47 swung toward her.

"This is my wife," JT answered, moving to protect her by positioning himself between her and the automatic weapon. He felt it would give her more protection if the pirates knew who she was.

"Wonderful," Raaxo said. "A nice big happy family." He nodded to one of his men. The pirate took the helm and steered southwest.

"Where are you taking us?" JT asked Raaxo.

"Hobyo," was the terse, one word reply.

At John's previous request, Carrie had keyed the radio mike open so that anyone listening might be able to hear conversations in the wheelhouse. Raaxo was unaware that the USS Roosevelt was listening and in pursuit.

"Captain, the Gulf Queen's destination is Hobyo, Somalia. Here, midway down the Somali coast, north of Mogadishu," the USS Roosevelt radioman said, pointing at the chart. "At 13 knots and from their last reported position, it will take them about sixty five hours to get there. At our full speed, it will take us nearly seventy hours to overtake them. We are in a difficult position unless they can do something to further slow their ship."

"Is there any unit closer to Hobyo that might be able to be of better help?" the destroyer captain asked. "Does Task Force 150 have anything in the area?"

"No sir. Not that I am aware of," came the reply. "The Carrier Group is two thousand miles to the east of them and can't be of immediate help either."

"Fine then, all ahead full. Let's try and catch these bastards," the Captain ordered.

♧

"Mr. Owner, or should I say Mr. President, what is the problem with your ship?" Raaxo asked.

"We have lost one engine and we are nursing the others to safely preserve way. We are at roughly two-thirds of full speed," JT answered.

"Push your engines to three-quarter," Raaxo ordered.

JT gave the order and the ship came back up to 13 knots. The Gulf Queen limped on with no further incident. JT and Carrie were ordered to sit on the deck and the Gulf Queen's captain and navigator were sent to the safe room to be with the other crewmen.

They were now just two hours from Hobyo, and land could be seen faintly through the shimmering mid-morning marine haze on the horizon. JT wondered what was to become of them. He knew that the pirates were going to demand ransom, he just didn't know how much. He put his arm around Carrie, who was still visibly shaken.

"Mr. Owner, you and Mrs. Owner will come with me to my headquarters in Hobyo. The remainder of your crew will remain on board under the guard of my men, and will remain there until our business is completed. No one will be harmed as long as things go well. Do you understand me?" Raaxo asked.

"Yes we do. We will do our best to hold up our side of the business," JT said, appearing to be cooperative, but all the time thinking how he might be able to turn the situation around. *They will, at some point, become lax. They will drop their guard and I will be ready*, he thought. *But for now, as long as the AK-47s are pointed at us, there is little I can do except protect the woman I love.*

They arrived in Hobyo's anchorage and JT and Carrie were immediately taken ashore in the skiffs as the Gulf Queen anchored one-half mile out with the mother ship tied off at her stern. Small pirate skiffs and other fishing boats littered the beach and the waters of the naturally formed harbor. Boat houses, sheds and awnings dotted the harbor area. After a twenty minute walk over the sandy and windblown tract, they came to Raaxo's villa and were placed together in a dirty outbuilding with a five gallon bucket toilet, a five gallon bucket of fresh water, two reed mats and two straw pillows to sleep on. There was one window that looked out onto a weed-ridden, windblown open area and a beaten pathway. They stood dejected, isolated and in shock as the doors closed and locked behind them. Their hearts sank and as they stood holding each other, they could feel their bodies begin to drain of self-reliance.

"At least we are together," JT said, squeezing his arms around Carrie to comfort her. He could see she was in shock, and he felt her trim body tremble. "We will get through this, I promise you."

"My God JT, how long do you think we will be here?" Carrie asked in desperation.

"The USS Roosevelt knows we are here, and I am sure that by now Double O knows we are here. Things should start happening pretty quickly, if I know my uncle."

20

TAKE THE REINS, SEIZE CONTROL

As soon as John received word from the US Navy, he swung into action. He called an office meeting and told them that his brother Joe would be in charge of the company business and that he, John, would personally deal with the pirate situation.

His second move was to call his old friend and confidant Trent McSpadden and ask him to come to the office for discussions.

"Bring a change of clothes, Trent. We will be meeting with some Naval Officers tomorrow at the Pentagon."

McSpadden said he would be with John within the hour.

"Trent, thank you so much for coming immediately," John said as he warmly shook his old friend, detective and security specialist's hand in welcome.

"Christ John, what a terrible thing to happen to JT and Carrie," Trent began. "How long ago did this take place?"

"Three days ago, Trent," John said with exasperation. "It's time to get going."

John laid out the whole picture to Trent, who sat shaking his head and taking notes. John related the story of how he had met and gotten to know Carrie and how their relationship had evolved to the point of adoption.

"Trent I don't care what we must do, how long it takes or how much it costs, I want my nephew and his wife back unharmed, safe and sound," John demanded.

"Believe it or not, I have been through a couple of these before myself. There was an oil tanker and a cruise boat commandeering. There were no family members involved, so it came down to dollars and cents for the ship and the crew and the companies eventually paid off. It took an average of four months to accomplish and there was no blood, by the way," McSpadden offered in comfort.

"I know it is asking a lot, but I want to be able to have your council on a moment's notice until this ordeal is over," John said.

"That is absolutely no problem John. I will be at the other end of your line anytime you call, day or night, and will be at your side as fast as distance and time will allow. We are in this together. We will get this thing done, and we will not fail. We have done it before, we will do it again," Trent pledged, and much of John's tension and angst was relieved by Trent's sworn oath.

"The Pentagon meeting is to be at 11:00 AM tomorrow morning, does that work for you?" John asked.

"Works fine John. I'll need to make a few calls, but count me in," Trent said.

The two men spent the remainder of the day studying maps of Somalia and reading up on Somalian pirates. They had dinner together at Henri's and Trent went home with John so that they could get an early start in the morning on John's company jet.

"Good morning Admiral Stimpson, it is a pleasure to meet you sir. I'm John Wingate, and this is my security advisor Trent McSpadden."

"Nice to meet you fellas, albeit a lousy situation that we meet under," the Admiral replied.

The Admiral was in charge of the World Pirating Defense Group for the United States.

"This is my adjutant, Commander Bellows and our Pentagon Communications Chief, Captain Holmgaard. Please have a seat."

The five men sat around the office conference table and Captain Holmgaard laid out the situation as it currently stood from the Navy's point of view. He projected satellite photographs of the Gulf Queen at anchor about a half mile off shore from Hobyo, with the pirates' mother ship tied off at her stern, and he showed close up photographs of the town and its natural small boat harbor.

They could make out fishing boats and pirate skiffs in the harbor. John could see that the Gulf Queen was fully laden and apparently undamaged. He could also see that the anti-piracy systems had been successfully deployed.

"John, we have made copies for you of everything we have here, and we will continue to do so and feed the intel to you on a daily basis," Captain Holmgaard offered. "All we ask in return is that you keep us informed of your plans and activity, and do nothing until we have discussed things fully."

"Thank you very much, that will help tremendously," John said as Trent nodded. "And we are committed to working together with you."

"Here is what else we know. Your ship lost its starboard bow engine, crippling her to 13 knots. Your company's president and his wife have been taken ashore and are more than likely being held in one of those three compounds," he said, pointing to the satellite photo and the compounds marked A, B and C. "We also know that your crew is still on board, being guarded by pirates. We have seen them outside twice a day for an hour or so.

One of our missile destroyers, the USS Roosevelt, is cruising twenty miles offshore, out of sight. She arrived in the area just three hours after the Gulf Queen anchored. It was close, but unfortunately not close enough," the Admiral reported.

"What a shame," Trent said.

"Have you, as yet, had any contact with the pirates?" asked the Admiral.

"We have not," John replied.

"Our communication set up is such that we can have you, your security advisor, my office and the Roosevelt on conference call almost instantaneously," Captain Holmgaard advised. "As soon as you are contacted, you should contact us immediately and we can all discuss what can be done."

"Why can't we just storm in and commandeer the ship and my family by force?" John asked.

"We can 'storm in', as you say, and commandeer the ship, but our standing orders do not allow us to go ashore, and the pirates know that," the Admiral replied.

"There is a good chance that the pirates will ask for two ransoms, one for the ship and one for the abductees," Commander Bellows offered. "Typically a laden RO RO cargo ship goes for 2.5 to 3.5 million dollars, depending on the cargo, and human ransoms vary widely depending on who the hostages are and their ability to pay. You can bet that their brain trust is making those calculations as we speak. The Roosevelt said they overheard a conversation between your family member and the pirate captain saying he was the owner of the ship and then correcting himself to say he was the president of the shipping company that owned the ship," Bellows finished.

"Mr. Wingate, I can order the Roosevelt to move in and take back the Gulf Queen by force, we have done that in the past. The pirates don't usually put up much of a fight in the face of a destroyer's 5-inch cannons and Chinook missile launchers," the Admiral said. "I am afraid that in doing so, however, we may put your family members in jeopardy."

"You are absolutely right; we need to think this all the way through completely, Admiral. I suggest we wait for the first contact and take it from there. I will be in immediate contact with you when that happens," John concluded.

"Not all pirates are the same Mr. Wingate, but the communication method of choice among the majority of them is e-mail through agents spread out in various parts of Europe and Asia," Captain Holmgaard advised. "Please forward everything you receive to us immediately. We are at your service. Here is all the contact information you need."

The five men stood, shook hands and said their goodbyes. The Admiral gave John a small pile of standard Navy publications regarding Somalian pirates and case studies of past hijackings and settlements; it was a formidable package of data.

"Get familiar with this information. It will give you a good base from which to make better decisions and plans. The Navy is here to help you, please take advantage of our resources and experience with these bastards," the Admiral offered. "They are a constant thorn in the world's side and we need to stand together to beat this."

"Thank you Admiral. We will keep in touch and as a multi-generation member of the maritime community, we do stand together and look forward to working with you," John said as he left the Admiral's office.

On the flight back to New York John and Trent studied the books, pamphlets, photos and other data. They were both intent on learning as much as they could before putting together their plans.

21

LEOS, MEOS AND PROOF OF LIFE

Rudely, the pirate guard broke in on JT and Carrie and led them to the Raaxo's villa. As they walked in the hot afternoon sun, JT noticed the proximity of his captive cell to Raaxo's villa, approximately seventy five yards, and noticed that the villa was well away from the other Hobyo compounds.

"Come in, come in," Raaxo offered from his seat on the floor and leaned back onto a large, firm, horsehair-stuffed diwaniya-style pillow.

"Why have you brought us here?" JT asked, still standing.

"I want to tell you that we have contacted your New York office, and they have indicated that they want to work with us to bring this business to an end quickly."

"That is good news," Carrie said.

"Women are not to speak!" Raaxo shouted harshly, green Khat spittle spewing from his mouth. "When and if I want you to speak, I will tell you. Then and only then will you speak in my presence."

Carrie looked down at her hands clasped at her waist. She held back a primal urge to retaliate regardless of the consequences.

"What is Mrs. Owner's name?" Raaxo asked JT with a mock pleasant smile.

"Her name is Carrie," JT replied.

"You get her under control, or I will," Raaxo threatened.

Raaxo put a new chew of Khat in his mouth and announced that as long as things went well, JT and Carrie would be allowed outside to walk around the side yard for one hour in the morning and one hour in the early evening.

"Another Mr. Wingate has asked for proof of life before he begins negotiations, so I am taking a video of you with my cell phone and sending it to him through my agent. Sit over there on the chairs and when I tell you, say only your names and answer my questions. Do not add anything to the conversation. This time, you may speak when spoken to, Mrs. Wingate," Raaxo said condescendingly.

Carrie seethed in silence, hatred sourly welling up in her throat.

"What day is it today, Mrs. Wingate?" Raaxo asked, a taunting smile could be heard in his voice.

Carrie answered the question and looked immediately down at her lap.

"Are you well Mrs. Wingate? Are we taking good care of you?" Raaxo goaded.

"Yes you are sir. We are being well fed and well cared for. We could not ask for better treatment. Thank you," Carrie answered without looking up, trying to stall and appear to go along with Raaxo's game.

"And you Mr. Wingate?" Raaxo asked.

"As Mrs. Wingate said, we are fine and wish to work together to bring this to an early end as coolly and calmly as possible," JT answered. "As you know Mr. Raaxo, we wish to cooperate."

John received the video and immediately sent copies to Admiral Stimpson and Trent McSpadden. Minutes after the video was sent, John received an e-mail from someone calling himself Hassan, demanding 2.8 million dollars for the Gulf Queen and crew, and 5 million dollars for JT and Carrie. John forwarded the e-mail to the others immediately as well.

"John, where did the e-mail come from?" came McSpadden's immediate call.

"As nearly as I can tell, it came from somewhere in Austria. The e-mail has an AT tag," John replied.

"John, I'm going to put someone on this immediately and see if we can track down the source. If we can, we might be able to squeeze some information out of him," McSpadden said. "Also, I don't know if you noticed, but JT was tapping with one finger on the side of his knee during the video. He tapped out; O K 4 N O W."

"Really?" John replied. He remembered playing with JT when he was a boy, teaching him Morse Code, which he himself had learned as a Boy Scout and mastered at the Double O ships' radios.

"Yes. We will ask for proof of life as frequently as we think we can get away with it. Maybe JT can get us something of real value," Trent said.

"Captain Holmgaard, what are the satellite run times over the Hobyo area?" Admiral Stimpson asked.

"The Navy satellites are MEOs, running every three and three-quarter hours, just over six passes per day," the Commander reported. "We can run normal photography during daylight hours and use heat sensitive photography after dark."

The Admiral instructed the Commander to have someone study the Hobyo runs looking for anything that might tell them where the Wingates might be hidden.

"Look for anything unusual. We need to know where they are," the Admiral said. "Have Roosevelt do the same thing. They know the area better than most. Get a four-way going with everyone, I want to tell them what we are doing and I want to know what they are doing."

"Right away sir."

John and Trent, along with the Admiral and the Roosevelt, began their first four-way conversation.

John told the group that he was distributing the e-mails and the videos as soon as he was receiving them, and would continue to do so, holding nothing back.

McSpadden told the group that his people had tracked down the source of the e-mails in Austria, and had a surveillance team watching the source's building.

The Admiral told the group he had two groups studying the satellite surveillance images looking for anything they could find.

"Mr. McSpadden, what are you intending to do at the e-mail source?" the Admiral asked.

"We thought that we might be able to squeeze the source for useful information," McSpadden offered.

"I think that it is a good idea to have eyes on the source, but I don't think that it is a good idea to intercept the source just yet," the Admiral said. "I will send you some contact information for NCIS people we have in the area. If need be, you can contact them and work with them using my name and offices."

"We will certainly follow your advice, Admiral," McSpadden said.

"How will you handle the ransom negotiations?" the Admiral asked of John.

"I really don't know at this point, any suggestions?" John asked.

"The ransom for the ship and crew is in line. The ransom for your family members seems a bit high. You might try to haggle the number, and regularly ask for proof of life. We need to try and delay this a little until we get a firmer handle on what is going on," the Admiral said.

"I believe you are right, but it has been my experience to act as quickly as possible. Situations like this have a way of eroding rather than getting better with time," John said, recalling his Iran incident twenty-one years earlier.

"I agree. I'm talking two, three, four weeks, maximum," the Admiral concluded.

"I'll do what I can," John said as he rang off. The Admiral heard the impatience and pique in John's voice. He knew he would have to work more closely with Mr. Wingate.

"Hey Charlie, look at this!" the Petty Officer, Second Class called to his workmate.

"What you got Jake?"

"This picture was taken at 0830 yesterday, this one at 1215 and this one at 1600 hours. The first one shows two people standing or probably walking in this yard. The second one nothing and the third one they are back again. Then the next day the same thing," said the PO2. "What do you think?"

"You need to keep a close eye on that, and you need to inform the Lieutenant of what you have immediately."

"Lieutenant, may I have a minute of your time to look at these photos sir?" Jake asked.

"Certainly Petty Officer, come in," the Lieutenant responded.

Jake showed the Lieutenant everything he had gathered on the Hobyo situation. He gave the Lieutenant his interpretation of the photos and asked if the Lieutenant agreed.

"I think you are on to something," the Lieutenant said. "These are our MEO's (Middle Earth Orbit Satellite Photos) aren't they?"

"Yes sir. They orbit every three and three-quarter hours," Jake answered.

"Do we have any current LEO's (Low Earth Orbit Satellite Photos) of the area?" the Lieutenant asked.

"No sir, but the Army does," Jake quickly replied.

"I'll get Washington to coordinate with the Army to see what they can come up with. We need ninety minute revolution runs, and we need to get it going today," the Lieutenant said. "Good work, I'll get back to you."

"General Hoffman, this is Admiral Stimpson, how are you today?"

"I'm just fine Admiral. What can I do for you?" the General offered.

Admiral Stimpson gave the General a quick overview of what was going on in Hobyo, and told him that he needed the last three days of LEO surveillance photos of the Hobyo area and then constant daily updates from there on. They shared communication sources, participant's names and contact information.

"Damn little monkeys are at it again," the General said. "I'll have the LEOs in your hands within the hour."

"Can you transmit a set to the USS Roosevelt, and continue to send them daily updates as well?" the Admiral further requested.

"I can, and I'll get it going immediately," the General promised then rang off.

"Wow, these 1.3 meter resolution LEOs are fantastic Lieutenant. You can almost see what they're having for dinner with these," Jake boasted.

Both men pored over the photos and came to the same conclusions, but this time they had pinpoint accuracy. They could actually recognize the difference in the dress of the two yard people versus the others at the harbor and other areas around town. They noted that one of the figures was male, the other female.

22

TALK IS CHEAP; OR IS IT

S itting in his cramped, dirty and rundown flat in Vienna's City Center, Hassan began to revel in his findings on John Wingate and the Double O Shipping Company. He had worked hard to gather the necessary data. The hours in front of his computer screen in this shithole of an accommodation were about to pay off. This time it would be different for him though, and he would not have to go through this again for a long time to come, if ever.

Raaxo demanded two million dollars for the Ro Ro and three million dollars for the Wingates. When all this was finished, Hassan would clear two point eight million dollars. The cursor blinked patiently as he pressed SEND.

John's e-mail beeped at 4:00AM, waking him. The e-mail was from Vienna, Austria with a 10AM time tag.

> *Mr. Wingate,*
> *We have not heard from you in some time and would like an update on your progress so far. Have you secured the ransom money?*
> *Hassan*

John looked at the e-mail and wanted to get on a plane, hunt down these worms and put an end to this game. However, he knew he had to swallow it all and deal with them as the enemy, and to win the war he must remain calm, calculated and smart.

> *Mr. Hassan*
>
> *We are in the process of amassing the money and it is taking us longer than we thought. I have sold personal assets, I have drained my cash accounts and I have pushed my borrowing limits to the maximum. I would like to request a reduction in the amount you have asked for the Wingates to a more reasonable and collectable sum. An amount of three million would be somewhat easier for me to collect on such short notice, and more in line. By doing this I could bring the matter to a close at the earliest possible date, otherwise I'm afraid this will drag on for some time.*
>
> *Please be advised that I am working at this as fast as I can. John Wingate*

Hassan opened his e-mail and read the information with disgust. He had studied John Wingate and knew of his company and its worth as well as his personal assets. He was sure that the company had ample amounts of money to pay the ransoms. His blood pressure had risen slightly with the balking plea from John Wingate. He knew he was on strong ground, and persisted with his heavy handed approach.

> *Mr. Wingate*
>
> *I have studied your company, its worth, its assets and its cash value and I know that you have access to ample sums to meet my client's demands. I suggest that you cease delaying the process and settle negotiations immediately.*
>
> *Hassan*

> *Mr. Hassan*
>
> *I do not own the company, and neither does JT Wingate, your client's hostage. We are shareholders and employees only. The ransom for the Gulf Queen and its crew will be met by the company, but the personal ransoms for Mr. and Mrs. Wingate will require personal funds that I do not currently have. I request that you make that clear to your client and ask him to either lower his demands or give me more time to amass the funds.*
>
> *John Wingate.*

Hassan sat and digested the latest e-mail. John watched the cursor pulsate on his computer screen. He waited thirty minutes before going back to bed. There was no further communication from Hassan that morning.

Hassan felt confused and irritated. He went back to the files that he had gathered on Double O and the Wingates and reviewed each page, one by one.

The day wore on and he saw no flaws in his assessment. John Wingate had millions in his own right, and the company was asset-rich and reasonably well off cash-wise. It was the successful company he had originally assessed it to be. Hassan also knew that Double O was well insured. Hassan decided to take a risk and create a ruse to undermine John's negotiating capabilities. He sat back down at his computer and composed the email he was sure would break the stalemate.

John's computer chirped with the new communication.

> *Mr. Wingate*
>
> *I am the bearer of bad news. My client is very upset with your last communication and tells me he is losing patience. He will no longer be so kind and he is taking away half of your family's exercise privileges. They will no longer be allowed to walk outside in the afternoons. The*

next punishment will be to take away eating privileges and if delays
continue, other punishments, primarily physical, will be administered
if necessary.
    Hassan

Hassan pressed the SEND button with a sadistic flare. He was positive that Mr. Wingate would wither. He went back to his squalid couch, stuffed his cheek with Khat and smiled up at the ceiling feeling tentative but satisfied with himself and the direction the negotiations were going. A week to ten days more and he would be a multi-millionaire.

"If I could get near these little bastards I would kill them with my bare hands," John said to his brother Joe.

"He is using the only leverage he has, and that is threats against our family," Joe Jr. said, sitting across the desk.

"That certainly makes sense to me," John answered. "Any suggestions on where to go from here?"

"The man has given you at least two more chances for more delay before they start to inflict possible physical harm to JT and Carrie," Joe Jr. said. "I suggest we continue the hard line for a while longer and see where it takes us."

John agreed but knew he had to be careful here, yet he also knew he had to remain firm.

    Mr. Hassan
    I am sorry to hear that your client will not negotiate with me. With
the three million I offer and the two point eight million for the Gulf
Queen, your client will clear nearly six million dollars which should
be satisfactory to him. I am continuing to try to raise the five million
and I will work at it as fast as possible. I can do no more than that.
    Also I require another 'proof of life.'
    John Wingate

"That should hold them temporarily Joe," John said. "Thanks for the input."

"John, don't you think you should engage a professional negotiator?" Joe Jr. suggested.

John was reluctant to let anyone else get between the negotiator and himself. His hands-on need for control was competing with his logic and he knew he was going to have to face the situation soon anyway.

John called the Admiral and asked for a four-way and was told that it would be arranged for the next day at 3:00PM eastern, because there were serious communication satellite problems.

The call came through the following day, as promised, and John began the conversation. He told the group of his recent e-mails with the Austrian connection and about the punishments that would and could be inflicted upon JT and Carrie.

"Mr. Wingate, when did you say you had the e-mail conversation with Austria?" the Petty Officer aboard the Roosevelt asked.

"Yesterday. Nearly thirty-four hours ago," John answered.

"That's interesting; today's photos show that nothing has changed in the walking patterns. I think that your contact is handling negotiations solo without consulting his client," the Petty Officer replied.

"The Austrian has probably set the ransom limits above what the client asked for to get a bigger cut for himself," the Admiral opined. "Where is he telling you he wants the drop made John?"

"He is telling us the drop will be made somewhere in central Vienna," John answered. "I'm sure it is close to where they are currently located."

"I'm thinking that the Petty Officer has nailed your problem," the Admiral said. "You are dealing with a rogue negotiator, and it is my recommendation you get some professional help."

"Please let me know as soon as you can tomorrow if the same situation continues," John asked. "This changes everything. Till next time gentlemen. I will keep you posted of any changes in the negotiations."

They all rang off.

John now knew he had real allies in his corner. He had a top notch team that was on their toes, doing their jobs with efficiency, accuracy and a joy of the hunt.

23

SEEDS ARE SOWN, IDEAS GROW

John immediately called McSpadden on his private line. "Trent, I have some ideas I would like to run by you. Can you meet me for dinner tonight at Henri's?" John asked.

"I can," was Trent's answer.

"Great, 7:00PM."

"Trent, I'm not overly excited about the delay the Admiral is talking about," John began as Henri brought drinks.

"I'm not happy with it either, but it does take some time to get the lay of the land and try to figure the best way is to defuse the situation," Trent answered.

"Have you had any experience with ransom dealings?" John asked the seasoned investigator.

"I have, but I used, and I also recommend you use, a professional hostage negotiator," he said. "I'm not talking about some lawyer either. I'm talking about a successful, seasoned, retired police hostage negotiator, and I know just the guy."

"My brother and the Admiral suggested the same thing. Would you ask your man to give me a call Trent?" John requested, and Trent made a note in his pocket pad.

The men continued to eat their dinner while talking about the amounts of dollars. Trent posed the hard questions. Was John prepared to pay the 7.8 million if the pirates insisted, and was he willing to take other steps should the situation call for it? John answered positively to all Trent's questions; he would take any steps necessary.

"I was thinking of looking into the possibility and probability of putting together a team of retired Navy Seals for a possible extraction operation," Trent blurted out. "A good hunting buddy of mine is a retired Seal; I know he will have great ideas."

"You mean remove them by force?" John asked doubtfully.

"Snatch and grab," Trent said. "It is one of the many operations that the Seals are particularly well trained for."

"How the hell can they walk into a small, remote, God-forsaken village like Hobyo without a sound and walk out with my family?" John said with consternation.

"The Seals' motto is 'slow and silent'. The operation will happen at night, and no one will be the wiser," Trent said.

"Trent, what about dogs, watchmen, guards, patrols and the like?"

"John, I don't know if you know anything about Somalis in their own country, do you?" Trent asked and John shook his head.

Trent went on to explain that the country, for a large part, was fundamentally lawless. Except for family codes and tribal rules, there isn't much control. It is a loosely knit government, incapable of controlling all of their dissidents such as the remote and lawless Hobyo clan. He further described the habit of the Somali male to chew Khat, and the side effects it has.

"Khat produces euphoria and at the same time excitement and talkativeness. It can also produce manic behavior and hyperactivity. There are reports it has side effects like constipation, dilated eyes, increased heart rate and high blood pressure," Trent said.

"My God," John said. "Does it produce all these effects simultaneously?"

"I suppose it can," Trent said. "The worse thing is that withdrawal produces lethargy, depression, tremors, loss of appetite, impaired liver function, greenish stains on the teeth, ulcers, loss of sex drive and, most worrisome, deep irritability. If you were to catch one of these fellas on a bad day, it could get ugly. For the most part however, most of the men are in a stupor at night, having chewed most of the afternoon and evening."

"Okay, that takes care of the male humans, what about the dogs?" John asked.

"Somalis hate dogs to the extent that the only living ones in Somalia are wild, cunning and therefore silent. Their fear of humans is so high that they run away quickly at first scent. Unlike our domestic dogs, they have no desire to proclaim their territory by barking and howling," Trent instructed.

John could see where Trent was going. The men were asleep and/ or in a stupor, the dogs were hiding, it was dark and the Seals were slow, methodical and silent. He was getting a much better picture. "Just what are you thinking?" John asked.

"I'm thinking we should put a team of twenty to twenty-four Navy Seal retirees together for a sneak attack and extraction. Remember, it is what the Seals are best known for; they are particularly well trained in that exercise. The US Navy would assist, but they can't get involved with the on-shore activities. The Admiral made that very clear. We will need to provide that arm of the scheme," Trent said. "If we can talk the Admiral into boarding and taking over the Gulf Queen, it would take that phase of the operation off of our plate and we could concentrate on JT and Carrie. If he won't, we'll just have to figure out how to handle everything by ourselves."

John liked the ideas Trent was putting forth. *A plan B is definitely required to deal with this wild and irrational bunch*, John thought.

"What do you think this will cost Trent?"

"These guys get two thousand a day, suited up, including the day before and the day after and eight hundred a day before and after that. I'm estimating a little over six hundred thousand total for the Seals. I'm guessing three-quarters of a million for gear and munitions. With my expenses, it would be somewhere around a million, six hundred thousand dollars," Trent calculated. "Add in your company costs, we are easily looking at two plus million."

"That's still a lot less than the ransom demands. Put together a complete working plan, and get handshake agreements from at least twenty of the best men you are talking about. You should probably make it twenty-four or twenty-five to cover attrition and changes in plans. Put together a list of gear you think will be required and let's get together again day after tomorrow, same time, same place," John said. "Will that work?"

"I have a friend, my hunting buddy, who will help me and I'd like to get him on the payroll immediately," Trent offered. "It will pay off in the long run."

"Go ahead," John authorized.

The two men finished their entrees. They both got up to leave feeling better about things than they had when they had come in. Both John and Trent were the type of men who needed to feel in control, and this was definitely a step in that direction.

"Trent, let's keep this between ourselves for the time being," John ended. "We'll get the Admiral on board when we have a sure-fire idea of what we want to do, when we can present him with a viable plan."

"That is my thought exactly," Trent commented as he walked to his waiting cab. "I'll have something put together the day after tomorrow."

Trent got to his office early the next morning. He called his close friend, James 'Jumbo' Reimer, MCPO US Navy Seals, Retired.

"Jumbo, this is Trent, how are you my friend?" Trent opened the conversation.

"I'm great Trent, what's going on with you?" he replied. "You want to go somewhere and decrease the buck population?"

"Sounds tempting, but I'm involved in a ransom operation, and I would like to hire you as a team leader and consultant. When can you get here?" Trent got straight to the point.

"Is tomorrow afternoon okay? I'm finishing up a task today and can be there on the first flight out of here," came Jumbo's quick and decisive reply. "There are ample flights out of Omaha," Jumbo remarked.

They talked for a few minutes more and rang off.

The next day James Reimer arrived at Trent's office at 1:00 PM. After greetings and offers of coffee, Trent got down to business.

"Jumbo, I have a friend whose nephew and wife have been caught up in a Somali pirate issue and are being held captive in a village in remote Somalia," Trent revealed, pointing to the many charts, maps and satellite photos he had pinned to his ops board.

"How long has it been going on?" Jumbo asked.

"A little over two weeks now," Trent replied.

"How can I help you?" Jumbo asked.

Trent showed Jumbo the layout of the land at Hobyo, pointing out the likely places that the hostages might be as well as the place they were suspected of being, and asked for Jumbo's initial assessment and what he thought might be a good approach to a snatch and grab operation.

"If we can pinpoint their location, say here where you previously pointed, I would launch a three prong attack, sending one team to this point, a second team here and the third here. Team one would perform the extraction while teams two and three would create distraction and cause mayhem and inflict fear. Once the hostages are clear, I would remotely detonate a line of land mines stretching from here to here," Jumbo said. "Letting any surviving locals know this is as far as they go."

"Beautiful," Trent said. "Simple and direct. How long do you think it would take to execute that plan?"

"Once the teams are ashore, no more than thirty-five, forty minutes. Ten minutes infil and set up, five minutes snatch, ten minutes diversion, five minutes mop up, ten minutes exfil. The only catch would be if the hostages were somewhere other than planned, shackled and/or drugged, and that wouldn't add more than five to ten minutes, which, by the way, can be a lifetime if the village is well armed. I suspect this one is, being as remote as it is," Jumbo added. "Shit, this place is in the middle of nowhere, one road in and the same road out. Talk about your wide spot in the road."

"What size teams, and how many do you envision?" Trent went on.

"Three teams of eight would be sufficient," Jumbo said.

"Do you have access to that many men?" Trent asked.

"I do, and I can have agreements from twenty-four by tonight, latest tomorrow morning. May I use your offices?" Jumbo said.

Trent got the retired Seal settled in one of his spare offices and gave him what he needed in the way of phones, secretarial help and supplies.

"What kind of time frame are we looking at?" Jumbo asked.

"You need to get commitments for the next three weeks, minimum, with a possible fourth," Trent answered. "I'll sketch out the plan that you outlined. If you could work on a list of equipment, materials and supplies that the teams would need that would also be extremely helpful," said he continued. "Spend money like it is yours, but don't hold back. List everything you think you will need."

Both men got to work immediately. Trent took a satellite picture and blew it up to 18 by 24-inch plan size.

He looked at the town layout and the areas where they thought the hostages might be. There were three likely villas located at the south end of the town closest to the harbor and well away from the main part of the village. All three looked like high quality villas with some outbuildings. There were several big, expensive and American-made SUVs parked in two of the three compounds, SUVs large enough and strong enough to make regular trips to Mogadishu to the south and Galkayo to the north.

He scaled the distance measurements from the three landing spots Jumbo had chosen to the sites where each team could, with as much safe cover as he could discern, perform their part of the operations. He noted all of the distances in feet.

"Goddammit, we are going to kick ass," he thought as he sketched out the plan.

24

DETENTION, APPREHENSION, TREPIDATION

"**A**re you awake?" JT whispered to Carrie.

"Yes, my love, I am," she sighed.

JT kissed her and cuddled her to him. She was warm and a little stiff from the night's sleep on their thin mat on the dirt floor. Her spirits were high, however, on this their thirteenth day of confinement and sixteenth day since the attack.

"We've overslept; it's nearly 8:30 AM. Let's go for our walk first today, and get rid of the cobwebs," JT suggested. He knocked on the door to alert the guard that they were ready for their walk.

They walked around and around the garden walls, hand in hand and often arm in arm. They had worn a path into the dry, hard-packed, sandy earth. They talked about their situation and wondered what was being done to save them. They had heard nothing since Raaxo told them negotiations were starting. They could smell the sea and could hear its pounding surf, and they longed for their freedom.

"It shouldn't be much longer now, if I know my uncle," JT comforted. "He won't let us sit here any longer than he has to."

The side gate to the garden opened, and in walked Raaxo.

"Good morning Mr. Wingate," he said, with a smile on his face.

"Good morning," Carrie returned.

Raaxo slapped her hard across the face, hard enough that she fell to her knees. "I told you women don't speak!" He screamed in a Khat-fueled frenzy, green spittle spewing from his enraged mouth.

In an automatic jiu-jitsu reaction, JT kicked Raaxo hard in the stomach, bending him over at the waist. He grabbed one of Raaxo's hands, spun him around and forced him to his knees, twisting his extended arm painfully.

"That wasn't necessary, she meant no disrespect," JT said, looking down at the infuriated black man with his long brown-green teeth protruding over his lower lip, eyes bulging and chest heaving slightly.

Raaxo's guard burst in, frantically pointing his AK-47 at JT.

"Stop!" Raaxo yelled at his guard. "Put down your gun, I am fine."

JT released his grip, letting Raaxo stand again. "You will never touch my wife again, do you hear me?" he hissed.

"I understand and forgive your well trained, automatic reaction to protect your property, but she needs to learn her place, and that takes discipline. Since you won't do it, someone must," Raaxo said, still smiling. "You are changing compounds today. Your guard will take you there, so go and gather your belongings and toilet and water buckets. You will wear this when you walk outside the compound," he said, tossing a head and upper body shawl at Carrie. It reeked of curry and body odor.

They walked to the next compound, which was just over five hundred and forty yards away and closer to the water's edge, JT counted. The building they were shoved into smelled of animals. They saw two goats at the far end of the barn-like structure. The garden area was similar to their previous location.

"JT, come look at this," Carrie said.

"Looks like tallies to me," JT said. "Someone keeping track of time like we do."

"Good God, there are over 170 marks here!" Carrie counted. "These poor souls were here for over five and a half months. God JT, I don't think I could take that."

"Don't worry my sweet, we won't be here that long," JT comforted.

The barn was somewhat darker than the previous cell had been. The only light came from knot holes and cracks in the dilapidated roof and a missing board or two high up in the siding. JT smiled and hugged Carrie. "It's not much of a honeymoon spot I admit, but at least we have each other. How is your cheek?" He caressed her as he spoke.

"Split my lip, the little bastard. You know JT, I just have the feeling that I will, somehow, have my day with that man," Carrie said with vengeance. "Thank you for trying to protect me, but it isn't wise for us to provoke them too much."

That afternoon they were let out into the yard for their walk. JT knew it was very important they keep up the walking. Two hours a day of walking paired with the yoga they did on their mats inside was keeping them in good mental and physical shape. After their walk, they went inside for their evening meal.

The meal consisted of a bowl of spicy meat curry and bariis (sticky rice), canjeero (a staple bread) and hot, sweet tea. They noticed that it was the same old food, but the preparation was slightly different; a little spicier they thought.

The food didn't taste bad, but the new cuisine was initially hard on their digestive systems and diarrhea cursed them for the first four or five days of their detention.

"We must be getting used to this stuff," Carrie said. "It seems to stick with us a little longer each time. I was starting to worry about dehydration. I think we have somehow built up an immunity to the local bugs and are taking this gruel in stride."

"I think you are right," JT surmised. "Also, it must be that Raaxo's crew members have to switch off cooking for us."

The PO2 Specialist aboard the Roosevelt studied the satellite photos closely. He noticed that the two figures were in the garden area in the morning but not in the afternoon and worried. With magnification, he patiently studied the surrounding buildings and yards. He noticed two figures in a yard closer to the water and called his superior.

"Sir, I think that they may have moved the hostages," The PO2 said. "They were here for the last two weeks and this morning, but now they are here. I am very sure these are the same people."

"Good work Petty Officer. I'll get the word out to all the parties at our next conference call," the lieutenant said.

"Gentlemen, how are each of you progressing?" the Admiral asked.

"I have had several e-mails from Austria, and have answered them, as you know. We are sixteen days into this now, and I'm starting to get a bit antsy. I have hired a professional hostage negotiator who I would like to introduce to you. His name is Vince Packard, like the old car," John said.

"John, I fully understand your current feelings, but please try to relax. These negotiations have been known to go on for months and months. How are you, Mr. Packard?" the Admiral offered.

"Very well Admiral, thank you. There always comes a time when the pirate captain or his crew start to get impatient and more dangerous," said Vince. "The money they get from one hijacking goes, in part, towards paying for the next and if they begin to run out of funds, things start to get more and more demanding. We have only been at it for a little over two weeks now, but we need to keep on track."

"You have done this before with the Somalis Mr. Packard?" the Admiral asked.

"I have sir, on several occasions," Packard answered. "A Korean oil tanker company hired me. Against my instructions, they played with the Somalis too long, and two of the crew ended up dead. It is rare when that happens, I have been told, but it does happen. It took weeks to straighten out that negotiation, but we finally got it back on track and succeeded in recovering the ship and the rest of the crew."

"Gentlemen, I think we have located the Double O hostages," the USS Roosevelt Lieutenant said.

Everyone on the call took a deep breath.

"We believe they are allowed out for a walk twice a day, and they are being moved around. That's how we figured it out. We will send you copies of the satellite photos for your interest and files. Compare them to the ones you received last week and you will see they are the same people only in a different location."

"Great going Lieutenant. Keep up the good work," John and the Admiral said almost in unison.

"Gentlemen, till tomorrow, same time," the Admiral rang off.

25

VIENNA

"Captain Holmgaard, how are we set up in Vienna?" the Admiral asked.

Captain Holmgaard went on to explain that McSpadden checked with the NCIS people from time to time, but that McSpadden remained in control and had agents watching the Somali negotiators' flat and following the negotiators when they came and went. He continued that there was only one man and one woman in the flat. The woman did most of the traveling to the markets and elsewhere. He explained that he felt McSpadden had been forthcoming with his intel.

"She appears to be Somali in European dress, except for the head scarf that she puts on as she leaves the building," the Captain added.

"Have they seen him?"

"Yes he comes out, walks around and visits one of the local Bistros where he has coffee and a smoke," the Captain answered. "They stay fairly close to the flat; they don't range too far off."

"I think we need to get more deeply involved. I'll call Wingate and have a discussion with him and McSpadden. I want to catch all of these monkeys and put an end to this den of thieves."

McSpadden, Vince and John spoke with the Admiral for half an hour, and they came to a mutual agreement regarding the negotiator and his female partner.

"Trent, I'll get NCIS to share your workload so we can begin working together. They will need to get up to speed. Besides, it will be good to have different faces hanging around the area," the Admiral said.

"That is fine with us Admiral, as long as everything is transparent and above-board," John said with Trent and Vince's assent. "And as long we are all moving in the same direction on this."

"Admiral, it is our intention to string them along, and then on the night we rescue the hostages you can drop the bomb on them and pick them all up," Vince said.

"I don't think it is wise that we get involved with the pick-up," Trent said. "I assume you will have local police with you when you make that grab."

"We have to be very careful that the locals don't screw up our timing. How do you think you can make that work Admiral?" John warned.

"That's a good point John, and when I meet with NCIS I will discuss that thoroughly with them. I agree we can't let anything jeopardize the safety of the hostages. John, I'll get on it right away," the Admiral replied.

"Admiral, we don't want to have a bunch of police walking around the area all of a sudden, either," John said.

"Agreed," said the Admiral and then he rang off.

"Hassan, how much longer must we live in this rat infested place?" Aamina asked.

"Not much longer now, my wife," Hassan reassured her. "We are very close now, two to three weeks, a month at the most."

She lay back on the mattress on the floor and stared up at the ceiling. She hated this place. A girl of her education and upbringing should not have to live this way. She had learned English, German, Austrian, French and Spanish. She closed her eyes and dreamed of finding a haven in Mexico, or even Central or South America for that matter. They would have plenty of money and live extremely well.

Hassan joined her on the mattress and started to remove her clothing. She did not resist, it was her obligation to give herself to him whenever he wished. He was usually very tender, and she didn't mind. She wished she could enjoy it more, but couldn't.

"Vince, I think you should take over with the Somali negotiator," John said. "Take this computer, and use my name. I call him Mr. Hassan and sign off as John Wingate. You can study the thread to get a feel for my use of language. I need to know what is going on as it happens or, at a minimum, immediately after it happens. We will string him along, plead with him not to let the hostages suffer too much and then one day we tell him we have the money and are ready to hand it over. God, I can't wait for that day to come."

"Please have confidence John, I have done this often. I fully understand your reticence to give up control, and I will keep you completely and immediately informed and, your time permitting, we will work out the issues together," Vince promised.

"Would you be averse to working here in this office? I can get you set up with everything you need," John asked.

"Not at all," Vince answered. "We usually work from the same premises as the ransom source."

"Very good then, we are set," John said. He pressed the intercom button and Pat got on the line. "Pat, I need an office for Vince Packard, can you set him up with one please?"

"Certainly John, I'll get on it right away," she answered.

"Make sure he has access to me at all times, you know my schedule better than I do," John said. "See that he has everything he needs please."

26

ASSUAGING AN ADMIRAL

"How are things moving on your end Trent?" John asked over his two fingers of Laphroig.

"We have the agreement of twenty-four retired Navy Seals," Trent reported. "When I say retired, I mean these men are between thirty-five and forty years old and in peak physical and mental condition."

Trent gave John a file with pictures and a short bio of each man as Henri approached the table. John was impressed with what he saw and read.

"I'll have the chicken tonight, please, Henri," Trent said.

"I'd like to try the lamb shanks. You choose the wine," John said, looking up at Henri with a smile.

"Very good sir," Henri said, and was off.

"These men look like they can handle the job," John remarked.

"John, these men make my typical security recruits look like Cub Scouts in comparison. They don't need any training, and they relish a good fight," Trent boasted.

They finished their dinner and rose to leave when Trent said, "John, let's go back to your office, I have something I want to talk over with you."

Back at the office, Trent went over three scenarios for a snatch and grab operation. They required about twenty to twenty-four men, one of John's RO RO's or LST's, three high speed rubber beach assault boats and a ton of courage.

"Trent, these are great scenarios," John said. "On a scale of one to ten, how do you rate them?"

"Number one, I call it the Stealth Plan, is a 10. The entire operation takes forty-five minutes, and not a sound is made. Only two teams are required. Number two, also a Stealth Plan, is an 8. We take only the hostages and leave everything and everyone behind, sleeping or dead. It takes only one large team. Number three, which I call the WWIII Plan, is a 15," Trent replied. "It's obvious that number three is the most aggressive: it carries the biggest punch, and it is sure to pass muster with the Admiral. There won't be a doubt left in the mind of a single villager that they have been had, and had good. Three eight-man teams are required."

"How do you rate them for risk, both to the hostages and to the men?" John asked.

Trent went on to explain to John that they felt number two had the highest risk. "The fewest number of men are involved, but the fewest number of bases are covered as well. If we are detected, we could have a hell of a time getting out of there."

They reasoned that number one was a little less risky in that there were two supporting teams and two routes of exfil.

"Number three we feel is the least risky, as we have all bases covered. We do a thorough infil, have ample men to ward off attack and to create havoc and confusion, and we have the big blast to escape behind. We really prefer number three," Trent said. "A little more expensive, but thorough in its execution."

"And lastly Trent, how do you assess their success rates?" John asked.

"Number three has the highest success rating, then number one and finally number two."

ॐ

"Good day gentlemen," the Admiral began the phone conference.

The Roosevelt Lieutenant reported that there had been no changes in the previously reported activities of the Wingates. "Things appear to be on an even keel, and we have no changes to report."

John and Trent reported that they had a Plan A, B and C started, and would send details to each member by e-mail. "We feel that Plan C has the most teeth and will send the strongest message to the pirates and cripple them. We also feel C has the highest success rating and the lowest risk," John concluded. "The e-mails, of course, are for your eyes only. From here on in, secrecy is of the utmost importance."

"John, we will review your plans carefully and give you our opinions as soon as possible," the Admiral promised.

The hostage negotiator, Vince Packard, reported that the proof of life data had just come through minutes before and that the Austrian agent was getting firmer in his demands.

"What do you mean firmer?" John asked.

"They have given us compliance dates," Vince answered. "They have given us thirty days to make the money drop for the ship, and an additional week to make the drop for the hostages. We also think we noticed the man in the video tapping Morse Code on his knee. He tapped M O V E D."

"Alright gentlemen, everyone on their toes. John, I would like for you and Trent to come to my office again, if you will."

"Certainly Admiral. When would you like us?" John said.

"Give us three or four days John. How about this Friday?" the Admiral requested.

"This Friday it is," John said, getting an approving nod from Trent across the desk. "Usual time Admiral, 11:00 AM?"

"Yes, that's fine." the Admiral rang off.

27

RAAXO, A MOST DESPICABLE MAN

"**M**r. Wingate, how are you and the Mrs. getting along today?" Raaxo asked as he joined them for their walk in the dusty, weed-ridden garden.

"We are fine Raaxo," JT said.

"Well I have some good news and some bad news for you then. The good news is that we have issued a compliance date for your ransom."

"What's the bad news?" JT asked.

"In twenty-six days, you will no longer be able to walk outside in the afternoon. You will have to get that portion of your exercise in-doors," Raaxo smiled his ugly, toothy smile and walked off through the garden to his villa. "And we are moving you back again to my compound," he said over his shoulder.

JT and Carrie carried on with their walk. They walked silently, both deep in their own thoughts. Carrie clutched his arm tightly as if she was worried about something.

"What's the matter my sweet?" JT asked.

"Why do you suppose they will be restricting our walking?"

"Probably so that they can keep a closer eye on us just before the payoff," JT answered. "I don't see it as an earth-shattering thing."

"I think that we should seriously try to get ourselves in the best shape we can over the next several weeks without changing our outward routine," Carrie said. "I want to be able to stand up to whatever these scurvy, scrawny little creeps have in store for us. I am not going to show any weakness."

JT hugged her tightly. He admired her spirit and grit.

She somehow felt better knowing there was an end date. It was like a light at the end of the tunnel. JT noticed a difference in her attitude and her bold defiance.

"The next time you see that filthy creep, see if you can't have our food ration kicked up a little. I notice that I have lost a little weight in my upper thighs," she commented.

"They look very nice to me," JT remarked.

She punched him playfully on the shoulder. "I didn't say they didn't look nice, you rake."

The move back to Raaxo's compound went smoothly. They noticed that there was very little activity in the area where they were housed. It appeared that they were located on the far southwestern outskirts of the village.

"I'm not going to miss those goats," Carrie remarked. "Ten to one, we all meet again though."

"I have a feeling they won't miss us either," JT added with a weak smile.

It was difficult to function everyday while continuing to wonder what was going on, what was happening with the company and what plans were in store. They nevertheless managed to keep their morale high, and JT knew he owed much of that to Carrie. He was falling more and more in love with her, and he secretly cherished the chance they were having to genuinely and deeply get to know each other. Defecating in a five gallon bucket in each other's presence with only shirt tails for privacy and propriety went a long way to create closeness, tolerance and mutual respect. He silently swore that nothing bad would befall her. He knew he could handle himself, being a black-belt traditional jiu-jitsu master. The numbers were overwhelming now, but in the end, if need be, he could and would protect her no matter what.

"Raaxo, I wonder if I might prevail upon you for a favor," JT said the next time they met.

"What is it?" Raaxo asked irritably.

"Would it be possible to have our meal allotment increased to three meals a day?" JT asked, his voice firm and unwavering.

"You don't want to get fat do you?" Raaxo said with his pinched grin.

"Actually, we have noticed some weight loss. We aren't asking for more than we need, we would just like to stay even," JT appealed. "Also, Raaxo, my wife is in need of some feminine items; her time of the month is here. We have supplies in our stateroom on the ship, if you will allow me to get them."

"I'll see what I can do. With the exception of your single, understandable outburst, you have been model hostages," Raaxo said and walked away to his villa and an afternoon of Khat chewing with his friends, in absolutely no hurry to appease his hostages.

Raaxo was born in Mogadishu approximately two hundred and seventy miles south of Hobyo, on the Somali coast. His family was well connected: his father was a ranking officer in the in the Somali Police Force in the 1960s during the fighting for independence. His father fought valiantly and gained the respect and the eye of the new army commander Daud Hersi and his successor Mohamad Said Barre.

As a result of his father's rank and training, Raaxo received an excellent education, learning the English language fluently at an early age. He was smart and ranked high in his class.

The country began a series of convulsive confrontations in attempts to draw the various clans and family factions together as one, united under one government. Clans revolted and the army did all it could to keep some semblance of peace. The army began to develop a shortage of manpower and in the mid-1980s, it elected to institute an obligatory military service requirement of its young men. Although Raaxo was a good citizen and the son of an army officer, he did not relish being conscripted to fight in skirmishes he did not believe in.

In 1985, Raaxo fled to Hobyo, joined the remote fishing community and soon found anonymity. He spent his time fishing and developing his stature in the Hobyo community until 1995 when the pirate movement began in earnest. His friends and fellow citizens praised him for his daring in chasing the foreign fishermen from their fishing grounds. Pirating was in its infancy.

Raaxo distinguished himself during the hijacks. He showed daring and skill and was soon assigned a crew. Part fisherman, part pirate, Raaxo lapsed into the quiet lifestyle of fishing, fighting, fucking and chewing Khat.

He took over as chief pirate in 1999 when he entered a dispute with his leader and killed him in a Khat driven fury. He was now responsible for five crews and feared by everyone in the village.

He singlehandedly escalated the pirating activities to such a point that leaders in Mogadishu to the south and Bosaso to the north became aware and concerned of his brazen escapades. So much so that they sent armed envoys to Hobyo to reign in the prolific pirate. All were thwarted and sent home.

The next day, Raaxo and his second-in-command came to take Carrie away.

"Where are you taking her?" JT demanded.

"We are taking her to the ship for her supplies, and then we are placing her in another shed until her period passes. A man should not sleep with or be around a soiled woman," Raaxo said.

"That's okay," JT said with a very worried look. "I don't mind."

"Nonsense, you will get her back when she is past her time."

"Nothing had better happen Raaxo," JT threatened.

"Everything will be fine. Don't worry."

They went out to the Gulf Queen in Raaxo's skiff and Carrie showed them to the correct stateroom.

"Nice, very nice indeed," Raaxo said, looking around the extravagant stateroom. "I think you should take a shower and have a change of clothing, don't you, Mrs. President?" Raaxo chided and goaded. "Take off your clothing and get into the shower," he demanded.

"No," was her single word of defiance.

Raaxo slapped her hard across her face and neck and she fell to the deck.

"I said, take off your clothing and get into the shower!" he yelled.

She stood unsteadily, turned away from him and began to unbutton her shirt. He sat on the bed and ogled her, a disgusting smile on his face. She removed her bra and slid her pants down over her hips, dragging her panties down with them. She removed her pants and panties and started for the shower.

"Wait," Raaxo demanded. "Turn around."

She turned partially, and in her absolute embarrassment she covered her breasts and crotch with her arms and hands as best as she could.

"Take your arms away and turn this way!" Raaxo shouted.

She dropped her arms in complete disgrace and faced him, looking up to the ceiling with tears welling in her eyes. He slowly looked her up and down and got up and walked toward her. Her heart jumped with fear and loathing at what was to come. Lowering his hand, she gasped and groaned. Wiping his finger on the white pillow case, he noticed a tinge of red. She was not lying, he thought.

"Alright, take your shower, and be quick, don't take all day," Raaxo said triumphantly, having humiliated and cowed her nearly to her core.

She walked away with her head bowed in utter shame and disgrace and took her shower. She silently dried, dressed and quickly gathered her feminine needs into a tote bag. *I will have my revenge,* she said to herself. *You can beat me with your fists, you sorry excuse for a human being, but you can't defeat me,* she said to herself over and over again.

"Get a change of clothing for Mr. President also," Raaxo ordered. "If there is anything else you need, get it now. You won't be coming back here for a while."

Back at the compound, Raaxo walked Carrie to JT's cell first. JT was shown that Carrie was unharmed, although in noticing her new change of clothing, he thought he observed that her right cheek was pinker than the left, but her damp hair was hiding much of her face. She gave him his change of clothing and a toothbrush and paste, and then she turned and walked away silently as she had been previously instructed.

"I love you," JT called.

She did not speak, still following previous instructions.

Raaxo watched the whole scene and was elated that he had succeeded in bringing the disobedient woman to submission.

Five days later, there was a knock on JT's door at an odd time of day. The door opened and Carrie walked in with her tote bag. As the door closed, she fell into his arms, releasing nearly a week's worth of stress and tension in one long sigh.

"Was he mean to you Carrie? Did anything happen while you were on the ship or in the other cell?" JT demanded.

"No my sweet, everything went fine. He didn't hurt me," she lied, not wanting to get JT agitated and upset. "Other than being lonely and wanting you every minute, I was fine. Come, let's lie down together, I need your strength."

JT felt something must have happened, but decided not to pursue it. If and when she wanted to tell him, she would.

28

GIVE 'EM HELL

"**A**dmiral, it is good to see you," John said as he extended his hand to the distinguished, heavily gold-striped and medal-festooned military man.

"Would you fellas like a cup of coffee, tea?" the Admiral asked.

"I'd like a cup of coffee, black, no sugar," John answered.

"I'll have the same," Trent echoed.

The Admiral made the order over his intercom and minutes later a very shapely and attractive Navy Ensign in service dress blues entered the room with the beverages.

"Thank you Ensign," the Admiral said. She smiled, turned and left the office. "One of the perks," the Admiral said with a sigh and a grandfatherly smile.

The Admiral called for Commander Bellows and Captain Holmgaard to join them. "Bring your own coffee," he said over his shoulder as he turned back to the two men.

The two officers entered the room without knocking. After the greetings, the Admiral opened the discussion.

"We have studied your plans and your personnel roster," he began. "We actually know, personally, most of the men you have engaged, and we like Plan C."

Trent looked at John with a knowing smile.

"That is the plan we prefer as well," John added. "As long as we are there, we might as well punish them."

"We agree, although I will never say that in public," the Admiral qualified. "If and when we see that we need to go through with this, we will do what we can do to help you within the purview of our capabilities and our orders. We can and will pose a threat, shadow your operations and seize your ship," the Admiral said.

John and Trent beamed at the Admiral's answers.

"I would rather spend my millions taking action than paying ransoms," John added. "It only fuels the pirate's fires and prolongs the piracy era, and in my business I don't need that."

"We feel exactly the same way," the Admiral concluded. "We will need at least two weeks' notice to obtain the proper authorities and move our assets in place. We will have at least two more meetings, one here and one aboard the Roosevelt to synchronize our plans."

"We agree completely Admiral," John said as the meeting came to a close. "We will get started immediately and we will let you know no later than tomorrow when we can have our people in place. Thank you very much Admiral, I want to start the two week clock as soon as possible."

"Mr. Wingate, be assured and forewarned that if anything goes awry on your end, we will salvage your ship and protect your other assets at sea, but that will be the end of our involvement. We will have nothing to do with the other part of your plan," the Admiral reiterated. "We will deny ever knowing of your plan. Do I make myself absolutely clear?" he said firmly and seriously.

"Crystal, sir," was John's simple yet comprehensive answer.

"Trent, let's get started immediately. Are you clear to move ahead with this now?" John asked as they flew back to New York in Double O's Hawker Beechcraft jet.

"It will take me a day or two to get the men pulled together, and I have a one-day task to complete before I personally can devote myself full time," Trent answered. "I'll go back to Fort Worth tonight and get my people moving. Why don't you gather your things over the weekend, and meet up with us in Fort Worth on Monday?"

Both men looked at each other with the same anxious intensity. Memories of the past came back in rapid succession, one after the other. They smiled at each other, knowing exactly what the other was thinking and feeling.

"That's a great idea Trent. Jesus, I can't wait!" John said, feeling almost giddy.

Charles met them at the airport to take John home.

"Anything special I should bring with me?" John asked.

"Your checkbook would be a good idea."

"See you Monday."

"Trent, I'll call the Admiral tomorrow and tell him to start the two week clock on Monday," John finished.

29

JENNIFER

At his office, John met with his Board and then met separately with the company executives. He told them that he planned to go to Fort Worth on Monday, and would return one more time before leaving on the mission.

"After that, if all goes well, I should be back no later than the middle, maybe the end of next month. Of course I will be available by phone should you need me," John announced to his brother Joe and the rest of the senior management. He intentionally didn't reveal all of his plans, only that the Navy was prepared to intervene to save the Gulf Queen and the Sea Queen should the need arise. "I am investing my money in this venture, along with Double O's. I believe we have shared interests."

John went home and sat daydreaming about the days and weeks to come over two fingers of Laphroig. He was nervous, but not afraid; happy, but not gleeful; excited but not blithe. He realized that his mind and body were gearing up for the challenges ahead and doing so in a quiet, aggressive and responsible manner. He liked the way he felt.

"Hi, Jennifer. I'm glad I was able to find you at home in New York," John said into his phone.

"John darling, how are you?" she replied.

"I'm sitting here feeling very lonely, and I hoped I might persuade you to have dinner with me," John said.

"Where and when?" she asked.

"My place, and as soon as Charles can pick you up and bring you here," John answered.

"Should I bring a toothbrush?" she asked in their personal code.

"You should."

John lifted Jennifer off of her feet in a warm embrace and a kiss as he met her at the door.

"That was nice," she said with a smile as she walked in.

"Here, let me take your bag. There is a glass of wine waiting for you in the living room," John said, taking her belongings back to his bedroom.

She wore casual slacks, a silken, sleeveless top and nothing else. Her breasts, still pert and firm, teased the front of her blouse. She had ageless sensuality, beauty and allure. She took care of herself. John desired her as much if not more than he had when they had met all those years ago. They had enjoyed a long and beautiful yet separated love affair with each other over the years, and there was a familiarity that brought joy to both. He always felt thrilled in her presence.

"What's the occasion?" Jennifer asked, sipping her wine.

"I'm going off on a little adventure next week, and I wanted, no, I needed, to spend time in your arms before I go," he answered.

"Sounds ominous," she said roundly in her English accent, getting up and walking to his chair. She sat down on his lap, put her arms around his neck, and kissed him warmly on the lips. "Will this do?" she smiled, hiding her concern.

"You betcha," John smiled back, rubbing his hand up and down her silken back, feeling her smooth, taut and lean body beneath.

"What is going on with you and your 'little adventure'?" she asked.

He went on to tell her about the hijacking, JT and Carrie's capture and the ransoms, but fell short of telling her what he planned to do. He told her that he and the pirates were negotiating and he would have to fly to their location and give them the ransom money personally.

She sat straight up in his lap with a look of disbelief on her face.

"John, how did all this happen?" she said, standing and going back to her seat on the couch, folding her long legs beneath her.

He told her about the honeymoon trip, how he had been concerned before they left and how he had talked himself into it, realizing the odds and the low likelihood that a hijacking would happen.

"I didn't want to burden you with the situation earlier. I wanted to make sure I had everything under control before letting you know," John said, looking her in the eye. "They have been in captivity for three weeks now; it is actually three weeks today. A deadline has been set for the handing over of ransoms. As far as we can tell, judging from the videos I receive as *proof of life*, they are still fine, but we aren't going to let things slide and risk a change in attitude. We have heard that the Somalis typically stand true to their dealings and rarely harm their hostages. We can't be positive it will be true in our case, however. There are no guarantees," John said.

Jennifer sat motionless, concerned and in deep thought. After several minutes she said, "I am having a very hard time getting all of this straight in my mind, John. Are you actually going to confront the Somalis or are you sending a proxy?"

"You know my feelings for JT and Carrie, who is now legally my daughter by the way. With the exception of her new husband, I am all that she has. I have to be at her side when she needs me," John confessed. "But I don't want to cast a pall on the evening. Would you rather go out or eat a Crab Louie that Rosa has made for us?"

"By all means the Crab Louie, light on the dressing," and Jennifer began to perk up.

He walked over to the couch and pulled her up by the hands. He hugged her and kissed her, caressed her backside and said, "It is

151

always you who I think of when I have deep, troubling problems. You manage to level me every time."

"I haven't done anything," she said.

"If you only knew how much your mere presence affects me," John rallied as they strolled to the kitchen. "Why don't you set us a table and I'll get this thing dished up?"

They both went about their agreed tasks and had a delightful meal, Jennifer sitting next to John with her hand resting on his thigh, removing it only to wipe her mouth or smooth her thick, lustrous, white/grey and shoulder length hair. She got up to clear the table, and John watched her hips rhythmically sway at her narrow waist as she moved from the dining room to the kitchen and back.

"How do you do it?" he said, pulling her down to his lap.

"Do what?" she smiled.

"Stay so drop dead gorgeous," he said, kissing her shoulder.

"Hours upon hours of exhausting work. And it isn't getting any easier, by the way," she admitted. "I am in a cutthroat business where looks count. If I were to rest for one minute, I would be so much 'dead meat' as you Americans are fond of saying. The eighteen-year-olds would devour my flesh," she said with a laugh in her rich, round and sensual British accent.

"Can you stay the weekend?" John asked.

"Only if you promise to ravage me," she said, throwing herself at him.

"Oh, I promise," he replied, and the memories of their youthful days streamed back.

The weekend went by too quickly, John thought. "I'm flying to Fort Worth tomorrow to meet with a group of men who will work with me on this venture," John told Jennifer on Sunday evening. "Let's go for an early dinner at Henri's so we can come home and sit together on the couch and neck until it's time to go to bed."

Jennifer loved his playful libido, still very active at sixty. She cherished every minute she spent with him. His strength, honesty and virtue were irresistible. If only she could find a way to settle down with him.

"John, when you get back from your trip, I want to sit with you and talk about us, our relationship and the future," Jennifer said to him.

"I would like to do that as well," he said, holding her tightly.

30

THE ULTIMATE BETRAYAL

"Mr. Wingate, I would like for you to have casho with me tonight," Raaxo said to JT.

"Casho?" JT asked.

"Dinner," Raaxo answered.

"What about Mrs. Wingate?" JT asked.

"Women have no place in a man's world. We will chew Khat and talk of men things."

"Very well, what time?" JT asked.

"I will send my man for you."

At eight o'clock, JT began to worry because there still had not been a messenger. Finally, he heard a knock and went to the door.

"You come," was the abrupt request.

John smiled at Carrie and told her to close and bar the door behind him as best she could. He told her to wait for his knock and not to let anyone in, and to scream loudly if anyone tried.

She strolled around and around her cell until she tired and then lay down on her mat.

JT walked to the main villa with the scruffy pirate. He counted paces and observed and made mental note of everything he saw.

"Come in Mr. Wingate. Welcome to my home," Raaxo said.

"Thank you for inviting me," JT said.

A slender, reasonably attractive woman entered the room with a plate with several bundles of what looked like spinach leaves wrapped in a sheath with their petioles sticking out. The six-to seven-inch long bundles looked, to JT, like giant green squids.

Raaxo tossed a bundle to JT and began to unravel a bundle for himself. The outer sheath was a banana leaf used to keep the Khat leaves moist, and the smaller inner leaves were the darker green Khat. Raaxo stuffed his mouth with the leaves until his left cheek bulged out and began a slow, cud-like chewing. John did not open his sheath and set it aside. Raaxo noticed, but didn't seem upset or concerned.

"Foreigners don't like Khat," Raaxo mumbled, slurring slightly with his full mouth. "It is an everyday ritual here in Hobyo among the pirates, the only ones who can afford the luxury."

"Please excuse me, but if you don't mind I'll just chew these peanuts instead," JT said.

"Not at all," Raaxo said, and JT noticed the slight slurring of words. The drug acted very quickly.

The woman returned with tea and more nuts. JT smiled at her and thanked her.

"It isn't necessary to thank her, it is her job. You foreigners are much too civil," Raaxo said.

After dinner, as the evening wore on with continuous nonsensical gibberish from Raaxo, JT noticed that the Somalian became more and more indolent. He was almost sprawled on the floor and his words were more and more incoherent. At one point, he noticed that Raaxo had nodded off and woke with a start and a grunt, choking and coughing on the Khat leaf residue in his mouth. *How easy it would be to cripple or kill this man now in his current state, steal his arms wherever they are hidden and run for our lives.* Unfortunately, JT knew there was no place to run, especially with Carrie in tow.

JT heard a loud scream and instantly knew it was Carrie. Something had happened. He woke Raaxo, and started out the door.

"Hold on Mr. Wingate, you go nowhere unescorted," Raaxo said while strapping his AK-47 over his shoulder. JT noticed three or four of them hanging on wooden pegs in the hallway off the living room.

Staggering slightly, Raaxo followed JT out the door, spitting out what was left of his Khat. JT started to trot as he heard the screams again and Raaxo picked up his pace as well. When they got to the cell, they noticed that the door had been forced open and Carrie stood in a back corner shuddering and holding the front of her blouse together with shaking hands. JT went straight to Carrie and put his arms around her, holding and shielding her.

"What are you doing?" Raaxo shouted at the pirate who said nothing in return. Raaxo butted him in his forehead with the stock of his AK-47 and the man went down. Raaxo kicked him hard in the ribs several times, and the man pleaded for mercy.

"These people are our bread and butter you stupid pig! If anything happens to them, we don't get our money and everything is for nothing. Don't ever let anything like this happen again, or I'll kill you. Do you understand me? I will cut your heart out and feed it to the sharks!" Raaxo ranted, still shouting.

The man nodded. His face was bleeding from Carrie's scratches and the head butt, and he got up and scurried out of the cell.

"I am sorry Mr. Wingate. This will never happen again," Raaxo said as he turned to leave without even a glance in Carrie's direction.

JT noted that there was no apology to Carrie. JT also noticed that Raaxo was reeling a little when the two of them had entered the cell, and that he jarred himself bouncing off the door jambs as he left.

Raaxo left the cell and staggered back to his villa. Inside, he hung up his AK-47 and roughly grabbed his woman by the arm, dragging her to his shambolic bedroom. He pulled up her skirts and roughly mounted her as she laid there motionless and unfeeling. He entered her mutilated and scarred genitalia (an occurrence in ninety-eight percent of Somali women) cruelly and forcefully.

When he was finished, he rolled off; she got up, smoothed her clothing, and left the room. He rolled over and fell into a mindless stupor.

JT slept holding Carrie in his arms. When she woke the next morning, she was still visibly shaken.

"It will be okay, Carrie," JT consoled. "They aren't going to try that again. Besides, I'll never leave you alone again," he promised.

The two went out for their walk and Carrie noticed, with disgust, that the offending pirate was watching them. She had had enough of these repulsive little creatures.

"That's his job sweetie; he has to keep an eye on us, more so now since he has been berated," JT said.

"I know it, but I don't have to like it. These scrawny, sweaty, nauseating little creeps make me sick just to look at them, never mind being touched by them," Carrie almost spat the words.

That noontime, Raaxo had a lunch meal served to JT and Carrie.

JT wrote a note to Raaxo:
> Your guard tore the buttons from the front
> of my wife's blouse and we need needle and
> thread to repair the damage.

Within minutes of the message being delivered, the guard reappeared with the items JT had requested.

"Seems as though contrition might be a part of the Somali ethos," Carrie said with a smile as she began sewing back the buttons and repairing the small tears at the loop holes.

Minutes later, Carrie stood and put her blouse back on. "There," she said, pleased with herself. "Good as new."

JT took the needle and thread and placed them on the window sill. *Might come in handy someday,* he thought.

The days and the hours seemed endless as JT and Carrie endured their incarceration. They unwittingly became creatures of habit.

Every morning, after breakfast, JT would scratch a tally on the wall, seven to a cluster, counting the days and the weeks. Carrie rose, ate her breakfast, brushed her teeth with the brush and tooth paste she had retrieved from the Gulf Queen, and then did several stretching exercises.

The two would then be let outside for their walking exercise. Around and around their fifty-foot by fifty-foot yard they walked, counting the revolutions, always ending in between 35 and 40 round trips before their hour was up. The path they walked was bare of weeds and thick with dust.

They would then be locked back up inside the hovel and do hatha yoga exercises together, and then they would sit and rest or nap if there were no breezes to cool them.

At noon, the guard entered with their lunch meal and they would sit on the floor and slowly chew their food, talking and comforting each other. JT was the most nurturing, noting that Carrie was getting more and more antsy with the continuing captivity. After lunch, they did more yoga exercises and then laid down to chat and rest.

At around 4:00PM, the guard entered to let them out for their afternoon walk. Hand in hand, they continued their laps around the yard. The tree-lined, CMU block walls were too high to see over, but they could hear the ocean's waves in the distance, and smell the sea breezes.

They ate supper at 6:30PM and spent the rest of the evening in each other's arms, talking, kissing, and often, like tonight, making love.

"Time for another *'proof of life'* video," Raaxo announced. "Mrs. Wingate, how are you today?" Raaxo asked, mockery lacing his words.

"I am fine," Carrie said.

"Are you getting enough to eat?" Raaxo went on taunting. "Especially since we added a third meal last week."

"Yes we are," She said, keeping her emotions completely in check and ignoring his nauseating behavior.

"Is there anything you need or want, Mrs. Wingate?"

"No, thank you," Carrie ended and looked down at her lap.

"And Mr. Wingate, is there anything you need?" Raaxo continued.

"No, thank you," JT said, also looking down at his knees.

John studied the video as he watched it over and over with Jennifer. JT was tapping on his knee again, but the photographer panned upward momentarily during the session, interrupting the coded message. B A C L A C E 1 was all that came through. He and Jennifer tried as many combinations as they could think of, and eventually Jennifer hit on BACK PLACE 1. *If this is the message,* John thought, *they are located at the first place the Roosevelt Petty Officer noticed the two walkers.*

John decided to call the Admiral with his find at the Admiral's weekend number. Within five minutes, the Admiral connected him to the four-way.

"In the proof of life video I sent you all this morning, my nephew is tapping on his knee again, and the message that I got was BACK PLACE 1. Did anyone else get that?" John asked of the group.

"I saw the tapping, but didn't put it together," the Admiral noted.

"Same with me," Trent confessed.

"We are on the same page Mr. Wingate. We came to the same conclusion, and have been watching the first villa more closely," the Roosevelt Petty Officer remarked.

"Thanks gentlemen, I'm beginning to feel a little better about this whole thing. Admiral, we are working on a final plan of action and will be getting it to you soon," John announced. "I would like to start the two week clock tomorrow."

"Very well John, we will start the countdown then," the Admiral said.

"Trent, give me a call when you hang up please," John said. "Thank you all for your attention, and sorry about the weekend interruption," John said and hung up his phone.

John's phone rang again almost instantly.

"Hello John, Trent," Trent offered. "Good discovery. We have been working on the final plan, and we have concentrated on the three possible villas at the south end of the village. We are targeting the villa we all suspect holds your family members now."

"Great Trent, I'll look forward to the briefing with all the men tomorrow," John said and hung up. "All right, I'm yours for what's left of the weekend," he said to Jennifer.

"'I'm beginning to feel better about this whole thing'?" Jennifer questioned. "'We are working on the final plan of action'?" she continued. "What does all that mean?"

"We just need to polish off the final details of how and where to get the ransom money to them. We need to make sure JT and Carrie are safely in our hands aboard the Gulf Queen at the same time we hand over the money," John lied.

"I feel so bad for JT and Carrie. They looked very brave in the video, but they must be petrified," Jennifer remarked.

"Jennifer, JT has a black belt in jiu-jitsu and has eerie self-control. If he thought he could get away from his captors and bring Carrie with him, he definitely has the capability and I am sure he would have made his move before this. I'm sure it is the remoteness that is keeping him from trying to escape," John said. "Don't count that young lady out either. She has strength we haven't begun to see the best of yet. Let's sit on the couch and hold hands."

After breakfast Monday morning, John told Jennifer that Charles would take her to her boutique or home, and John would continue on to the airport and the beginning of his adventure.

31

HULK, CHUNK, JUMBO

John's trip to Fort Worth was uneventful, and Trent was at the airport to meet him.

"John, good to see you. Here, give me one of those bags," Trent offered.

"Thank you, Trent," John said, handing him his Hartmann garment bag.

"How is everything stacking up?" John began.

Trent told John that he had brought the three team leaders to Fort Worth for the initial briefings.

"I think we should allow each team leader to pick his own crew of seven men. They belong to a fairly small and elite community, everyone knows, or at least knows of, everyone else," Trent opined.

"That's good thinking," John replied. "It will integrate the individual teams as well as the group as a whole."

"After we have completed the initial briefings and you have gotten to know and approve of the leaders, I will have the rest of the men join us for final briefings, and off we go."

There was Charles 'Chunk' Farrington, a six-foot five-inch, two hundred and thirty pound bruiser from South Carolina. He had a very soft, calm and self-assured voice that demanded your ear.

There was Erik 'Hulk' Hendersen, a six-foot four-inch, two hundred and twenty-five pound Scandinavian from Minnesota. He had a number one haircut that reminded John of the Norse Vikings he studied as an elective in university. Erik said little, but when he did speak, he made complete sense, speaking only to the core of the matter with substance.

Lastly there was James 'Jumbo' Reimer, one half-inch shy of six-foot six-inches, hailing from heartland Nebraska. His hands were like hams, his arms were like clubs and his smile was infectiously disarming. Always time for a joke and a laugh, but never time for error.

Even with his six-foot four-inch, two hundred twenty pound frame, John felt dwarfed in their collective presence.

"It's a pleasure to meet you men. I'm glad we're meeting here in this well lit room rather than some back alley in Fallujah, however," John greeted the men, eliciting a chuckle. "I want very much to get to know you three on a one-to-one basis."

It was John's intention to spend as much time with each man as he could, have meals together and share drinks together in the evening. He would observe the men's team capabilities during the briefings and the daily workouts. He would assess their leadership capability when the rest of the crews showed up.

The memories of John's earlier days at the Fort Worth facility came rushing back as he worked out with Trent and the three Seals. Trent and John were obviously straining at the workouts while the Seals were taking it all in easy stride. Trent's regimen wasn't a tenth of the training a Seal received from the US Navy. All three Seals were in top physical condition, capable of conquering anything that Trent had to throw at them with ease.

"Chunk," John called, realizing how apropos the crew name was. "Run with me this morning, please."

The big man swung in beside John at an easy lope as the two took on the four hundred meter asphalt track.

"Do you run every morning, sir?" the Seal asked.

"Yes, I try to, and please call me John," he answered.

"Yes sir," was the reply.

They jogged on and John picked up the pace to a run. He noticed that his exercise partner wasn't even breathing hard. John picked up the pace to a sprint and the Seal followed suit, realizing this was some sort of test or drill. John pulled up to a jog again and the Seal kept sprinting until he rounded the track and caught up with John again.

"Smart ass," John said. "Showing up a sixty-year-old."

The Seal smiled, his chest heaving slightly, small beads of sweat beginning to form on his tanned, muscular and smile-wrinkled brow. They jogged and talked for another twenty minutes before they went to the house for breakfast. John watched the Seal put away at least fifteen hundred calories of fried eggs, bacon, pancakes and milk as John ate his yogurt, fruit and two scrambled eggs.

"Where did you serve?" John finally asked.

"Mideast mostly. Iran, Afghanistan and I trained fighters in Pakistan," Chunk answered. "We mainly did extraction work and kills on extremist militants."

"Purple Heart?"

"Three."

"Kills?"

"Didn't keep track, sir."

They finished their meal and went to the briefing room. Trent had charts, satellite photos, equipment lists and crew lists tacked up on the front wall. The Seals went up to study the data close-up and John noticed that they spent the majority of their time at the crew lists, no doubt looking for buddies and potential crew members.

"Snatch and grab," Trent announced to the trio. "We have a hostage situation, and we have a nasty little bunch of Somalis to deal with."

The satellite photos had three circles drawn on them and the letters A, B and C written next to them. The C circle now had a big X through it. John noticed only expressions of curiosity on the Seals' faces; there were no signs of fear, anxiety or distress. *These men are the real thing*, John thought.

"Please study everything for the next hour or so, and then have a seat," Trent instructed. There were four easy chairs arranged in front of the room.

Trent and John left the room and went to Trent's office in the turret.

"Great bunch of men, Trent," John offered. "So far they are very impressive."

They talked over the extraction plan in detail and went back to the waiting Seals.

"Fellas, I'd like you to list your crew preferences in the following categories: must have; will take; can't work with," Trent said. "As you can see, there are twenty-five names on the list and we are thinking that we will require three crews of eight each."

The men got to work, and within five minutes they had completed their lists. Trent gathered them up and projected them up on the screen that electronically lowered over the front wall, and the men sat back with smiles on their faces.

Each list had only seven names, none of the names were repeated and all were listed under 'Will Take' only.

"Well gentlemen, that was easy," Trent said. "I had visions of us going back and forth for hours trying to fill out the lists."

"It was a no brainer, sir," Hulk said. "We all agreed while you were out of the room."

"Why only 'Will Takes'?" John asked.

"Sir, a Seal Team motto is 'Ready to lead, ready to follow, never quit,'" Hulk answered. "They are all Seals, so there are no 'Can't work withs.' They are all of equal abilities and all Seals act as one, so there are no 'Must haves.' Our choice was that I took the first seven, Chunk took the second and Jumbo took the third. Simple, no fuss, no muss. Everything is neat and tidy and in alphabetical order as well," Hulk smiled. "We did fudge Wilson in, however. He is having some major financial issues with a very sick child and really needs the money, so we chose him over Uthman. He also happens to be one of six ace night snipers in our group."

"What is the problem with Wilson's child?" John asked.

"Cancer, sir," Hulk answered.

John wrote a note to himself.

"I will contact these men, and we will have them arrive on Wednesday," Trent announced.

"We noticed that there is no night vision equipment on your lists. Does this mean we will do this job in broad daylight, sir?" Chunk asked in a firm, fearless voice.

"No, it doesn't," John interrupted. "That was an oversight on our part. Thanks."

"If we can, we would like to suggest four-barrel NVGs for the point-men and snipers, double barrels for everyone else," Jumbo added. "We understand the expense."

"Note taken," Trent said. "Let's break for lunch and our afternoon workouts."

"Expense isn't an issue, if you think everyone should have four-barrel NVGs," John said as he started to stand.

"Not necessary, sir," Jumbo said.

John had underestimated the integrity, work ethic and capabilities of these men. He was getting more and more excited.

"Fellas, I am not at all interested in paying ransoms, and I would rather spend my money on you and your capabilities and punish the hell out of those people in the process. Even though this is personal, we in the shipping industry are getting sick and tired of these renegades upsetting our daily business. This has personally put me and my president on hold for over a month, and we have a large, successful business to run and can't afford that type of interruption," John announced. "I know there is risk to you men, but it is calculated, and if everyone does their part we will be safely victorious."

"Hooyah!" the three Seals answered in unison.

"I was extremely impressed with you fellas during the crew selection process," John said to Hulk as they ate their lunch.

"How so, sir?" came the reply.

"I just thought that in such an elite outfit, there must be strong bonds formed that would drive your selection process."

"There are strong bonds formed sir, but those bonds have no place in combat. We were trained to put everything aside except the mission and the objective. If you find out that you have been assigned to a team along with a good buddy, that's fine, but there is no room for emotion of any kind in the CQ type of battle we do," Hulk offered. "Close quarter kills, sniper attacks, bombings; we can't spend time worrying about each other. Only the target gets our full attention. We have each other's backs, sir, but that is instinctive. We don't really think about it, we just do it."

The afternoon completed the briefing session. John liked the plan very much and couldn't wait to put it into action. On Wednesday, the remainder of the men arrived at DFW and Trent had a shuttle waiting for them. John had told Trent he wanted everything first class for the men. He wanted them to feel special about the mission.

Thursday morning, all twenty-four men had gathered in the briefing room and Trent decided to let the crew leaders lead the briefing. The men listened to the plan intently.

"Day or night operation?" one of the men asked.

"Night," Jumbo answered.

"Any rules of engagement?" another questioned.

"None," said Hulk. "Part of the plan is to punish these people. That should help answer your question."

"Are there local or national militias operating in this area?" a third inquired.

"We haven't seen anything like that in the three plus weeks we have been observing the area," Trent answered. "It looks like a very isolated spot to us. Probably four or five large extended families at the most. There can't be more than a few hundred people living in the village, and there is nothing for hundreds of miles in any direction."

"Have you spotted any night guards posted around the village or down at the harbor?" another Seal asked.

"Good question," Trent said. "We haven't gotten any input on that from the Navy, but then again we haven't asked. I'll bring that up with the Admiral at our next get together."

"Can I ask who the Admiral is sir?" requested one of the seals.

"Admiral Stimpson," John answered.

"Good man sir, one of the best. You are sure to get full coopera-tion from him. He hates the pirates more than most. He has been fighting them for some time now. Most of us have served under him at one time or another," the Seal said.

The questions continued and by the end of the day, all the men ap-peared satisfied with the planning, the manning and the equipment.

32

A LAST FAREWELL

"Hello Admiral, nice to see you again," John said as he and Trent entered the Admiral's office for the last time.

"Mr. Wingate, Mr. McSpadden, welcome," the Admiral said.

After the usual greetings and formalities, John told the Admiral that the pirates had upped the ante to $6 million for his nephew and wife if we don't set a 'drop date' immediately. He further told the Admiral that he had no interest in paying those kinds of dollars without a fight.

"Admiral, we have put together a group of men with solid backgrounds," Trent said. "We have briefed them and we have, with their help, fine-tuned our scheme to the point that it is almost foolproof. We are leaving for Oman on Saturday to practice the whole thing, with the Sultan's permission, on the ground under very similar conditions on the west central side of Masirah Island."

"Getting the Sultan's permission may be easier said than done," the Admiral said, knowing the Sultan's integrity.

"I have met the Sultan many times and have worked with him personally. If there is a chance, I will find it," John interjected.

Trent went on to say that they would need escort from Oman to Hobyo, assistance with the recovery of the Gulf Queen and its crew and escort back to Bahrain.

"I have promised you that I would do what you ask, and it will take me several days to get a destroyer to the Oman and have the Carrier Task Force swing south within range of your operations," the Admiral said. "Again, we can have nothing to do with your ground operations. You must launch from your vessels and return to your vessels. Roosevelt can provide a fear factor, but that is it as far as our close-up operations will go."

"By the way Mr. Wingate, one of the reasons we like your plan so much is that you have managed to gather most of the best men we have ever trained," Captain Holmgaard commented. "We know many of the men personally, and if anyone can pull this off, that group can."

"I have just spent the last week working with them, and you are preaching to the choir. I am amazed by those fellas," John reiterated. "They are not overconfident, arrogant or machismo; they are only self-assured, you feel it the entire time you are around them. I have no regrets about investing my money in those men. By the way, they had very high praise for you and your team, Admiral."

"Captain, one of the team members asked if we had done any night infrared studies to see if there were guards posted around the village or at the harbor area," Trent added. "Do you know?"

"You know, Trent, that is a great question, and I'll get into it right away," Captain Holmgaard promised. "I'm amazed we didn't think of that earlier."

"Mr. Wingate, I will contact you as soon as I have received confirmations from all of our participants. It will probably be sometime later today," Captain Holmgaard said.

All the men stood and shook hands.

"Good hunting everyone," the Admiral said as John and Trent filed out.

"Are you coming with us, Trent?" John asked on the flight back to New York.

"I think it would be wise for me to stay with you through the launch of the Masirah Island effort, but after that I think you are on your own," Trent said. "Unless, of course, you think otherwise John."

"No, that sounds right to me," John said. "I'm flying out tomorrow to Oman to grease the skids with the Sultan, and then off to SOAF Air Force Base on Masirah Island, if he gives us the go-ahead. You need to check and double check our equipment and supplies, make sure we have an excess and get them and the men to Oman as soon as you can."

John had his pilot fly Trent back to Fort Worth. Both had a full plate and there was no time to waste.

"So that is where we stand at the moment," John said in conclusion to the board and the company executives gathered for the final briefing. "The cost breakdown is all laid out for you in the file I have made up for you. The ransom amount demanded for the Gulf Queen is 2.8 Million, so I feel that Double O should pick up at least two-thirds of the cost, which would naturally include the offsetting value of other company asset costs we will be using. I'll carry the remaining million of the cost myself."

"No John, JT is my son. I'll split the remaining costs with you," Joe offered.

"Thank you Joe," John smiled, shaking his older brother's hand. "Is the board happy?"

"We think that your offer is more than fair John. We have extensive piracy coverage policies, I believe, and we will work with the insurance companies to see where we stand with them."

"Very well then, I will keep you all informed and we will have a complete tally of costs when the operation is concluded," John finalized. "I leave tomorrow to get the ball rolling. Are there any other issues you would like to discuss before I leave?" he asked.

"All we ask is that you communicate with us as best you can and keep us informed of your actions. We will have our attorneys research the legalities of our actions," one of the directors said.

"The communication I will deal with, but I don't want our plans to be out in the open until we have completed the operation. I want you to promise that you won't bring in attorneys at this juncture. The top house legal only, if you must, and he needs to be sworn to absolute secrecy. Don't talk with the insurance company either until you get the word we are all safe. Too many good lives hang on the secrecy of the endeavor," John emphasized. "I will sign a waiver and resign from the board if you feel that will be necessary."

The directors spoke amongst themselves and decided to shelve the issues. John's plan was sound, he was approaching it in a professional manner and he had a history of strong and sensible decision making.

"Resignation won't be necessary, John, we just want to make sure the company's best interests are preserved," Joe said.

"I understand," were John's last words, miffed at the circumstances.

With the board's blessing, John left for the remainder of the day to prepare for his venture.

33

THE SULTAN OF OMAN

The trip to Oman was long but comfortable in the Oman Air First Class seating, and John was able to fine tune his proposal to the Sultan, Qaboos bin Said Al Said. He decided that the best approach was to be completely open and honest with his plan. He had met the Sultan personally several times in his early years in shipping operations and remembered him to be a fair-minded, even-handed, just individual, one of the few such leaders in the Gulf. He was concerned that the Sultan's neutral foreign policies might get in the way, and John had worked out a few scenarios to speak openly without confrontation.

A private vehicle was waiting for him at Seeb International Airport. It was a forty minute trip down Sultan Qaboos Street through Muscat, Al Mina Street, and Al Bahiri Road to Al Alam Palace.

"Your Majesty, thank you for seeing me," John said as they sat in the formal receiving room.

"It is my pleasure Mr. Wingate. We haven't seen each other for some time now, and if I remember correctly, the last time was 1996 when you personally supervised the shipments of earthmoving equipment to Masirah Island," the Sultan reminisced. "I remember our meetings well, you and me knee deep in the shallow surf watching your ships offload piece after piece of heavy equipment."

"I remember it well too, sir," John smiled. "Like it was yesterday. Those were the days."

"What brings you back to my country, Mr. Wingate?" the Sultan inquired.

"First, thank you for allowing us to mobilize our efforts at your port," John began.

The Sultan smiled and nodded.

John explained that his nephew and daughter had been taken hostage by Somali pirates and that he would like to practice their extraction plan in a similar environment on Masirah Island.

"The western beach areas, four or five miles south of the RDF Base near where we offloaded in 1996, if I remember correctly, would be a perfect spot to practice," John said. He laid out the plan in detail, beginning with the landings and ending with the race to the successful finish of the operation. All the time he spoke, he noticed that the Sultan made mental notes, looked down at his folded hands and then back to John's eyes. At one time the Sultan furrowed his brow slightly and then went back to his calming, smiling demeanor.

"Mr. Wingate, the Somalis and the Yemenis are our neighbors and we have commercial ties with them and we will do nothing to harm that relationship," the Sultan said as John shifted in his seat to await the Sultan's refusal. Qaboos sat pondering for nearly one or two minutes, looking at his knees, and at one time even looking at his watch. "So let me understand this correctly. You are making a movie about US Navy Seals, and you would like to use an area of Masirah Island to ensure authenticity. Is that correct?"

"Aaah that is absolutely correct sir!" John smiled in relief. The Sultan had found a way to grant the permission he knew John desperately needed and that the Sultan himself wanted to grant.

"Very well then, I will notify the Commandant at the Island to let him know of your presence and the length of your stay. We will not be able to help you in any way, but feel free to stay as long as you need," the Sultan assured.

The two men stood and faced each other. John took a half step toward the Sultan, leaned well forward and offered his hand. The Sultan took his hand and placed his other hand on top of their shake in a warm and infrequently made gesture.

"Good shooting my friend," the Sultan said, and he then winked, turned and strode with regal bearing from the receiving room.

John couldn't hide his elation as he left the Palace. He was driven to Muscat Port to meet the Sea Queen and her captain for the short 200 mile, ten hour trip to Masirah Island. The Seals had been assembled and all of the operations materials were on board, ready for whatever was to come.

"John, how did it go with the Sultan?" Trent asked.

"Well Trent, he had me worried for a few minutes, but he gave us the approval to 'shoot a movie about US Seals' on Masirah Island," John said with a big, cocked-mouth wink.

"Fantastic John! What a man he is. I was concerned about this one last hurdle. I know the Sultan is a fiercely honest man, and plays by the rules. One of the few here in the Gulf," Trent answered. "I also read somewhere, however, that he is staunchly anti-piracy and speaks out openly about it at the Arab summit meetings."

"Trent, when I first met the Sultan as a young ruler, he had to fight for everything he had and then fight to hold onto it as well. He completely understands our mission. He may be short in stature, but he is a giant in courage, mettle and understanding."

"John, you sail at 20:00 hours. I'm leaving you now if there is nothing else you want of me," Trent said.

"No. Have a safe trip back, and thanks for everything my friend. Again, I couldn't have gotten this far without you," John said, shaking Trent's hand and giving him a warm, rare hug. "Don't forget that other operations we talked about. Don't let me down now."

"I've got that under control, John, and if you run into any snags or find yourself wanting something, anything, you call me and I, or it, will be here in a heartbeat," Trent finally offered before turning and leaving the ship.

John sat and ate with the men at dinner that night and he asked the three team leaders to join him in his stateroom that evening for last minute discussions. He told the men that they were on Masirah Island to make a movie, and all three crew chiefs immediately understood. John offered drinks. All three passed as they held up their coffee mugs and water bottles.

"Thanks anyway, sir," Hulk said. "We have a long challenge ahead, and yesterday started the final preparation. From here on out its coffee, water and milk."

"Have you gone through your provisions and equipment to make sure you have everything?" John asked.

"We have sir, and we are ready to go. We will lay out the course on the beach tomorrow and take a few runs at it tomorrow as well," Chunk added.

"Do you think that will do it for you?" John asked.

"We will have to run it until we can do it blindfolded. We think that we should have things wrapped up on Masirah Island in three days, and then, if you are satisfied sir, it is off to Hobyo," Jumbo said.

"The Navy said they would need three days to get to us, so that dovetails perfectly," John said. "Thanks fellas, and if there is nothing else, I'll get on with my communications and see you in the morning. Is the team settled and ready?"

John had his Bahrain office outfit the Sea Queen with twelve two-man housing units, two eight man shower trailers, two eight-man toilet units, and then wire and plumb all of them up on the cargo deck. The housing units were eight feet wide by twenty-four feet long and completely air-conditioned. The shower units and the toilet units were the same modular size, making the configuration easy to set up and remove. There were also four eight-by-twenty conex containers for the equipment, supplies and munitions. A canvas roofed eating area tent kept the men shaded. The accommodations for the Seals were first class.

"Hooya, sir. Hooya," Jumbo said as they left John's stateroom. The Seals appreciated John's thoroughness, professionalism, kindness and genuine concern for their well-being. He was treating them with dignity and respect.

John went up to the wheelhouse and met with his captain, Nabeel. John requested that the bridge be cleared and then discussed the next three days and the Sea Queen's participation. He discussed the trip to Hobyo and the Sea Queen's responsibilities there, as well.

Nabeel, one of Double O's best Gulf Sea captains, nodded his head in complete understanding.

"You won't be in danger at any time, as we are being shadowed by the US Navy the entire way. They will be at our side within minutes should we need them," John said.

"That is certainly good to know Mr. Wingate. I'm not afraid sir, I only want to perform our tasks perfectly to your satisfaction and to the needs of the fine men you have brought aboard," Nabeel praised.

"Nabeel, I chose to speak with you in private because it is imperative that we maintain secrecy. We can't risk leaking our plan," John said. "You can tell your crew we are making a movie about Seals on Masirah Island, which will get us through the next three days. Then it is up to you who you tell and what you tell them. We will keep the radio equipment locked from here on in. It might be a good idea to collect cell phones. If any of them have emergencies, we can accommodate them somehow."

"I understand your concern sir, but the crew is very loyal to Double O. All have been sailing with me for years. I trust them," Nabeel said. "We know all of the Gulf Queen's crew; they are our friends and we all want to help."

"Nonetheless, I still ask for your discretion," John repeated.

"I will be, and my crew is at your service," Nabeel proudly said.

John completed his communications with the Admiral and Double O and went back to his stateroom for a final night cap and reflection on the days to come.

34

PRACTICE MAKES PERFECT

The teams were simply named 'Alpha', 'Beta' and 'Charlie' in keeping with the 'no muss, no fuss' character of the Seal team leaders. John's respect for the team leaders and members was still growing by the hour.

"Today we will accurately lay out the targets and then do a couple of walk-throughs, sir," Hulk announced to John. "Everyone is familiar with the target layout sir, and ninety percent of the time we don't get the luxury of trial runs. We will take full advantage of this opportunity."

The 90°F temperature coupled with the 80% humidity and the 83°F dew point took its toll on John as he and the men walked through the operation. At the end of the first walk through, John was flushed, nauseated and bushed and he had to take shelter from the oppressive weather in one of the temporary tent targets the Seal teams had laid out and constructed to the correct scale and location.

"It will be a little cooler at night sir, but with all due respect we feel you should rethink your participation in the ground work portion of the operation," Jumbo said to John. "We fully respect your desire to be hands-on involved sir, but we all feel that all of our efforts will be best served if you opt out of the snatch and take on a less strenuous role back at the beach."

John appreciated the straight talk he was receiving from the men, and he wisely decided to take a back seat. It wouldn't be fair to the other men to have to worry about him and their perilous jobs as well.

"You're right Jumbo, and thanks for the sugar coating," John said with a weak smile. "I can follow you fellas on the radio and be of possible help that way. I will remain with Alpha 1 at the beach."

"Fair enough sir," Jumbo said. "We know you are disappointed."

The men completed the second walk through and went to meet with John again at the tent. Even the youngest among them appeared sapped after the second run-through.

"Tonight we will do our first dress rehearsal sir," Hulk announced to John. "The men will cool down and rest up until it's time to go."

"We'd like to discuss a few things with you first though sir," Hulk continued.

"Certainly," John said.

"First, we think that the diversionary tactics we have devised are well thought out and will be very successful. We need to make sure that everything happens at the right time though sir. In order to keep the confusion going, we have to do things in a seemingly random order so that they never figure out where the attack is coming from. We hit them in the north first, north central next, south and then finally south central and keep hammering until it's time to leave."

John agreed and they discussed their thoughts in detail. John was again amazed by their capabilities and insight. He knew that the men were not going to make the operation any harder for themselves than necessary and their ideas were brilliant in their simplicity.

"Secondly, we think we should try to do the snatch first, or at least get Alpha 3 next to the target before all hell breaks loose," Hulk continued. "If these guys are hopped up on that stuff they chew, we don't want to risk any accidents."

"You are absolutely correct," John said. "My family will need some forewarning and reassurance. Good thinking, men."

"Thirdly, we were studying the satellite photos last night and noticed a situation we have all overlooked so far," Hulk said.

"What is that?" John asked.

"In the trees and brush just south of where Beta is forming, there is a compound that appears to be a pen in the satellite photos, but we can't be sure and need to clear it before getting the larger operation underway," Hulk said while pointing out the location to John.

"I see," John said. "You are right. That could be a deal breaker if there are people there."

"There are several compounds near where Charlie will be forming up and operating, and we need to allow time for Charlie to clear those structures before going on with the plan as well."

"No question," John confirmed. "How much time do you think this will add to the overall scheme?"

"It shouldn't take us more than eight to ten minutes to deal with everything we have talked about," Hulk estimated.

After dinner, the men dressed in their full beach assault gear and gathered on the Ro Ro's deck. Each man was fully armed, equipped and ready for the mission. The Ro Ro angled itself with its stern to the shoreline some four miles away. When the stern ramp had completely deployed, the men pushed their assault boats into the churning sea, one at a time, and jumped aboard. All three boats were outfitted for silent running. They shoved off, two headed right and one headed left for the shore.

John had left earlier and was positioned in the temporary tent that coincided with the point where JT and Carrie were last seen on the satellite images. It was cool, dark and eerie as John sat alone waiting for the action. Even though he knew the plan as well as any Seal on the team, he saw and heard nothing until two green faced men burst into the tent behind him, wet, breathing deeply, fierce and determined.

"Alpha 3 in place," Chunk spoke into his radio. There were several short conversations back and forth on the radio, then John was whisked up and he and one of the men began jogging. John heard sporadic gunfire, and then a larger explosion about one hundred yards behind him as well as dogs barking well off in the distance. The other two Seals soon joined them and they jogged to the waiting assault boat.

Within minutes, the remainder of the men could be seen jogging for their assault boats and everyone successfully returned to the Sea Queen, whose stern ramp was down and ready to receive the teams. Drenched and happy, John gathered the men on deck and congratulated them.

"From my perspective, that was perfect men. How do you all feel about what just happened?" John inquired of the group.

"There was no opposition sir, so it is difficult to assess how things will go down based on a practice run," Hulk offered.

"What about the barking dogs I heard off in the distance?" John asked.

"There is one thing I have recently learned, and that is that Somalis hate dogs and want nothing to do with them. The only dogs in Somalia are wild and silent like Seals. Now, goats may be a different story. What I'm trying to say is that if we are careful, it should be a pretty quiet night until we blow the shit out of the place. You heard Omani dogs."

"The thing we did learn this go around, sir, is that every man knows his job and what we are doing there. Agreed men?" Chunk added.

There were nods, words and other sounds of agreement from everyone.

"A couple of more night runs sir, and we feel we are ready to go," Chunk said.

"Good enough," John said. "Clean up, get some rest, and we'll do it again tomorrow evening." John started heading off to his stateroom. He was pleased with the day's efforts, but something nagged at him and he couldn't put his finger on the issue. Was the plan too easy, was it too fool proof, was it missing something?

He rolled out the drawings and written scenarios and pored over them. Step by laborious step, he went through the plan, once, twice and on the third time it hit him.

"That's it," John said aloud. "Damn it!" *Thank God for the gut*, he thought.

35

JUST PUT ON A SMILEY FACE

J ohn rose early the next morning and went to the wheelhouse. Nabeel greeted him with several messages the radioman had received between 06:00 AM and 06:30 AM that morning.

"Sir," Nabeel said. "Yesterday I had a talk with the crew and told them we were on a mission of great importance, and that every man would receive a bonus if the mission was successful."

"That's fine Nabeel, how much is the bonus?" John asked.

"One month's pay, sir."

"Very good Nabeel, I should have thought of that, thank you," John said as he began to read his communications.

The USS Roosevelt will arrive Masirah Island 09:30 AM today.

The Admiral asks that John Wingate and the lead Seals board the Roosevelt for a conference.

Joe Wingate would like an update.

John contacted the Roosevelt and told them he and the Seals would be ready at 10:00 AM for the Roosevelt Captain's Gig.

John encoded an email letting Joe know exactly what was going on. Without giving their plans away completely, he let Joe know that all was well.

"Captain, it is a pleasure to finally meet you face to face sir. I am John Wingate, Chairman of the Board of Double O Shipping Company. These fellows are retired Seals Charles Farrington, Eric Henderson and James Reimer, our team leaders," John said with an extended hand as he entered the bridge.

"Welcome gentlemen," Commander Harrison shook each civilian's hand in turn.

John explained what had transpired over the last week and brought everyone up to speed. "Have there been any changes in the location of my family members at Hobyo?" John queried.

"We have confirmed their present location, sir," The PO2 said while handing John several satellite images. "You see these two people here and here?"

"Yes I do Petty Officer," John replied.

"Their patterns of movement are very strong indications that they are your family members," the PO2 continued. "They are moved back and forth between these two points on a regular ten day to two-week basis. We don't know why they are moved, but we do know they are the same people."

John was somewhat relieved to see the walking figures in the satellite images.

"We see very little movement elsewhere in the village, and we have seen no night movement near the beaches and boats you see here, with the exception of an occasional fisherman or what appear to be supply boats going back and forth to the Gulf Queen. We have noticed sporadic vehicle movements, mostly here and here. You can see the road they travel on here," concluded the PO2.

"How often are the boats going out to the Gulf Queen?" John asked.

"Our intel says two or three times a week, and always in the daytime," the PO2 answered. "Also, sir, we have completed an extensive infrared night search of the area and have detected nothing other than the sporadic movement of people in the village and some night movement here in this boat house. We haven't seen any sign of an organized guard system."

The Seal leaders studied the images carefully and asked if they could hold on to the photographs. The PO2 looked at the Captain, who nodded his head.

"Anything they want," the Captain said.

"You are sure of the current location of the hostages?" asked Chunk, the Alpha leader.

"That is correct, this one here," the PO2 answered, pointing at the photo.

"How long have they been there?" Jumbo asked.

"They were brought there day before yesterday," was the PO2's reply. "If the pattern holds, they should be there for at least eleven, twelve days."

"Can we get a broader view of the village?" Hulk asked.

"Yes you can," the PO2 answered. "I'll go get them for you right now."

The men talked for a while longer about the coming days and their individual roles in the operation.

"We have a Seal Team aboard as well who will be responsible for liberating your ship and crew. We will not do anything until your team is completely clear of the area and safely back aboard your ship. We would like you to stay for a question and answer period with them regarding your ship and its layout," the Captain interjected. "We will rendezvous ten miles out when all operations are completed."

The Roosevelt's active Seal team leaders filed in and there was no need for introductions. The three men knew John's Seals and had a mini-reunion before they started with their questions.

"Mr. Wingate, what is in the containers stacked on the cargo deck of the Gulf Queen?" The Roosevelt Seal asked, pointing to the satellite photo.

"I believe the containers are loaded with hard goods from Europe. The Gulf Queen came through the Suez Canal to Sharm el-Sheikh to pick up my nephew and his wife," John surmised.

"Are the containers strong enough to support the weight of a Sea Hawk?" was the next question.

"They look like standard, unreinforced containers to me. I don't think so, unless you can come to rest with each wheel directly on a reinforced corner, or somehow spread the weight to the corners," John answered. "It will probably be best to hover during your operations. If you were to accidently bounce, the container would endure the short, quick blow. They are designed to withstand short term loadings," John said, his engineering background kicking in.

The Seals also wanted to know where the Safe Room was; if the men held hostage were armed or not; were there any secret passages or hiding places; did the ship have a closed circuit surveillance system; what kind of locks did the doors to the bridge have?

"I anticipated this meeting and brought with me the marine architect's drawings of the Gulf Queen. Here is a copy for you," John offered.

After thirty minutes or so, the Seals thanked John, said farewell to their old buddies and escorted them all to the waiting Captain's Gig for their return trip.

Back on Masirah Island, John sat in the temporary tent on the beach that was meant to be the location of his nephew and adopted daughter. He looked up at the stars and marveled at how many could be seen in the clear skies over the island. There were no lights observable in any direction, but the starlight and the moonlight gave his visible surroundings a clarity he had not expected. He made a mental note to speak to the team leaders about that.

No sooner did that thought pass than the two Alpha 3 team members burst into his tent. He rose immediately and followed the two men exactly as he had done the night before. They re-gathered back at the Sea Queen and prepared for the third run.

"Hulk, I couldn't help but notice how bright everything looked through the clear star and moonlit skies on the island," John said.

"That makes it perfect for us sir, and if there is cloud cover when we actually deploy, our night vision gear will take over. If not, we go in low, slow and silent. A minor change in tactics is all that's required," Hulk answered.

The men always had an immediate, plausible answer for all of John's questions. Their training was so ingrained that they had an instinctive response to everything, which allowed them to automatically change and adjust as they went along, always keeping the end result in mind.

"Very good then, I'm headed back to the tent for the final run," John said. "Also, there is one other thing that has been bothering me from the start." John went on to explain his concerns. Hulk recognized the gap in planning immediately and thanked John for his perceptive insight.

"I will have a word with Alpha Team right now and we will close that gap straightaway and practice it on this last run. It will add five minutes to the infil and exfil is all."

"Carrie sweetie, it's time to go for our evening walk," JT said. "I've got something I want to try."

"What's that JT?"

"Come on, I'll show you."

They walked out into the pathetic garden and began their evening stroll. Their guard looked at them casually and went back to his Khat. JT went to the middle of the garden area, and with his heel he dragged out a ten-foot long arched furrow into the sandy soil and then stepped back to Carrie's side. On their next lap, JT picked up a large black stone and placed it near the furrow. He did the same thing on their third lap and walked back to Carrie with a smirk on his face.

"What was that all about?" she asked.

"On our next go around, I'll tell you when to look."

They rounded the far corner of the garden and JT said, "Okay, look."

Carrie looked at JT's enigmatic effort, and all of a sudden she broke out into a hand muffled chuckle. JT pulled her to him, burying her face in his shoulder. Carrie kept giggling into JT's shoulder and when he finally pulled her away, she had tears of laughter in her eyes.

"Pretty funny huh?" JT smiled.

They completed their walk and went back to the shed to do their yoga exercises. JT was maintaining his weight and muscular structure, and Carrie had actually gained back a little weight thanks to the third meal.

"Lieutenant, have a look at this intel sir," the PO2 said the next morning.

"What have you got there?" the Lieutenant asked as he took the satellite image in his hand.

"We have complete, confirmed proof, that's what we have sir," the PO2 smiled. "Came in less than 5 minutes ago."

"I'll get this out to everybody immediately. Great work," the Lieutenant said as he went to the bridge, chuckling.

"God damn it," the Captain said, seeing the LEO photo. "That is funnier than hell. Risky, but still funny."

36

OFF WE GO INTO THE WILD BLUE

The Roosevelt took the lead in the ocean convoy and the Sea Queen followed by one mile. It was a beautiful morning; the seas were relatively calm, the skies gave off a cloudless crystal blue glow, the men were charged and ready and John was relieved to get started as the operation was formally and finally launched.

John had asked his team leaders to join him for coffee and rolls in his stateroom. "Fellas, if you don't mind, let's go over our checklists one more time. Hulk, the boats?" John asked.

"All have been inflated, fueled, checked for leaks, fully loaded and made ready sir," Hulk affirmed.

"Jumbo, how about the plan?" John asked.

"With last night's confirmation--can you believe a smiley face? I can't wait to meet your nephew sir," Jumbo said. "After adding yesterday's additional clearing actions and your eleventh hour realization, we are cast in stone sir," he smiled. "We are set and ready to go."

"And Chunk, how about provisions, equipment and munitions?"

"Night vision goggles have been checked. We took the precaution of replacing all of the power supplies, cleaned and inspected the image tubes, checked all eye pieces for defects and checked all buckles and straps," Chunk reported. "Everyone has shown me and checked off his personal gear list. Camelbacks are filled and ready sir."

In addition to his uniform and brain bucket (helmet), each Alpha Team member carried the following:

Armor plate and carrier vest

Four Barrel NVGs (102 degree Night Vision Goggles), for the four Point Men and the three Snipers

Two Barrel NVGs (70 degree vision) for the rest of the men

Fixed blade knife and sheath

Spiked breaching axe

IR Chem lights (visible only to NVG's), white and red

Two tourniquets

Gerber APT (All purpose tool)

Water bladder back pack (Camelback)

HK M-4 Assault Rifle, with ammunition, Suppressor and Armasight Gen-2 Night Vision Scope Attachment

HK M45C Tactical compact pistol, with ammunition and Suppressor

Two breaching charges

Beta and Charlie Team members carried the same as Alpha Team except for the breaching Axe and breaching charges.

In addition Alpha Team carried the following:

Two extra helmets and NVG's for the hostages

Frag and smoke hand grenades

One bolt cutter (36 inch) (Made in Russia), to be left behind at the site, a game the Seals loved to play on these exercises

One sledgehammer (ten pound) (Made in Russia), to also be left behind at the site

Teams Beta and Charlie carried two M224 60-mm mortars plus HE (High Explosive) frag and smoke mortars and Armasight Gen-2 Night scope attachments. Alpha Team carried sixty Remote Activated Mines (RAMs), Beta had fifty-four RAMs and Charlie had forty, a total of one hundred and fifty-four.

Raaxo lounged in the afternoon shade, chewing Khat and talking with his second in command.

The annual average temperatures in Hobyo are around a balmy 82°F; it is the average 73% relative humidity and the average 73°F dew point that makes the area uncomfortably hot and sticky. Of course, the Somalis were acclimated, but the hostages still suffered.

"Khaalid, my trusted friend, we are coming close to the end of this thing. Within the next ten days or so we should have our money," Raaxo said.

"That is good to hear, Raaxo. When do we plan our next operation?" Khaalid inquired with a look of delight.

"We will do so immediately. This sitting around chewing and fucking can get on a man's nerves. We need something to get the juices flowing again," Raaxo reported.

The two men lay back against their horse hair pillows and closed their eyes. Their emaciated faces belied their physiques. Both men were in excellent physical condition; lean, muscular, sinewy and lithe. They were somewhat out of condition due to the three week plus hiatus, but both knew it wouldn't take much to get back into fighting shape.

"Soon we must shake out these cobwebs," Raaxo said. "Tomorrow we will get the men together and begin our road back." He got up and walked toward his villa. "For now I need a fuck," he said as he walked into his villa, leaving Khaalid behind to nap and only dream of fucking. He didn't have a woman.

"Joe, any word from John?" the board member asked.

"Yes, Peter. Just this morning we got an e-mail saying that the preliminaries were done and he is on his way to the rodeo," Joe cryptically answered. "His words exactly."

Admiral Stimpson met with his adjutant and communications officer. He was satisfied that everything was moving properly.

"Admiral, we just received this from the satellite intel sir," Captain Holmgaard said.

"What have you got there?" the Admiral asked.

They both looked at the image and noted the symmetrical group of dots, circled with a black felt pen and located between the beach and nearest villas.

"What's this?" the Admiral asked.

"Looks to us like a group of men in an orderly gathering," the Captain answered.

"Alert the Roosevelt. See if they have similar intel. Send a copy of the image to Wingate as well with a note detailing your thoughts. I want to keep them tightly in the loop," the Admiral ordered.

"Aye, sir," the Captain said, leaving the office.

"Also Captain Holmgaard, I want to order a full 24-hour LEO surveillance of the area for the day before, the day of the extraction and the aftermath," the Admiral said. "Notify Wingate of our intentions. Eyes only."

The Captain nodded and left the room.

"Jumbo, Hulk, Chunk, what do you make of this?" John held out the satellite image to the three team leaders.

"Looks like the boys are getting restless, sir," Hulk offered. "They are probably anticipating the big pay-day and getting revved up for the next adventure."

"You really think they do that sort of thing?" John asked.

"We never underestimate these little monkeys, sir," Chunk said. "It takes strength and stamina to do what they do. We always give benefit of the doubt where that is concerned. This is a good thing though, they will be tired after the days' work and sleep better at night."

"I'll get your thoughts off to the Roosevelt and the Admiral. Bring your guys up to speed," John said as the men left his stateroom.

"My thoughts exactly," the PO2 said to his Lieutenant. "They smell the money and have ended their holiday and are getting back into shape."

"Do we have any other intel on this?" the Lieutenant asked.

"No sir, but I will keep my eyes open. By the way Lieutenant, I haven't seen the Wingates outside since this morning, and its past time for them to be out walking."

"I'll spread the word, thanks Charlie," the Lieutenant said and headed for the bridge.

"I'm very sorry Mr. Wingate, but you will have to begin getting your evening exercise indoors from now on," Raaxo announced. "You may continue with your morning walks, I know how much you enjoy them."

"Why is that? Are we being punished for something?" JT countered.

"Not at all Mr. Wingate," Raaxo said. "We are doing some different operations and I can no longer stand guard at the villa all day. I will have to secure you in your cell so I don't have to worry while I am away from my compound."

"We certainly aren't planning to go anywhere," JT offered.

"Sorry Mr. Wingate, I have heard that one before," Raaxo said with a smirk, and he was off.

As Raaxo left, he ordered the compound to be locked down from 10:00AM on.

37

GO GET 'EM TIGER

Raaxo ordered his men to be assembled each day at the boat harbor for exercises. He told his men that he expected to have the ransoms for the Double O ship and hostages within the next week. Negotiations were underway, and they were outlining details for the drop. A date and time had been agreed upon. Both the ship ransom and the personnel ransom were to be made simultaneously, once the payers were satisfied that the hostages were safe.

"Okay, enough of your laziness," Raaxo chided his men. "I want you to jog up and down the beach for the next hour, and report back to me here when you are finished. And stay in formation, no straggling."

The pirates groaned and went up the beach in a jog. It was hot, but not so hot they couldn't carry out their exercises. They ran in their bare feet. They ran in a phalanx or five rows and four columns, twenty sweaty men in all. The sand was medium-coarse and Raaxo knew the bottoms of their feet would again be perfectly calloused by the end of a few of weeks of daily runs.

The next exercise was at the harbor. "I want these five boats pulled out of the water, sanded, re-caulked and painted with three coats of paint. You need to make sure that all of our boarding equipment is in good repair, and that our personal gear is working properly and is stowed at the boathouse. At 5:00 PM, you may stop and go home," Raaxo ordered. There were groans from the men, but all bent to their task.

"Sir, I noticed that the hostages were out walking in the morning again, but not in the evening. The targets spent their day running up and down the beach in the morning and working on their boats during the day," Jake said to his Lieutenant.

"How many of them are there?" the Lieutenant asked.

"I counted twenty men running, and five less working on the boats," Jake added. "My opinion is the boat captains don't do menial work and sit out the day elsewhere, chewing Khat and talking of important things."

"I'll pass the word on Jake, thanks," and the Lieutenant was off.

"John, Vince has been in steady contact with the negotiators and has them convinced that the drop for the hostages will be made six days from now, and the drop for the Gulf Queen will be made later that day when the hostages are safe aboard the Gulf Queen, as we have requested," Trent said into the four-way communication system.

"Great Trent, we need them to be convinced that the money is definitely coming," John answered. "What's going on in Austria?"

"They are sitting tight, but I don't know for how long now," Trent answered. "I would imagine that their work will soon be over and they might stay on there or move to another location. Actually, if we aren't going to roust them and try to get intel, I think that our work is done there."

"I get your point Trent," John said. "Admiral, how do you feel about that?"

"Yes John, I understand," said the Admiral. "How much longer will your negotiator be with you?"

John told the Admiral that the negotiator would be available full time until the operation is complete and everyone is safe aboard the Sea Queen, but that he didn't feel that the surveillance needed to go on from John's side.

"I agree John. I will have NCIS take over the surveillance, and we will apprehend the negotiators only if they show signs of leaving or at the safe return of your family, whichever happens first." The Admiral wanted to do as much as he could to decimate the entire rogue Hobyo network.

"I agree completely Admiral, but I strongly stress we shouldn't do anything more than follow the negotiators until such time as we have the hostages in hand. I don't want to risk a tip-off," John cautioned.

"We respect your wishes here, no contact until we get the 'all clear' from you. Is everything ready to go John?" the Admiral asked.

"Yes it is sir," John answered. "The men are geared up and enthusiastically ready for a fight. The atmosphere here is one of calm readiness."

"Calm before the storm, so to speak," the Admiral added.

"Exactly," John said finally. "As soon as we have completed our portion of this affair, I will immediately contact Roosevelt and let them know we are safe and they can swing into action."

"Good enough John, the Roosevelt won't let you or the operation down. Believe me, they have crack crews aboard that will do their jobs," the Admiral said.

"I know sir, I met many of them today at a briefing, and like my crew, they epitomize the Seal motto. Silent and ready," John said.

"Good hunting John. Come back safe. Our thoughts are with you, your family and your men," the Admiral remarked. "I'd give a left anything to be with you."

John could hear all of the men on the call echo the same senti-
ments and he thanked them for their blessing and their great work in
support of his quest.

"Go get 'em John," Trent said.

"We're right behind you," the Roosevelt Captain offered.

38

STORM THE BEACHES

The stern ramp of the Sea Queen yawned open with creaks and groans to the level position. The men stood around their boats, some checking straps and connections, some checking the boats, all calmly smiling as if spoiling for a fight.

The night was overcast and dark with blocky clouds that occasionally let the stars' light peek through, the quarter-moon darting in and out of the clouds like a cork bobbing on a fishing line.

"Charlie team to the end of the ramp," Chunk, the Alpha Team point man, announced the first order of the operation. "Charlie goes first, then Beta and then Alpha, on my go." The ramp lowered into the water, and the Charlie boat pushed off and was afloat.

"Charlie go." The 55Hp silent-running engines jumped into life and charged off in a muffled hum. The ramp recycled and Beta boat moved to the front. Two minutes later, "Beta go." Again, the engines pushed forward. The Alpha Team Seals moved to the front of the re-raised ramp and straddled the tubular inflatable sides of their Zodiac FC-470 EVOL 7 boat one behind the other, three Seals on one side with John the last in line and four Seals on the other side. The helmsman knelt on the hard rubber deck to handle the tiller. They looked like close-quarter bucking bronco riders in a rodeo, hanging on for all they were worth. Slowly and deliberately the ramp lowered a third time and Chunk lowered himself into position with the rest of the men, grasped his hand holds firmly and cried, "Alpha go. Earn your Trident again today."

The sea spray immediately hit John so hard he had to hide his face in his armpit. He imagined what it must be like for the first man in line. The sea was relatively warm and warmed further as they approached the beach.

They had negotiated the ten mile distance in just under twenty five minutes. There were no discernable lights on shore, and the mottled cloud cover added to the eerie darkness. John heard the waves breaking at the shoreline, and before he knew it the boat ground to a stop on the coarse sandy beach.

Alpha 3 sprang from the starboard side of the boat and crouched together, arranged in guard position at the bow.

Alpha 2 bounded from the port side of the boat and did the same. Alpha 1 and John stood almost waist deep in the water on either side of the boat, holding it steady as several of the men reached in for pre-packed knapsacks and the remainder of the required supplies, equipment and munitions in the two-man carry packs.

John could hear his heart pounding rapidly in his earbud. His senses were heightened as the operation unfolded in front of him. He was afraid, but displayed no fear. He was nervous but had no anxiety. He was ready.

"Alpha beached and ready."

"Beta beached and ready."

"Charlie beached," came the last call and two agonizing minutes later, "Charlie beached and ready."

All the men crouched very still and from a guard position, searched with their NVG's for any signs of life in the flat, treeless moonscape ahead of them.

Chunk turned his head back to look at John and gave him a thumbs up. This was, as John had insisted, his last chance to decide yea or nay on the operation. He quickly crossed himself and cried, "Operation go!" into the troop net radio.

"Alpha 2 (the three man sub-team) for boat houses," came the first whispered call. Everyone else waited in guard position, scanning for movement of any kind. The boat houses and beach had to be cleared before anyone else could move.

"Alpha 3 (the four man sub-team) waiting on your go," came the second call. Everything fell silent except for the faint, nearly noiseless swooshing and crunching sounds of Alpha 2 jogging through the gritty surface toward boat houses one, two and three. Within minutes, the three Alpha 2 Seals were in place.

There was a light in house one, flickering like a candle. The three Seals stealthily approached the sheds and boat house one by one.

"House 2 is dark," whispered one Seal.

"House 3 is dark," whispered the other.

John heard the faint squeaks and thuds of doors opening and closing in his earbuds.

"House 2 clear."

"House 3 clear."

The third Seal carefully peered into the old, weathered and wind-blown boat House 1 with his M45C drawn, his NVG revealing the interior. At the sound of the squeaking hinges a startled man jumped from a grass mat on the floor and started for the Seal invader. A second man looked out from his hammock, his eyes straining to see the intruder as he grabbed for an AK-47 hanging on the wall beside him. Squirt, squirt, squirt, squirt spoke the Seal's suppressor. Four shots, one in each heart, one in each head, two men instantly dead.

The man from the floor slumped to his knees and lurched forward as blood began to ooze from the gaping exit wound at the back of his skull. The hammock man hung suspended from his sagging bed, swinging in an arc, back and forth, dripping blood from a similar wound to the back of his head, AK-47 clamoring to the dirt floor. Satisfied that no one else was in the house, the Seal snuffed out the candle in the anguished, tormented mouth of the hammock swinging Somali, planted his RAMS, bounded from the boathouse and closed the door behind him.

"House 1 clear."

"Alpha 3 go," Chunk said immediately. "Beta and Charlie go."

The four Seals of Alpha 3 took off in a fast jog, leaving John and the Alpha helmsman alone at the boat. Within seconds, nothing could be seen or heard except the surf lapping at the shoreline and the telltale glows of the IR Chem lights that were dropped every one hundred to one hundred and fifty feet and at each planned turn in the thirty-one hundred foot long assault path to the target villa. The ground was thankfully smooth and easy to traverse, which would make it easier on the hostages on the return trip. Alpha 3 dropped its two-man carry bags at the Alpha meeting place and continued on to their primary target.

After placing RAMs in as many of the boats as they could access, Alpha 2 picked up their two two-man carry bags and jogged off to the Alpha meeting place, fifteen hundred feet away, and laid on their bellies, fanned in guard position and waiting for phase two of the plan to be announced. They located the other two-man carry bags and looked back and noticed the Chem light trail Alpha 3 had laid, delineating their return trip.

"Alpha 2 in place."

After several minutes more jogging, Alpha 3 moved with caution across the gravel Mogadishu road and on to Compound A where two of the Seals placed breaching charges at the east wall near the suspected hostage cell. Then they moved back and waited, crouched behind a pile of CMU blocks and old boards. The two other Alpha 3 Seals moved to the front of the compound and took up position to deal with anyone trying to leave the Compound from that direction.

"Breaching charges set. Alpha 3 waiting. Phase 2 go."

"Front covered. Alpha 3 waiting Phase 2 go."

Alpha 3 team poised and waited for word from the rest of the teams. They all knelt and caught their breath, and then they methodically, in a 'matter of fact' manner, checked their gear and supplies, hydrating from the camel back.

♆

Beta team leader Hulk and Charlie Team leader Jumbo simultaneously waved forward two fingers for Beta and Charlie Teams to takeoff. Both Teams lurched from their crouch at the bow of their assault boats. The men jogged at a good clip with the two-man carry bags filled with RAMs and other munitions toward their prospective tree groves some nine hundred feet from the landing point, and crouched to observe the scene before them. One Seal from each team, crawled through the trees and shrubs to the far edge of the grove to set up his sniper rifle with night vision scope, waiting to observe and kill anyone who might try to leave the village in the direction of the beaches. Set-up preliminaries were completed and all men were in place, ready to go.

Beta 2 Seal team leader Hulk moved toward the recently observed compound south of their protective grove of squat trees and shrubs. The compound was small and smelled strongly of animal piss and dung. Hulk raised himself to the top of the block wall to have a look. A startled goat bleated and something dark moved in the corner. Hulk ended the bleating with one shot and he noticed a man moving toward him from the corner. Two quick shots and the man went down.

Hulk jumped into the pen and systematically executed all five remaining goats and moved toward the inside structure. He tried the door which opened with a squeak. He went in quickly and crouched on the floor. He scanned the room rapidly and noted there was only hay and water barrels, no humans. He placed two RAMS and left.

Three Charlie Seals simultaneously went off on a similar mission to clear recently noted buildings near their grove of trees. The structures they encountered appeared to be restaurants or cafes, empty in the early morning hour. Jumbo took no chances and sent one Seal into each of the structures. Quickly the cadence of, "One clear," "Two clear," "Three clear" rang into his earbud until the final "Six and Seven clear." The Seals placed RAMS in each of the seven structures and went on to their next chore.

Alpha, Beta and Charlie Teams began furtively placing their RAMS along a twenty-two-hundred-foot long line isolating the village from the shoreline. The RAMS were placed every twenty feet, which would create a wall of sand, gravel and smoke when the C-4 detonated that would hang in the air for long minutes, making it impossible for anyone to see the shoreline, much less want to run in that direction. The noise alone would strike fear into the bravest man.

Soundlessness, stealth and invisibility marked their movement as they worked; crouch, place, run; crouch, place, run; crouch, place, run; until the task was complete. No attempt was made to bury the mines, they would be detonated remotely and no one, except the retreating Seals, was expected to be anywhere near them. The late generation M18 Claymores were light, effective and deadly. They were detonated by a cell phone-like detonator that received its signal from a single push button. All one hundred and ten devices on the twenty-two-hundred-foot line, plus the twenty-four placed at the boat houses and in the boats and the twenty at the grove clearing areas A and B would explode in a single black-red cloud of flames, smoke, shrapnel and destruction. The town would not know what had happened.

"Amiin, I think I just saw someone running across the beach," Hamid, the Somali boy called in a whisper to his friend. They had been sleeping out on the sand to try to cool themselves in the night sea breeze.

Amiin, the older boy, woke and rubbed his eyes and looked around. He saw no one. "Go back to sleep Hamid, I don't see anything," the boy said as he rolled over on his side.

"No Amiin, I see someone, there, look!" Hamid said, now standing and pointing. A running Seal was silhouetted in the effervescence of the surf well beyond. Amiin rose and went to Hamid's side to take a look. Within seconds, both boys dropped lifeless to the ground, each with a small hole in his forehead. The sniper swung back to continue his scan of the area between the village houses and the groves.

John knelt at the water's edge, holding the boat in one hand and pressing his earbud with the other, listening intently for any word from the crews. His heart rate had slowed, his intensity had heightened, his mind cleared as he prepared for the next phase to begin. It seemed like hours had passed since he heard a transmission.

"Beta 2 in place. Waiting Phase 2 go," John heard in his ear bud.

"Beta 3 in place. Waiting Phase 2 go."

"Charlie in place. Waiting Phase 2 go."

With all preparations complete, all of the men silently lay or crouched, rested and caught their breath. One man looked at his watch; one took a suck on his camel back while the others waited calmly and cautiously for the next command.

"Phase 2 go." Chunk announced. He was anxious to get his own operations going again, but had to wait until Beta and Charlie had completed their much more time consuming and difficult preliminaries.

It was three-thirty in the morning and not a sound came from the village. Only a few far-off kerosene lanterns betrayed the village's presence. Generators were shut down for the night; it was eerily silent, deathly dark and strangely peaceful.

39

OH, THANK GOD

"Alpha 3 go," the helmsman barked into the radio.

The sound of breaching charges could be heard almost instantly. The four-foot wide by five-foot high hole in Raaxo's protective mud, brick and stone wall collapsed in a heap and the Seals leapt through the jagged opening and sprinted to the suspected hostage cell. A man at the entrance to the cell groggily stood, groped for his weapon and just caught his balance as the first Seal stabbed him with his straight blade knife just beneath his ribs and pulled upward, stopping a scream that made it only part way to the guards voice box. A second swipe to the neck finished the job, and both Seals were at the door of the cell. Breaching charges were set and the door fell off of its rusty, nearly useless hinges. The two Seals raced into the cell and found JT and Carrie, recoiled and cringing, together against the far rear wall in their underwear and bare feet.

"Not to worry folks, we are your rescue team. Please do as we say and do it now. Put on your clothes and shoes, tie them tightly and knot them," the Seal said with a pleasant smile on his large, burly black, brown and green camouflaged face.

Carrie put on her jeans and shirt and knelt quickly, as did JT, and got to work on their shoes. Their hearts raced and their breathing was quick as they stood for the next order.

"We wait here at the door for our next orders," Chunk told them as he knelt down and sliced off the excess of their knotted shoe laces and Carrie buttoned and tucked in her shirt.

"Here ma'am, put on this helmet," Chunk said and he snapped its straps under her chin. "Look alternately at the ground in front of you and at the lights we have placed ahead in the return path, like this," Chunk said, bobbing his head slowly up and then down. "When you see two lights close together, one white one red, turn in the direction the red light is pointing and quickly search for the next white light ahead. Remember to alternately look down at the ground in front of you, don't get fixed on the lights or you'll probably trip or twist an ankle if you do."

Carrie looked worried and confused, but his big handsome smile, southern accent and broad shoulders calmed her immediately.

"Why am I in the lead?" Carrie asked.

"We need to be as free as possible to deal with anything that might come at us from behind, and you look to be a capable leader," the other Seal said.

"Sir, here is your helmet," Chunk said calmly. "Did you hear my instructions to the lady?"

"I did," JT answered. "Don't fixate on the lights, watch the ground as well. What do the lights look like?" he asked for his sake as well as Carrie's.

The Seal pulled two IR Chem lights from his vest, one white, one red and lit them. He tossed them toward the other end of the room. They were of US manufacture but free of labels.

"Which direction would you turn seeing those lights?" Chunk asked Carrie.

"To the left?" Carrie answered questioningly and pointing to the opposite wall.

"Correct," Chunk said

"Okay, I get it," JT said, looking at the lights.

"Okay, is everyone ready?" Chunk queried to his small group patiently. Heads bobbed up and down. "Alpha 3 has cargo ready to ship," Chunk finally announced. "Waiting Phase 3 go."

Tears welled up in John's eyes as the anxiously awaited words came into his ear buds, in a sudden spasm; releasing hours of tension from his shoulders, arms and legs. "Oh, thank God," he said, looking over at the helmsman with a worried smile on his face.

At the sound of the first breaching charge, Raaxo leapt from his bed, still groggy from Khat, grabbed an AK-47 from the hall and ran into his villa's entry area. "Get back in your bedroom woman, close the door and hide," he barked at his wife. He stood poised in front of the door, ready to shoot anyone who might come through. The steel door he had recently installed for his own safety and protection was now working against him. He would have to wait for whoever was out there to enter.

The two Alpha 3 Seals at the front of the house tired of waiting for an escapee and placed breaching charges at the hinges and the hasp and blasted the steel door open. Raaxo reeled backward as the door flew at him. The Seals broke through the doorway in a low crouch. Wild erratic bursts of AK-47 fire met them as Long John, the first Seal to enter, dove low into the shooter, head on, and knocked him completely on his back as Raaxo continued aimless, erratic shooting into the upper walls and ceiling, reeling backward. The second Seal kicked Raaxo's weapon from his grip and threw frag and smoke grenades into the other rooms. Then both Seals fled with the dazzled pirate chief Raaxo dangling, inches above the ground, between them. Outside they threw him harshly on the ground, face down, and zip tied his wrists behind him. Painfully they jerked him to his feet and ran with him toward the hostages waiting at the breached hole in the perimeter wall.

"Alpha 3 has pirate, all secure and ready to return," Chunk barked into the radio.

"Beta has a go."

"Alpha 3 has a go."

"What the fuck was that?" Khaalid cried as he jumped from his bed at the sound of the first breaching charges. He stepped into his pants and ran toward the front door, grabbing an AK-47 as he made his way. The pirate, housed in Compound B, then ran, dazed through his front door with his AK-47 strapped to his back, buttoning his pants as he ran. He was three steps outside of his door when a club like arm and elbow smashed into his face, breaking his nose and upper jaw and flipping him to the ground. He lay moaning on his back, kicking his legs, thrashing in agony, grabbing for his weapon and bleeding from his nose and mouth, teeth, gums and lips, red with gore.

"No you don't you fucking little worm," the seal murmured, kicking the automatic rifle well to the side. "Your shooting days are over asshole."

Hulk threw a frag, an incendiary and a smoke grenade into the building as the other Seal picked up the groggy pirate, zip cable tied his hands behind his back and ran toward the other two Beta 3 team members.

"Drag that scum back to the boat and wait there, we'll soon be right behind you," Hulk said to the towering Seal as he and the other two ran off to support the Beta 2 team.

"Beta 2 set, waiting Phase 3 go."

"Beta 3 set, waiting Phase 3 go."

"Captain, it sounds like the Seal teams are having great success. Both the hostages and two of the pirates are in hand ready to be extracted," the Roosevelt radioman said to his Commander.

"That's good to hear," the Captain said, and ordered his Seal Teams to get aboard the helicopters and get ready for launch. The men swung into action with proficiency and made ready to do their part in the operation. "Report to the Admiral and to Double O as soon as you can, they will want to hear the news."

"Charlie, Phase 3 go," rang into the ears of every man in the operation at once.

On Jumbo's go, Charlie Team unleashed a mortar and grenade attack on the north central and northern end of the village. They fired round after round into the mélange of tinder dry huts and sheds that burst into flames as the incendiary grenades smashed into them. Choking smoke rose in plumes and people could be seen running helplessly in all directions, no one knowing where the attack was coming from. A few people ran from the village in the direction of the groves and the beach and were quickly mowed down by Beta 2 HK M-4 sniper fire. Shots began to ring out in the village as confused people fired at anything they thought might be attackers.

"Beta, phase 3 go." Beta Team let loose a similar mortar and grenade attack on the south central and southern end of the village. The noise from the attack was deafening. Everywhere someone in the town tried to run, they were met with explosive resistance. Raaxo's villa took a direct hit from the mortar fire and burst into flames.

The blaze could be seen and the explosions could be heard from the Gulf Queen, and the hostage crew wondered what was going on. The pirate crew saw and heard the massacre as well, and they wanted to get ashore to help their friends and families. They knew that was impossible, and prepared for the worst by closing themselves in the wheel house.

Alpha 3, with the hostages, ran past Alpha 2 waiting at the meeting point, and followed the IR Chem lights to the beach. They passed off the pirate Raaxo to the Beta Team Seal waiting there and kept on running.

JT had fallen, badly twisting his ankle. He was being assisted by two of the Seals. Carrie was jogging sure footedly, gazelle-like, just ahead of the men, correctly following the IR Chem lights and her instincts. She was the first to reach the boat. She ran directly into John's open arms. They silently hugged, and immediately John hoisted her and gently tossed her into the boat.

"Lie down and stay down Carrie," John shouted as he moved to help the two Seals lift JT into the boat.

"Cargo loaded. All teams, Phase 4 go," Chunk barked into his radio. "All teams report when clearing the beach."

40

BOOM!!!

Alpha 2 completed mop up in their area and began the one thousand five hundred foot run for the boat. A few shots could be heard from the village; confusion still gripped the residents. As the three remaining Seals approached the boat, the helmsman jumped in and started the engine. The last Seal jumped aboard and Chunk announced, "Alpha team and hostages have cleared the beach."

John knew that he and his family were home free now, and worried about the rest of the men still on the beach completing the task.

Halfway to the Beta Team boat, Raaxo wriggled free from his captor and stumbled off, awkwardly, hands behind his back, bare feet chafing in the coarse sand and brush, head reeling from the Khat and the night's events.

"Damn it," the Seal murmured as he reached for his HK M45C and shot Raaxo once in the leg that dropped him like a stone. "Shit, now I have to carry the little prick the rest of the way." He got back on the lighted path and ran as fast as he could, his burden draped like a deer carcass over his shoulders, Raaxo's tethered arms flailing wildly and painfully in their wake.

Reaching the boat, the Seal literally threw Raaxo in, lobbing his pain-wracked body like a medicine ball. The thud landing forced the air from Raaxo's lungs. He lay completely still in his agony. The last Seal leapt onto the side of the boat and after two agonizing minutes getting the prisoners trussed, tournequited and settled, "Beta Team has cleared the beach with two hostiles," Hulk announced.

"Charlie Team has cleared the beach," Jumbo declared, and all three teams began the twenty-five minute trip back to the Sea Queen.

Smoke, flames and dust were still rising from the demolished town as the three boats broke through the surf for open sea. An RPG shell landed very close to Alpha's boat, splashing the boat's occupants.

"Shit that was close!" Chunk yelled. "John, hit that detonator."

John placed one of his hands on Carrie's shoulder. He wasn't sure if he was trying to assure her or himself that everyone and everything was okay. "Do you two want to do the honors JT? Carrie?" John said as he handed them the detonating device.

"If this is what I think it is, you know we do," JT, smiling at Carrie, with his thumb on top of hers, they pressed the red button on the device together.

One hundred and fifty four RAMs went off simultaneously, lighting up the Hobyo skies with a Fourth of July-like display, dazzling the returning Seal teams. Raaxo stared at the carnage in a Khat induced stupor. He had little or no idea what had just happened to him. Khaalid looked wide-eyed into the flaming sky that now completely hid the town of his birth from his view. A wall of dust, sand, gravel, flames and smoke was all that could be seen. Both men began to cry as the Seals roughly shoved their heads down to the hard rubber floor of the Zodiac.

"Hope you have good memories boys, because you are never going to see that shit-hole again," Hulk barked at the pirates. "Home sweet home has gone bye, bye."

All three teams reached the Sea Queen at nearly the same time, tossing a monkey-pawed halyard to one of three of the waiting crewmen.

The ship's crews pulled the boats partially up the ramp and the Captain raised the ramp to level allowing everyone to safely roll off of the boats and move to safety.

"Roosevelt, we are all secure. You have a go," John joyfully announced into his radio. "Please contact my negotiator Vince Packard and tell him to 'make the drop', he'll know what you mean."

Within minutes, three helicopters whizzed overhead and past the Sea Queen on their way to the Gulf Queen.

41

MAKING THE DROP

Vince got Roosevelt's message and immediately called Trent McSpadden. "It's done Trent; they made it out without a scratch."

"Wonderful, oh Christ I'm glad it's over," Trent said. "It's time for you and me to swing into action now. Have you got everything set up and ready to send?"

"I do," Vince said.

"I'll call you right back."

Within five minutes Trent called back. "Go," was his simple instruction.

※

"I love fucking you Aamina," Hassan whispered in her ear as he rolled off of her slender, young black body and pulled himself free of her mutilated vagina.

Having suffered the mutilation years before she was married, she had never experienced joy in sex. It was strictly a duty to her, to lay there while he satisfied himself. All she got was the sad satisfaction of being a good Somali wife and a smelly vagina.

"I love fucking you as well Hassan," she lied.

She stood and dressed slowly in front of him, as he told her he liked her to do. It aroused him to watch her bending, stretching and sliding into her panties, bra and other clothing.

"Slowly, my sweet," he said.

He heard his computer e-mail beep.

"Who can that be? Bring me my computer," Hassan ordered. She was hooking her bra behind her.

He opened the e-mail; it was from Mr. Wingate. 'Please see attached.' There was a video that automatically started when the email was opened.

There was a large World War II bomber, silver in color, cruising in the far distance. The camera panned up close to the writing, diagonally positioned just below the cockpit, which read '*Enola Gay*'. The camera panned back as a large silver object dropped from the midsection of the plane. A big banner suddenly appeared that read:

READY TO MAKE THE DROP

Next a mushroom cloud erupted on the screen, red flames, black smoke and gray clouds streaming upwards into the sky. A second banner appeared, fluttering like a flag, that read:

HAVE A NICE DAY

He sat staring numbly and dumbly at the image in front of him and wondered what was happening.

At that moment, the door to the apartment came off its hinges and four Vienna policemen and a policewoman burst in. Two NCIS agents took up the rear.

"Stand up and face the wall, both of you," the policeman shouted.

A policewoman brought terrified Aamina aside and told her to put on her clothes. One of the men reached down and picked up the computer from Hassan's mattress on the floor.

"Have a look at this, people. Ready to make the drop, indeed."

They all had a good laugh as Hassan was allowed to put on his clothes.

Hassan and Aamina were given their *Letter of Rights*, handcuffed and shoved to the door.

"Come with us, scum," said the policeman. "We want you to '*have a nice day*'."

"If you don't mind, we'll take the computer, phone and the files," the NCIS agent said. "We will press charges within twenty-four hours."

42

OUCH!

"Is everyone okay?" John asked of the three team leaders.

"We suffered two palm cuts; one bruised arm, you should see the other guy, and a hangnail I think, sir," answered the always jovial Jumbo. "I think we kicked some bad ass there and I'm sure those little bastards will think twice before going on their next raid."

"Someone take this filth out of my sight and get them ready for transfer to the Roosevelt. I can't even stand looking at them," John said. "And they don't deserve to be in our presence."

"Wait a minute please John, I have something I would like to say to this one," Carrie said, pointing at Raaxo. He was being held, on either side, by two burly, sweaty and camo-faced Seals. Raaxo limped on his tourniquet-tied right leg, red stains all up and down, still dripping a mixture of sea water and blood. He looked pathetic and beaten. Carrie, devoid of empathy, didn't care.

"What is it dear?" JT asked.

Carrie strode from her position at JT's side to the wretched looking pirate chief, half dangling between the two Seals.

"Mr. Raaxo," Carrie said, standing defiantly in front of the pirate captain, hands on her hips, speaking loud enough for all to hear. "You have managed to upset me very deeply. You are now standing amid a group of people who recognize a women's right to speak. I want to exercise that right to tell you that you are one of the lowest forms of filth I believe I have ever, in my life, been associated with."

Raaxo looked at her straight in the eyes with a defiant, smug, superior and green-toothed smile on his face.

"And this should wipe that surly smile off your face," Carrie said as she unexpectedly, with a place-kicker's hop, squarely and firmly kicked him, full force, between his unguarded legs. She felt his genitals crush under the force of the blow.

Raaxo doubled, coughed, grimaced and fell to his knees, puking yellow-green bile from his mouth and nose. Tears welled in his eyes; he was humbled, shamed and beaten.

Carrie looked down at the now shaking Somali and said, "I'll bet you're not feeling too *pleasant* now are you *pleasant one?*" She accentuated 'pleasant' for effect. The two Seals dragged the pathetic mess away.

As the ramp reached its full vertical position, Cookie burst out on the deck, pushing a trolley with a tub of iced down champagne and a plastic bag of red Solo cups. Each of the Seals grabbed a bottle and began shaking it. Corks went off in all directions as they doused and squirted each other with the frothy contents. They finished by holding up the bottles and joining in a resounding HOOYA, drinking whatever remained in the magnums.

John simultaneously laughed and cried as he watched the men celebrate as hard as they fought. "Men, this is only the beginning of the celebration. As soon as the Roosevelt finishes their work and rid us of our filthy cargo, and we are all back safely on our way home, I am treating you all to a party you won't soon forget."

43

LIBERATING THE GULF QUEEN

The three six-man team Roosevelt Seahawk helicopters hovered over Gulf Queen's cargo deck with their lights glaring, rotors chopping, door gunners strafing as Seals descended to the cargo containers below on fast rope insertion extraction systems (FRIES). They advanced to the forward superstructure and immediately surrounded the bridge. There was no resistance with the three Seahawk Helicopters now hovering on three sides of the bridge, cannons and search lights aimed squarely at the pirates within. Weapons dropped, hands and arms raised, the four remaining Somali pirates knelt down on the wheelhouse deck and bent forward as if praying to Allah.

The Seals burst through the wheelhouse door in seconds, pointing their HK MP5's into the terrified faces of the surrendering pirates. The Roosevelt silently loomed into sight off the port bow, pointing her forward floods and aiming her five inch forward cannon at the Gulf Queen's bridge.

"How many more pirates are still onboard this ship?" the Seal yelled.

"We are all that is left," a shaking pirate said. "You killed two."

"Is there anybody aboard the mother ship that is tied astern?" the Seal yelled again.

"No, everyone, except us, is ashore," the blubbering pirate said.

"Where is the ship's crew?" the Seal barked at one of the pirates.

"In the safe room," the pirate replied. "They are all well, no one has been harmed. Please don't hurt us."

The Seal stock butted the pirate saying, "You should have thought about that before you pirated this ship. Maybe you'll think twice next time, if there is a next time," the Seal threatened. The kneeling pirates began to snivel and tremble, anticipating an undesirable end.

Two of the Seals broke away to head for the safe room that was located within the engine room. They banged on the door yelling, "Seal Extraction Team. You are all safe now." Seconds later, the door squeaked slowly open and one of the crewmen peered out. He pulled the door full open in recognition of the liberators.

"Allah Akbar, we are glad to see you," said Nabeel, the Sunni Pakistani Captain.

"How many of you are there?" the Seal asked.

"We have eight men here," Nabeel answered.

"Is everyone alright?"

"Yes, we are fine. Tired and scared maybe, but fine," Nabeel said.

The Seal explained that the ship had been taken back from the pirates and that the chief mechanic was to start the engines and make way as soon as possible.

"I understand," said the Captain. "Okay men you heard the man, let's get this ship to sea."

The Captain, navigator, radioman and Bo'sun returned to the bridge, weighed anchor and began the process of getting under way. A hand severed the lines holding the mother ship.

One of the helicopters broke position and moved back to the cargo area, hovered above the conex boxes, and extracted its team of Seals and two of the pirates. With that completed, the second helicopter moved back and did the same. The third helicopter removed its crew and the two body bags, and all three units began their return to the USS Roosevelt.

Before leaving the area, the third helicopter swung around and faced the mother ship beginning to drift away from the Gulf Queen's stern. The pilot fired a Penguin into the broad-beamed vessel. Within minutes, the fated ship sank to the bottom.

"Gulf Queen this is the Roosevelt. Over," came a radio call.

"This is Gulf Queen. Over," the Captain answered.

"What is the condition of your ship? Over."

The captain explained that they were operating with only three engines and that fuel, water and provisions were getting dangerously low. He told the Roosevelt that he thought he would be able to manage to push a sustained twelve or thirteen knots out of the engines.

"We will start off with you in first position, Sea Queen in second position and we will take up the rear. Once out to sea, we will meet our oiler and you can refuel and take on fresh water and provisions. Over," the Roosevelt ordered.

"Sea Queen, did you copy?" the Roosevelt asked.

"Yes sir, twelve or thirteen knots, second position. Over," came Sea Queen's reply.

All three ships swung into position and began the 2200 mile, seven day trip to Manama, Bahrain. The weather was clear, the seas were calm, morale was extremely high and Hobyo still smoldered off the port stern quarter horizon.

Within thirty minutes the US Navy's Fifth Fleet oiler USS Platt, which had just finished servicing the Roosevelt, pulled alongside Gulf Queen and began the refueling operation. She transferred enough fuel, water and provisions to insure a safe trip to the home port of the Fifth Fleet.

A Seahawk Helicopter hovered over the Sea Queen's cargo deck and lowered two sling chairs to the deck. The Seals quickly placed Raaxo and Khaalid in the seats and strapped them in, zip cable tying their hands and feet, making it impossible for them to jump or get free.

"Although we will probably have to attend some sort of criminal trial for those two, it is good to have them out of our sight," John said to JT and Carrie.

44

THE LONGEST KISS

The seven day trip to Manama was savored by all of the men. They rested, exercised, read books and ate like they were running out of food.

"My father, your uncle, is one of the most amazing men I know," Carrie blurted out to JT in their stateroom.

"I agree, but why do you say that, all of a sudden and out of the blue?" JT questioned.

"It just came to me; he doesn't seem to ever fail at anything. He sees, he plans and he acts. Bing, bang, boom. Simple as that," she answered back.

"You have hit the nail on the head, Carrie, but understand that it isn't simple and that he does all three phases completely and competently. When he sees, he sees everything. He sees the problem and all of its aspects and complications and weighs all of the consequences. When he plans, he includes every detail he and his advisors can think of and more. He has a plan A, B and C. When he acts, he does so with conviction, determination and singular resolve. I have seen him do this time after time for years now, and I have absorbed his lessons most seriously," JT went on.

"You must revere your uncle," Carrie commented.

"I wouldn't call it reverence, as much as respect and admiration, which I know is splitting hairs," JT said. "There is a difference in my mind's eye however, and I consider myself very fortunate to have him as a tutor and benefactor. I know he will be watching me like a hawk as his father did him, and like John, I will be thankful for those seasoned, hardened, watchful eyes."

"Let's get dressed and go join John and the men. I have something I need to do," Carrie said.

As she and JT walked out on the cargo deck, she loudly called, "Good morning men." She was showered, fresh and full of life, love and energy. She relished being back among right-thinking, right-acting human beings, at the same time realizing that much of the ill treatment she had suffered was cultural and not all evil. She still, however, felt she had experienced the dregs of humanity.

They all turned toward her and smiled. "Good morning ma'am," they said almost in unison.

She pouted, "Ma'am?" she shouted. "I'll show you ma'am."

She walked up to the nearest Seal, who jokingly crossed his legs and covered his crotch area with both hands as she approached, causing everyone, including Carrie, to let out a howl. She had to jump up to throw her arms around the tall man's neck, but she did so, pulled herself up, almost shinnied, and kissed him squarely on the mouth. It was a long, crushing, dry kiss. She held on to his neck and squeezed with all her strength and whispered "Thank you so much" in his ear. She dropped back down to the deck and looked up at him with a teary smile, "I will never forget you and what you did for us."

She walked to the next man and did the same. He grinned a broad, engaging smile and said, "All in a day's work ma'am, uhh miss, uhh pretty lady."

Each man in turn received a special hug and a kiss; they began to line up, not to be left out. By the time she got two thirds of the way through the line, she said to the next man, "You are going to have to help me up here, I'm starting to get a little weak." With their joyful assistance, she managed to do the same with all twenty-four men. When she was finished, her clothes were rumpled, her lips and cheeks were red from the two days' growth most of the Seals sported, and her arms were drained of strength. Her tear-filled eyes were swollen with joy and she could not stop her breathless, ear-to-ear smiling. The Seals stood beaming, humbled and in full respect and admiration of her powerful effort to have her feelings known to all of them. They surrounded her, talking, smiling and accepting her gratitude.

"What are you fellas doing for exercise today?" she asked, wiping her eyes and tucking in her blouse.

"We work out right here on the cargo deck. We jog around the perimeter; we do calisthenics and play touch football. You are welcome to join us," Hulk offered.

"I'd like to run with you all if you don't mind. I think I can keep up," Carrie said.

"We'd love to have you ma'am, uhh miss, anytime," Hulk answered. "We are about ready to start now."

"I'll go get my runners on and catch up with you," she answered excitedly.

Carrie returned to the cargo deck, did half a dozen stretches and ran to catch up with the runners. Her blond ponytail bounced playfully at the back of her head as she got up to speed, which was between a jog and a run.

Smiling at the first Seal she met, she asked, "What is your name?"

"My given name is Richard, friends call me Jake," the Seal said.

"Jake it is. And I am proud to call you friend," Carrie said with a broad smile, offering him her hand, which he shook warmly.

"My name is John; the team calls me Long John," the Seal, diminutive by comparison to his mates, said, looking her in the eye from his five-foot-nine stature, certainly the shortest man in the group.

"Long John, why have they nicknamed you that?" Carrie asked.

"Well ma'am, uhh miss, it has nothing to do with my stature or anything else physical. Long stands for **L**ong **O**n **N**arley **G**rit," the Seal said as he jogged along.

"A pleasure Mr. Grit, nice to know you and damned glad to have you on my side," Carrie countered.

"My name is Benjamin. You can call me Ben, or anything you want, for that matter," said another Seal to her left.

Carrie, with a deep chuckle, laughed and said, "Ben you are. It is a wise man's name. Are you wise?"

"Can't be too wise ma'am, playin' insane games like the one we just pulled off yesterday," the Seal smiled back, shaking her hand.

The fifteen or so joggers continued their rotations around the deck and Carrie made it a point to meet all of them. She was taken aback by their stoic calm, silent assurance, matchless strength and unruffled senses of humor. Her sense of safety and well-being was tremendous in the nearly three tons of male presence.

After completing the run, Carrie joined in the calisthenics. She felt a little weak-kneed having been without this type of exercise for the last three weeks, but soon got back into the swing. The Seals were patient and helpful to her; they all knew what she had been through.

John watched Carrie from behind his dark aviator glasses and marveled at the ease with which she handled the men. He had a constant smile on his face, a sewn-on look that he couldn't shed. She saw him looking at her and she smiled broadly.

"Why are you sitting here alone, doing nothing?" Carrie said, trotting up to John.

"I'm observing you, and that's not nothing, believe me. It wears me out just watching," John answered. "And by the way, where is my hug and kiss? What am I, last year's model?"

She playfully jumped onto his lap and squeezed him hard around the neck. She kissed him and buried her head in his neck and chest.

"JT and I love you so much," Carrie said.

John squeezed her tightly, not wanting to ever let her go.

"We have come a long way together, you and I, and we have a long way to go," John said. "We can't and won't ever let anything destroy our love for each other. I will go to whatever extremes necessary to hold us together. Since that first day that I picked you up off of your knees, I knew that we were somehow connected."

"I did as well John," Carrie answered. "I couldn't put my finger on it at the time either, but I knew that our meeting was meant to happen."

John smiled down at her.

"By the way, Daddy dearest, I haven't told anyone yet, not even JT, but I think I'm pregnant," Carrie announced.

John pushed her back gently by the shoulders and beamed at her. He pulled her back to him and squeezed her tightly, being careful not to crush her.

"Now don't get all mushy on me, I don't know yet for sure, I only know how I feel. It is still very early yet," she said. "As soon as we get home I'll see the doctor. Meanwhile this is our little secret."

He squeezed her again. She knew he was speechless. The grand-child he had always wanted.

JT walked up to them embracing in the deck chair. "Ahem. What does a husband have to do around here to get some attention from his wife?" he playfully asked.

"All ya gotta do is whistle, big boy," Carrie playfully parodied in a sexy, deep Lauren Bacall voice. "You know how to whistle don't you? Just put your two lips together….. and blow." She got up and took JT by the arm and led him in to their stateroom, John smiling after them.

Later, the last evening before arriving in Bahrain, Cookie prepared his nightly cocktail hour before serving dinner on the cargo deck for those who wished, which was usually everyone. Carrie, as was always the case, was the center of attention. All the Seals monopolized her time. JT stood by proudly, watching her entertain and host this crowd of battle-hardened men. They were like big powder puffs in her hands. They would stumble over each other getting her drinks, hors d'oeuvres, and anything else she wanted.

After drinks, they all plied the buffet trays that Cookie had prepared. It was Indian Food night and he had prepared several spicy curries, a tasty Dhal Makkani, Basmati rice, chicken tikka and even naan bread. They all sat around the large table presentation, talking, joking and having fun.

John tapped on his glass to get the group's attention. "Men, Carrie, JT, I have to say this is probably the happiest day of my life. The joy that I am feeling right now, having my nephew and my gorgeous daughter back, is inexpressible," John's voice cracked slightly. "When you ran into my arms on that God-forsaken beach Carrie, I nearly exploded with a crazy mix of relief for your escape, anger and rage at your captors, respect for these brave and honorable men and joy for being reunited with you and JT," John shakily went on. "In the wake of success, one shouldn't talk about failure, but I don't think I could have dealt with failure." John raised his glass. "To you JT, and my hopes for your future. To you wonderful, wonderful men. And to you, my beautiful darling daughter. Thank God you are all safe.

"Hear, hear," echoed the men.

"Failure was never an option sir," Jumbo chimed in.

"One more thing," John injected before sitting down. "Tomorrow we are getting on a plane for a one-stop flight home."

45

PARTY TIME

The Gulf Queen and the Sea Queen pulled lazily into their side-by-side berths at Mina Salman, Port of Bahrain, and the Roosevelt sailed on to their Fifth Fleet headquarters. The Seals had just finished breakfast and were packing their belongings and assembling on deck. John's Bahrain office arranged for a customs and immigration officer to provide special clearance for the Seals, JT, Carrie and himself from the port directly to a Gulf Air flight about two miles from the port. The men rued the eleven hour flight, even though John had purchased nearly the entire number of available First and Business Class seats for their comfort. John knew from experience that six-foot-four, two hundred and thirty plus pound frames fared badly in normal airline seats designed for an average body weight of one hundred and seventy pounds.

"JT, may I sit next to Carrie for a while? I promise I won't monopolize all her time," John said.

"Certainly Uncle," JT happily replied, getting up to move to John's seat at the front of the first class area.

"How are you feeling young lady? Do you still think you are pregnant?" John asked, holding Carrie's hand.

"I think I know," she answered. "My body feels very different. It has to be pregnancy."

They each had a drink, Carrie her orange juice and John two fingers of Laphroig, and talked on for some time.

"I have arranged for you to see a doctor when we land. We aren't going straight home as you will see, and keep that to yourself as well," John said. He kissed her on the forehead and he rose to go back to his own seat.

As the aircraft began its descent for landing, the men with window seating looked perplexed at the view below. Nothing but ocean as far as they could see, no land in sight. Soon there appeared a small spot of ocean-lapped land, and before they knew it they were on the ground.

"Where the hell are we?" one of the Seals questioned.

"Damned if I know," another replied. There were no signs identifying their landing location.

"Holy crap, I'd swear I just saw my wife and kids," Hulk said to his travelling companion, looking out the window.

The men filed into the breezy open-air terminal and were instantly surrounded by their families. All the families met their men with hugs, kisses and leis of many different colors. The kids jumped up and down, tackling their fathers, who whisked them up and hugged them, showing all of the healthy signs of fatherhood and family.

Only two of the men were without wives. John had a special plan for them. One man's brother came to welcome him and spend the week with him. They hadn't seen each other in ten years. The other man's estranged seventeen-year-old son and fifteen-year-old daughter joined him for the remainder of the week.

Standing mysteriously alone in a far corner of the terminal area was a tall attractive woman, wearing a very colorful, body-hugging, floral design, sarong style wrap around, aviator sunglasses and a beautiful tan on her lean, lithe body. In the melee, John hadn't noticed her when he entered the terminal. She walked up behind him with a lei, a mixture of fragrant cream colored plumeria and raspberry orchids, and tapped him on the shoulder. He turned and she placed the lei ceremoniously around his neck.

Jennifer learned everything about the extraction from Trent while waiting for John's plane to land. Upset that she hadn't been told the complete truth, she understood why John had withheld it from her. Had she known, she would have been a nervous wreck. There was no need for her to have fretted and worried, but she would have been upset and confused if anything bad had happened.

"Welcome home, my conquering General," she said, pulling herself up to kiss him. "Aloha Au la 'Oe," she purred in Hawaiian with a British accent.

"Jennifer, what a wonderful surprise. How did you know?" John asked.

"A little bird named Trent McSpadden called me, and I couldn't resist. I have been here almost a week now and I can't get enough."

JT and Carrie walked up to hug and greet Jennifer, as did Trent McSpadden and his wife Gabriela, a lovely Latina. Trent had a special van for the six of them, and the rest of the men and their families boarded a chartered bus to take them to the Island Shores Hotel where Trent had lined up rooms for everyone and ocean view Penthouse Suites for himself and his wife, JT and Carrie and John and Jennifer.

Before the men and their families could leave the bus, Trent boarded and announced that the remainder of the day was free time for everyone, and that there was a cocktail party and private luau scheduled for everyone that evening and everyone was expected to attend and to assemble at the bus no later than 6 PM.

"There is a folder with information for the week in each of your rooms," Trent continued. "Only the luaus are mandatory attendance functions, and there will be two of them this week. The first one is tonight, and the second one will be on the last night we are here. There is a charge card in the folder that you are to use for golf, boating, hang gliding, horseback riding and other various nearby functions in which you may wish to participate. Eating and drinking at 505 right next-door is also included, eating and entertainment away from the hotel, you are on your own. The folder will explain everything. Enjoy, and we will see you all back here at 6PM sharp."

"Jennifer, I am so glad that you and Trent cooked up the idea to have you join us here," John said as they went out on the penthouse suite veranda to lounge and sunbathe. "I didn't think your schedule would allow it."

"I don't have a schedule where you are concerned, you big oaf. You should know that by now," Jennifer taunted. "Haven't you ever thought it strange that I am always available when you ask? Often it takes me hours to rearrange things, this time was no exception."

Jennifer laid on her chaise in a solid black string bikini bottom and nothing else. Her body had hardly aged since she and John made love that first night in Chabahar. She lay partially propped up on her elbows, glistening with tanning oils and looking out at the beach and the families enjoying their time together in the sun.

"You are a picture my love," John said, bending to hand her a Mai Tai and kiss her on her bare, protruding shoulder. She turned her head to him quickly and playfully kissed him on the lips.

"Scoot over," John said

John stretched out on the chaise next to her and they held hands, talked and wooed as they sipped their fruity and flowery rum drinks.

"You don't have to give me all the gory details General, but tell me about the operation you and those hunky men succeeded in implementing."

John tried to relate the story as clearly as he could, and Jennifer listened intently, enthralled and wrapped up in the drama. He tried not to leave anything out; he knew she was interested in it all.

"Apparently Carrie's captor was a typical Arab chauvinist. He had slapped her hard a couple of times for speaking before being told she could speak. Actually split her lip once," John related, and Jennifer perked up and turned toward him on one elbow, a look of disdain angering her otherwise flawless features.

"I think I know how this story is going to end," Jennifer said, mustering a smile.

"After we had captured the pirate and brought him back with us to the ship, Carrie confronted him on the deck in front of all the men assembled there. She had strong words for him and then she kicked him squarely between the legs with such force he went to his knees, choking and barfing."

"Yes!" Jennifer cried. "I knew it."

"Twenty four hunky, as you call them, square jaws dropped open in disbelief," John went on.

"She is all woman John. Not afraid to take her lumps, and strong enough to dish it out when necessary," Jennifer praised. "I have taken several self-defense courses, and I'll bet she has as well. She is responsible, relentless and unforgiving. She finds it difficult to turn the other cheek. No shrinking violet she."

That evening the families gathered at the bus, on time, for the trip to the Old Island Luau John had planned. It was the oldest running luau on the island. The women were in colorful, flowery sarongs, men in Aloha shirts, and the children in shorts and 'I Heart Maui' T-shirts. At the luau they were greeted by shirtless, sarong-wearing Hawaiian men, plumeria and orchid leis and rum drinks. The families stood around and talked while the children played in the sand with life guards watching out for their safety. None of the men appeared the least upset, concerned or traumatized by the earlier extraction operation. It was as if they had spent a day at the office and were now out enjoying their families. *What interesting men*, John thought.

There were two hundred or so other guests at the luau, grouped around the three-tiered, semicircular stage, with swaying palms and the blue Pacific as the stage backdrop. John's group of one hundred was all together at the center of the crowd.

After cocktails, the group was ushered to the seating area where tables had been placed. In orderly fashion, they were led to the buffet tables where they helped themselves to the authentic Hawaiian feast and sat eating, laughing and drinking.

When the dinner was completed, John walked up on the stage and asked for everyone's attention. The group slowly quieted and John began to speak into the microphone.

"Ladies and gentlemen. Undoubtedly you have noticed the large group of rather burly men and their lovely wives and children sitting in the center section there," John said, pointing at his group. "They have just completed a hair-raising hostage release, saving my nephew and daughter from despicable pirates. Tonight we are celebrating the success of the mission that has been in planning for the last month," John went on. "Please bear with us for the next thirty minutes, and we will then get to watch the show we all came here to enjoy." John strolled to the center of the stage and began his tribute. "I'm sure I don't have to tell all you men again, but I'm going to anyway. Thank you so much for giving me my daughter and my nephew back," John said as the group broke out in loud applause. "Fearless, determined, courageous and brave, you all discharged your duties perfectly and saved the day. Most important of all, no one, except those two dirty little *you know what's*, and I am sure many of the villagers, was seriously harmed or killed. JT is still limping a little from his twisted ankle, but he will mend just fine." The group chuckled, and the rest of the crowd looked on with interest.

"If you are able JT, I'd like for you and Carrie to join me up here for a minute."

JT, still limping slightly, followed Carrie up on the stage. As she walked across to John, the men cheered and whistled and shouted her name in unison, "Car-rie, Car-rie!" She smiled and waved to them and blew them all kisses. She shouted out to the men, "Hooya!" The Seals returned the shout at full volume.

"For those of you who don't know, Carrie is my beautiful adopted daughter, and JT is her loving husband and they both have just been liberated from a month's long captivity by renegade Arabian Sea pirates, by the brave and courageous men you see sitting there," John said to the crowd and pointing to the Seals.

John hugged Carrie tightly for several moments, then shook JT's hand and stepped back away from them, handing them the microphone.

"Men, we can only echo my uncle's praises and thanks. Even though at times we were afraid things might go badly, we never lost hope and knew our day would come. When we saw your big, scary black, green and brown camouflaged faces our hearts leapt," JT said. "Thank you."

"All of you wonderful men know that I love you with all my being, and will always have a special place in my heart and prayers for each and every one of you. God you are powerful human beings, how fortunate we are having you in our lives and how fortunate this country is to have men like you and your comrades. Thank you ladies for letting us borrow your amazing husbands," Carrie said.

One of the wives stood raising and waving her hand for recognition and said, "Hang on Carrie, don't give them too much praise, they are almost impossible to live with as it is!" The families in the throng laughed raucously and the crowd, now fully engaged, chimed in.

"I have something else I would like to say," Carrie said as she grabbed JT's hand. "I've been feeling kind of strange lately, not quite myself. I met with a doctor this afternoon who told me a tiny alien organism has invaded my body. I am going to be the proud mother of your child in about eight and a half months." The entire crowd roared.

"Captivity wasn't so bad after all, was it, JT?" one of the men chided from the crowd as JT beamed and took Carrie in his arms. John stood in silent, joyful and grandfatherly smugness.

"We aren't done yet folks," John said as the group settled back down.

"There is a particularly gorgeous lady here with us tonight and she is sitting right there," John said, shielding his eyes from the bright stage lights and pointing out at Jennifer. "And I'd like her to come up here and join me please."

Jennifer stood in her figure-caressing Hawaiian gown and the spotlight picked her up as she walked up onto the stage. To avoid tripping, she had to hoist her full length skirt, which parted to mid-thigh, as she walked up the stone steps, baring long, tanned legs with shapely ankles, calves, thighs and a sexy supermodel's walk. As she strolled across the stage, the men whistled and hooted like GIs at a Bob Hope USO Show in appreciation of her extraordinary beauty. She waved to them and blew them kisses as well. She was, as always, in full control of the crowd.

John intercepted her with a hug and a kiss, and with her arms around his neck, she returned firmly, to the delight of the brawny men. John stepped aside, held out his hands painting Jennifer's aura and the entire crowd clapped wildly as she curtsied and bowed.

John covertly reached into his pocket and knelt down on one knee in front of Jennifer as the crowd fell suddenly silent. Her hands went to her face in complete surprise as she bent slightly, looking down at him.

"Jennifer Middleton, will you marry me?" John blurted out into the microphone.

"Finally, after all these years, you are going to make an honest woman of me, you rake!" she said with a smile. "Of course I'll marry you; I'm partial to debauched, elderly men." She laughed, as did the gathering.

One of the ladies in the crowd yelled out, "That's Jennifer Middleton, the supermodel and clothing designer!" Everyone cheered with recognition.

John stood and placed the ten carat, emerald-cut diamond on her left ring finger.

She held up both her hands and showed off both of her rings, glittering green and white in the bright stage lights. "It took me just over twenty extremely patient years, but there you are folks, a matched set." She threw her arms around John's neck and kissed him eagerly as the house came down around their joyfulness.

"Still not done yet everybody, simmer down, bear with me," John said, holding Jennifer close at his side. "I'd like MCPO Harold Wilson, US Navy Seals, Retired and his family to come up on stage."

The crowd quieted to pin drop silence as Harold "Hard Head" Wilson escorted his wife and daughter and pushed his infirmed son's wheelchair to the stage. Two Seals stepped up and carried the young boy and his chair up on the stage.

"Come over here, Wilson family," John said as JT, Carrie and Jennifer embraced the entire family in welcome.

"It is my understanding that your son Kyle is a baseball fan, am I correct?" John questioned, getting his answer in the young boy's broad smile.

"Who is your favorite team Kyle?" John asked.

"The Anaheim Angels, of course," Kyle proudly said into the microphone with a teenage boy's ever-changing voice.

"Well that is an interesting coincidence," John said. "There is a fellow here by the name of Tony Grosse who wants to meet you."

The crowd stood and cheered as Tony, the four-time All Star, walked up on the stage and stood next to the young boy. Every one of the men knew who Tony was and of his career contribution to his teams, batting a lifetime .245, with 320 home runs and 950 RBI's and of course, his contribution to the season-winning Angels this year.

"Son, I am a big fan of Anaheim fans, especially those like you who come to our games whenever you can. I am happy to meet you Kyle, and I feel personally honored for the opportunity to invite you and your family to be our guest for the home games of the World Series," Tony announced as the crowd cheered.

"Really?!" the 14-year-old cancer victim said. "Holy cow, I don't believe it," his teenager's voice cracking in his excitement.

"We can't have you sitting in our box without the proper uniform. Here is an Angels Hat and shirt that is must-wear attire at every game," Tony said.

Tony wheeled the boy aside and knelt and talked with him on stage as John ushered Harold and his wife to the microphone stand.

"Harold and Greta, the men here don't know it yet, but each and every one of them has donated $1,000 of their earnings from this venture to the Kyle Wilson Cancer Foundation." All of the men stood, cheered, applauded and whistled at the news. "I personally have matched their donations and Double O shipping has matched all of our donations. We have started a foundation for Kyle with $98,000 dollars." The entire crowd went wild.

Trent McSpadden yelled up from the crowd. "I'm a little upset you left me out John! McSpadden Security Partners is in for ten percent of where you are right now, so that puts us well over the $100,000 mark." More cheers.

"Mr. Wingate, my name is Tom Beuhner and I am the Manager of the Island Shores," the man announced from in front of the stage.

"Yes Mr. Beuhner?" John said.

"The Island Shores Hotel would like to contribute 10% of its profit from your function this week to this young man's cause. We appreciate your choosing to stay with us, we hope you enjoy yourselves."

"John, Jennifer Middleton Styles Inc. would like to contribute $7,500 to the worthy foundation," Jennifer added, leaning into the microphone, garnering more cheers.

John hugged her tightly. "Thank you darling."

JT stepped up to the microphone. "John, Carrie and I would like to become a part of Kyle's Foundation and pledge $5,000 per year for the next five years."

The entire crowd was in a frenzy.

"Mr. Wingate," a man shouted from the crowd.

"Yes sir," John said, "Quiet down folks, let the man speak."

"Mr. Wingate, I have no idea what you and you group have been through for the last month, but I can imagine it was pretty harrowing," the man began.

"Harrowing is a good definition," John said, laughing.

"I would like to suggest that you give us all a chance to donate to your young man's cause, and I am sure that if everyone else has been as moved by your plight as I and my family have, there should be a fat increase in your foundation," the man continued. "I would like to start off by saying that my foundation, The John Kenneth Woodhouse Foundation, would like to offer your foundation $25,000."

"Sir, would you mind coming up on the stage?" John asked.

The man wound through the crowd as they cheered his generosity.

"What is you name sir?" John asked as the man approached.

"Phillip Woodhouse," the man said.

"Phillip, why would you make such a generous donation?" John asked.

"I lost my son John to cancer 20 years ago, and vowed to do whatever I could to help as many people as I can," the man offered. "It is a terrible disease, and we all need to do what we can to eradicate it. My foundation usually offers money to research groups, but I couldn't resist this opportunity."

"Bless you Phillip," John said, giving the man a genuine hand shake and hug.

A man rushed up on stage and walked over to John and asked for the microphone. "Folks, I am the manager of the Old Island Luau. If anyone else would like to donate to the Kyle Wilson Cancer Foundation, we have set up a table at the front entrance where you can do that. Please come up at your leisure. Any amount will be appreciated, I am sure. We here at Old Island Luau are offering the entire entrance fee for the Wingate group, and hope that you all enjoy the rest of your evening with us. Good luck to you all, and good luck to you, Kyle," the man said and left the stage.

"What a marvelous outpouring," John said, choking up slightly. "Thank you so much everyone for letting us interrupt your evening, and thank you so much for your generous donations."

As the jubilation died down, John stepped back to the microphone. "Enjoy the rest of the evening and the show everybody," John said as they all left the stage. "Trent, would you mind giving Jennifer and I a lift back to the hotel?"

"Why don't you just take the van John, there is plenty of room in the bus," Trent offered.

"See you tomorrow," John said, and the two drove off.

At the hotel, Jennifer went into the bedroom to change out of her clothing as John fixed them a night cap. She walked out onto the veranda wearing only her heels and her rings and John pulled her to him.

"You have made me a very happy man tonight, Jennifer Middleton, soon-to-be Wingate," John said.

"That makes two of us," she replied. "And to prove my happiness and sincerity, and this has been in my thoughts for several years now, when we get back to New York I'm going to franchise my London and Paris outlets, and pare things down to a size that a happily married woman can manage. I want to stay in the business, but the travel no longer excites me and I want to be close to you always."

"I think you should stay active, Jennifer, it keeps you young and in touch with what's going on in the world," John said.

For the remainder of the week, John, Jennifer, JT and Carrie mingled with the families and played with the children when they could be corralled. The joy and happiness they saw on the faces of the families was more than enough reward for John. He had succeeded again; the function was a raving success.

Carrie was often spotted jogging with the men in the mornings, sipping Mai Tai's with them at the poolside bar, and visiting the men's tables at dinner time and chatting with them and their wives.

"You have won the hearts of every bozo here," one of the wives told Carrie.

"I hope so," Carrie said. "I love them all so much."

When the final night arrived, they all met at the bus for the last luau and final get together of the week, a private affair near the hotel. John, Jennifer, JT and Carrie mixed through the crowd. John handed each man an envelope, shook the man's hand robustly and gave him a one armed hug. Each envelope contained a check for $28,000, except for Jumbo's who had put in an additional ten days in the planning stage, plus a personal hand written note from John and signed by John, JT and Carrie. John noted the deduction of one thousand dollars for the Kyle Wilson Cancer Foundation, so the men would get the tax deduction. The men folded the envelopes and put them in their pockets. They knew what the envelope contained.

Later that evening, Erik "Hulk" Hendersen came up to John with his envelope in his hand, and said, "This is too much money."

"It's not enough by half, considering what I got out of the deal," John said. "Please understand that I am fully satisfied with everything and I have been the one who has been overpaid," John went on. "You men have been an inspiration to me."

"Sir, if ever again you find yourself in need of our services, I for one will be front and center to answer the call," Eric said. "You are one hell of a stand up individual, I'd follow you anywhere."

"Thank you Eric, you have no idea what that means to me."

EPILOGUE

Years prior to this, the waters off of Somalia and Yemen were rife with ocean life. There were more fish than either country could harvest and they treated the fishing grounds with the respect taught them by their fathers and their fathers before them. It wasn't long before Chinese and Japanese fishermen began to ply the area, their own trawling grounds seriously and dangerously over fished. The foreign fishermen overfished the Horn of Africa waters quickly, much to the dismay of the Somalis and Yemenis. To compound the issues, in the early 1990's renegade Somali warlords were allowing foreign governments to dump toxic waste materials in Somali fishing waters and charged the offending governments millions for the privilege.

Somalis and Yemenis complained to their ineffectual governments and tribunals but nothing was done to stop the practices. The fishermen seethed and resorted to self-rule to solve their problems. At first they attacked the foreign fishermen strictly to drive them away from their waters, but the practice soon evolved into piracy and grew to the seriousness it is today. Piracy is still growing drastically. Not only were the attacks more often, but with the introduction of the mother ship, they were extending further and further from the Somali and Yemeni coasts deep into the Indian Ocean.

Somalia and Yemen, for years, were lawless outposts for warlords and pirates and both soon were marked pariahs of the Arabian Sea and the Gulf of Aden. The reaction of the lawful countries was to fight the pirates, rather than to help them police their fishing grounds.

Although piracy has been going on in the area since the 1990s, it really didn't start to catch the world's eyes and ears until 2000, and it has grown more and more serious every year.

It is for each individual to decide whether the Somalis and Yemenis are blatant criminals or the defenders of their seas. The argument for each side is virtually equal.